Defending Her Wolves
Hungry for Her Wolves, Book Seven
A Reverse-Harem Paranormal Romance
Tara West

LOVE SHOULD WITHSTAND anything, but I don't know if it can survive this.

We made it out. We survived. But we didn't know then that Dimitri and I did not escape the haunted forest unscathed. He risked his immortal soul to save me, but we've returned different.

Inside us spider demons are taking over, and our lives will never be the same. Relationships broken, lives destroyed, and worst of all, our family will be forced to kill us if we can't get rid of the demons.

We'll do anything to make this right, even make a deal with a tricky djinn.

Dedications

CARY, THANKS FOR HELPING me with my rusty Spanish. You rock!

Thanks again to Pamela for your insight and wisdom. You are amazing. I'm so glad our paths crossed, sister, even though an unfortunate circumstance brought us together.

Thanks to Sheri and Laura C.E. for finding my oopsies! My bunny brain can't keep track of all these characters!

Thanks to Theo, God of Grammar, for wielding your magical red pen of shame on my manuscript. It looked like my MS vomited blood, but that's okay. It's in much better shape now.

Thanks to Deb, PA Goddess, for keeping my head on straight and taking care of important tasks, so I can focus on my books.

Finally, thanks to my readers, for supporting this series so that I can pay my mortgage, and for patiently waiting for this next book. Sorry I left you on a hook. Hope this was worth it!

Prologue

"OPEN UP BEFORE I BANG the door down!"

Tatiana winced at the sound of Dimitri's booming voice on the other side of the door, which rattled at his assault. His Romanian accent was thicker when he was angry.

She searched the mirror once again for any more signs of the demon. The demon had looked just like her, with long, dark hair and high cheekbones, but instead of having the darker skin of her Native American ancestors, its skin had been sickly gray and its eyes blood red. How could she leave the bathroom, knowing she could be a danger to her mates?

"Dimitri, what's going on in there?" Dejan, her younger mate, asked.

"Tatiana screamed in the bathroom." Dimitri pounded on the door again.

"Just a minute!" she hissed, searching for clothes. All she could find were towels. If she walked out wrapped in one of them, they'd suspect she was hiding something.

Great. Dejan would see the marks on her shoulder and breast from her violent lovemaking with Dimitri. An image of her scraping her nails down his back, his flesh curling under her fingers, flashed in her mind. Her hand flew to her mouth. What had come over her?

"Tatiana, are you okay?" Dejan asked, while Dimitri banged louder.

She wanted to scream.

After heaving a shaky breath, she threw open the door and marched past her gorgeous blond mates, one arm slung across her bare breasts. She ignored Dimitri's beautiful muscular nakedness and the long appendage hanging between his legs and snatched her jeans off the floor. She flushed, remembering all the wonderfully bad things he'd done to her with his big cock, and how many more bad things she wanted him to do to her.

She bit her lip, stalling. What was she supposed to say? "I'm fine," she lied and stepped into her underwear, wincing at the soreness between her legs. Why had she begged Dimitri to be rough?

He was behind her, breathing down her neck like a bear in heat. "Why were you screaming?"

She grabbed her flannel shirt off a chair, scowling at the rip Dimitri had made on the collar. Covering her breasts with her crumpled clothes, she turned to him, unable to meet his eyes. "I-I think I'm turning into a demon." She regretted the words as soon as they were spoken. What if her mates thought she'd gone crazy? Or worse, what if they believed her?

He scowled. "Why would you say that?"

She jerked away when he grabbed her elbow. Even that simple touch hurt. Every muscle in her body ached as if she'd run the Iditarod. Great Ancients! Why had they been so rough?

"Answer me," he said forcefully.

His tone did nothing to ease her aggravation. Why was he being so hostile? The thought popped into her head that his guilty conscience was making him act that way. She searched his eyes for any sign of deceit. "I saw red eyes in the mirror." She was not comforted when he released her and looked away.

He was hiding something.

"Tatiana, come here," Dejan said soothingly, giving her one of his big, bear hugs while rubbing her back. "You're not turning into a demon. You have PTSD from your time in the forest."

She clung to him, praying he was right.

He let out a hiss when he brushed her heavy, dark hair off her shoulder. "What happened?"

"I-I don't remember." She knew perfectly well what happened. Dimitri had bitten her, drawing blood like a vampire.

Dejan arched a brow. "Dimitri, did you do this?"

He scratched the back of his head, his cheeks flushing red. "I didn't mean to leave a mark." Liar. He couldn't look either of them in the eyes.

"I think you both have PTSD." Dejan pulled back, rubbing his chin. "Maybe you need counseling."

Dimitri laughed. "Where are we going to find a shifter shrink, Dejan?"

Dejan blinked at him. "Tatiana's family will know."

"We *are* her family," Dimitri snapped, his pale blue eyes turning an ominous gray.

Dejan shrugged, acting as if his brother shooting eye lasers at him was no big deal. "Let me see you," he said to Tatiana, prying the clothes from her hands.

She fought him at first. She didn't want him to see her bruises.

He finally snatched the clothes away and swore. "Tatiana, your boob is swelling." He cast Dimitri an accusatory look. With a curse, Dimitri turned his back on them and shrugged into a pair of tight denim jeans.

She froze in shock. It looked like a rabid cat had attacked his back. Bloody raised furrows were already forming scabs on his pale skin.

"Your back is bleeding." Dejan clucked his tongue, scowling at them both. "Great Ancients, you two."

Dimitri responded with a dismissive laugh and slipped a jersey over his head.

Slowly lowering onto the edge of the bed, she said, "Do you think we're possessed?"

Dimitri shook his head. "Eilea and Amara would've cured us."

Gah! She felt so guilty for hurting him. "Then what's wrong with us?"

"Nothing." His laughter sounded forced. "You think we're the first couple to have kinky sex?"

Her shoulders fell. This was worse than kinky sex. His injuries would most likely scar unless Amara healed them. "I hope that's all it is."

Sitting beside her, he cupped her chin in his hand. "We're fine. No demon, no curse, is ever coming between us again."

If only they could be sure. "You're too confident."

"Tatiana," he said, his eyes sparkling with an odd gleam. "I'd wager my very soul."

She prayed it would never come to that.

Chapter One

AMARA SAT UP IN BED, propped against a pillow and breastfeeding baby Astrid. She was exhausted and still jet-lagged after returning yesterday from a ten-day trip to Romania. She couldn't wait to put the baby to bed and take off her heavy robe. She wore a little black nightie underneath. Her mates had bought it for her for Valentine's Day. She knew it drove Drasko wild, and she loved it because it covered her old pregnancy stretchmarks. Even though she had healing powers, strangely they didn't extend to stretchmarks and sagging breasts. Maybe because nature thought her body was flawless as it was.

She'd had one baby every year she'd been with her mates, five total. Luckily, shifter pregnancies only lasted five months, otherwise she would've felt perpetually pregnant. She hadn't stopped breastfeeding since Hrod was born, though. Another reason she loved that black nightie so much; tight stitching made her boobs look perkier. They'd lost a little more elasticity with each new baby. Her mates swore they were perfect, just like with her stomach. The muscles there had softened quite a bit, but her mates repeatedly told her that her body was beautiful. Still, she liked to pretend every so often that her breasts were still perky.

Rone came out of the bathroom, towel-drying his wet hair, another towel wrapped around his waist, which had widened after five years together. Humans called it dad-bod. She loved his body, for it reflected his love of cooking and taking care of his family. Raising five kids was challenging work, but Rone was an amazing gamma, up before everyone getting breakfast ready and then last to bed when he tucked the kids in for the night.

"Come to bed, baby." She patted the bed. "You look exhausted."

"I am," he said, "but I wanted to get a jump on spring cleaning."

"With five kids underfoot?" Drasko grinned as he entered the room, stretching with a yawn. "You're spinning your wheels."

Amara was pleased to see Drasko smiling again. He'd been pissed off most of the day after soaking himself several times with freezing water while fixing the plumbing on the hot tub. It was the second time this winter it had broken. At one point, she'd feared he was going to shift into a protector and throw the entire tub in the lake, but he knew how much she loved soaking her back and feet after healing tribe members all day. Not that she couldn't have healed her sore muscles herself, but soaking in the tub with her virile mates was far more fun.

"I actually got a lot accomplished," Rone said, holding out his hands to Amara. Astrid had fallen asleep at her breast. "Come here, *pui de lup*." He took the milk-drunk baby from her and kissed her on the forehead before lifting her and smelling her bottom.

"I already changed it," Amara said.

"You did? Is it on straight?" he teased.

"Straight enough." She refrained from rolling her eyes. It was no secret she still couldn't get a diaper on right.

She slipped off her robe, flashing them a coy smile. "Come to bed, guys, before we're all too tired to make love."

Drasko sat beside her, stroking her cheek with calloused knuckles. "I'll never be too tired for you."

A soft moan escaped her when he ran his hand down her neck and cupped a breast while nibbling on her ear. She craved his touch as if it were a drug. Out of all her mates, he was the most skilled in seduction.

"Hey, cub," Rone said. "What are you doing awake?"

Her middle child, Evin, barely out of diapers at three years old, was standing in the doorway, holding a stuffed wolf cub to his chest. His eyes were wide and glossy, his thick mop of hair sticking up in all directions.

She and Drasko jerked apart like two teens caught making out. "What's wrong?" she asked.

His bottom lip trembled. "Auntie Tati stab Uncle Dimi. She kill him."

"What?" Drasko snickered. "You must be mistaken."

Rone scooped Evin into his arms. "Baby, are you sure you didn't have a nightmare?"

Evin had been gifted with the ability to see things before they happened, but they'd just returned from visiting Eilea, who'd cast a spell on Amara's sons to mute their powers, which were becoming too strong, too soon. Their powers weren't completely diminished, just weaker. Would Evin's powers be strong enough to see Tatiana stabbing Dimitri? And why would she stab her mate?

A single tear slipped down his cherubic cheek as he made a stabbing motion. "No, she hurt him in heart."

Amara clutched her throat. "Why?"

"Tati angry." Dropping the stuffed wolf, he clutched Rone's neck. "Her eyes red."

Red eyes? Amara clutched her throat. Why would Tatiana have demonic eyes?

"That doesn't sound right." Drasko jumped from the bed, his features as hard as granite. "Stay here, Amara. I'll go over there."

"Are you crazy?" She slipped on her robe. "I'm not staying here when my brother needs me."

Drasko hastily shoved boots on his feet. "He had a nightmare."

Evin was still clinging tightly to Rone's neck. His premonitions had never been wrong before. She fixed Drasko with an unwavering glare. "I'm going."

TATIANA ADMIRED HER full breasts in the full-length mirror while slipping into her red nightie. Her mates loved her in it almost as much as they loved taking it off her. Constantine had bought her the flimsy lace garment for Valentine's Day two weeks ago, and she'd worn it to bed almost every night since, knowing it drove her mates wild. Constantine and Hakon, her oldest brother and also one of Amara's mates, had finally gone back to work in the oil fields, but that didn't stop her from teasing Dimitri and Dejan. If only Andrei could see her in it. After being gone for over two months, she missed him terribly. He only had two more weeks left of basic training, but they would drag on forever.

She came out of the bathroom, winking at her mates as they waited for her with ravenous eyes.

Dimitri scooped her into his arms and laid her on the bed before peeling off the nightie in record time.

She swatted his chest. "You didn't even get to enjoy the nightie."

"I only care about what's underneath."

She arched into his hand when he squeezed her breast. Grasping the roots of his hair, she slammed his face to hers, groaning into his mouth when he squeezed her harder. Over the past few months, his foreplay had become rougher, but she dared not complain. She was starting to like it that way, his fingers branding her skin with every pinch, squeeze, and slap.

The bed dipped and the mattress springs squeaked, and she knew Dejan was there. She briefly worried that he felt like the third wheel, since she usually paid more attention to Dimitri, but she couldn't help herself. Dejan wasn't like them, and she needed Dimitri's seed to make eggs.

What? Where had that thought come from?

Dimitri pushed her onto her back with a growl. Dejan crawled over to her, smiling, the dimples in his cheeks and his innocent, wide eyes reminding her of a lamb at the slaughter. How easily she could bite off his head with one snap of her teeth. No, wait.

She shuddered. What was wrong with her? Where were these dark thoughts coming from?

When Dimitri pinched her nipple hard, flattening the peak between thick fingers, she scowled. *Show him who the real dominant is,* a sibilant voice hissed.

Grasping the back of his head, she shoved his face toward her pussy with surprising force and smashed his lips against her dripping cunt. "Suck it," she commanded in a voice that sounded harsher and darker than her own.

He licked and slurped, driving his tongue into her, then pulling out and swirling the tip along her engorged bud. She cried out, thrusting against him while Dejan toyed with her nipples, tenderly circling her hard peaks with wet fingers. A part of her appreciated his gentleness, but another part resented his weakness. As the gamma, he was the most tender of her mates, the one with the softest hands and least defined muscles. He wasn't as strong as Dimitri, who could shift into both a wolf and a mighty protector, a large hairy white beast that resembled a Sasquatch.

Dimitri can also turn into a demonling, said a voice in the back of her mind. A what?

She fought the urge to slap Dejan off her, his dull foreplay making her nipples feel raw and sore, but then Dimitri speared her pussy hard with thick fingers, his sharp nails digging into her weeping, swollen flesh and making her orgasm without warning. She thrust her hips into him while her tight sheath contracted around his fingers, splashing his hand while he let out a low chuckle against her abdomen that reverberated across her skin, making her flesh rise with goosebumps.

Before she'd had a chance to savor each little quake, he flipped her onto her knees and speared her in one fluid thrust. She lurched forward, pain lancing through her spine as he dug his nails into her back.

"Go easy on her, Dimitri," Dejan said.

She ignored her gamma, meeting each of Dimitri's hard thrusts with equal vigor.

"That's right," she said, feeling as if someone else was speaking through her. "Give me your seed. Breed me with your spawns."

"What are you talking about, Tatiana?" she thought she heard Dejan say.

She closed her eyes as he gaped at her, wishing it was just her and Dimitri in the room. *He will try to stop you,* a voice echoed inside her skull. *Kill him first.*

Kill Dejan? What? No! What the fuck was happening to her?

Dimitri's groans grew louder, and he slammed into her harder, giving her every inch of his long cock and making her insides ache.

"Fuck that pussy," she cried through a hiss. "Fill me with your essence!"

Their bodies slapped together so hard, she felt something tear inside her, but she didn't care. She didn't know why, but she needed the pain. He came, his cockhead throbbing so much inside her, she thought she'd die from the agony, even as she strained against him, her release hitting her like a bullet. Blood rushed through her body toward that one aching spot of desire, swelling and bursting with the force of a thousand ice storms.

It's Amon's blood you need, not his seed, that sibilant voice said to her. *Your blood must combine.*

Who the hell is Amon? she thought.

Dimitri released her, and she slumped forward, then curled into herself, feeling as if a knife was stabbing her insides.

"What the fuck, Dimitri?" Dejan cried.

Her thighs were smeared with blood. Had Dimitri done that? Dimitri stared at her with a look akin to horror. His cock and thighs were wet with her blood.

"Are you having a menstrual?" Dimitri asked.

She shook her head then cringed as another wave of pain went through her.

"No, you asshole!" Dejan spat. "You fucked her too hard." He grabbed a towel from the hamper and wedged it between her legs. Stroking her face, he looked at her with a creased brow. "Do you need me to call Amara?"

"Amara?" she gasped. "So my brothers can beat the shit out of Dimitri?"

"Tatiana, I'm so sorry." Dimitri raked a hand down his face. "I don't know what came over me."

"It's okay." She winced. "It's not like I tried to stop you."

"I thought you were enjoying it." He frowned. "You orgasmed."

She managed a weak smile as another wave of pain washed through her. "I did. I didn't even realize you were hurting me."

"Something's wrong with you two," Dejan said.

He knows about us, the mysterious voice said. *We must kill him. Then kill Amon and take his blood.*

"I'm not killing anyone," she answered aloud.

Dejan arched a pale brow. "Who are you talking to?"

"No one."

Kill him!

Ignoring the pain in her abdomen, she slowly rose, hands clenched into fists, not caring about the blood that soaked the sheets. Her attention centered on Dejan, and for a moment, she didn't look at him as her mate but as her enemy. Someone who meant to destroy her.

He must have sensed that she was onto him, because he slid off the bed, holding out his hands in a defensive gesture. "Tatiana." His voice rattled. "I saw red in your eyes."

Kill him now!

Screaming, she launched at him, knocking him to the floor with amazing force. She glanced into the full-length mirror on the wall and red demon eyes looked back at her. She punched her reflection with a screech, ignored the pain in her bloodied hand, and thrust a shard of glass toward his heart. Yelping, he shifted into a wolf and jumped out of the way. Her hand landed on the wood floor, and the shard shattered.

Fangs extended, she grabbed another piece of glass and spun on her knees, ignoring the sharp edges of the broken mirror that ground into her skin. Dejan jumped behind Dimitri with a whimper. Dimitri looked at her with a feral gleam in his eyes, his skin taking on the gray hue of a decomposing corpse. Dejan howled and Dimitri panted like a wounded animal, his ribcage rapidly expanding and contracting with each breath.

His eyes went from red to blinding white and back again. "Morana, you can take my blood without killing me."

"I'm sorry," she said. "If I don't kill you, you will eat our offspring."

"I won't," he answered. "I will leave you in peace."

She shook her head. "My offspring will need your corpse for nourishment."

Dejan bounded out of the room, the sound of his paws racing down the stairs echoing in her skull.

You missed your chance, the voice said. *Now he will tell the others. Take the demonling's blood before it's too late.*

She picked up another piece of the broken mirror and leaped on Dimitri, marveling at how he didn't even fight her when she knocked him down. She drove the shard into his chest, then yanked it out, pleased when blood spurted from his cavity. She stabbed him again and again while he shook like a fish gasping for air.

Drasko's roar filled her skull like a freight train was driving through the room. "Drop the fucking blade, Tatiana!"

She dropped the piece of glass and rolled off Dimitri. Her brother shifted into his giant protector form, a ten-foot-tall hairy beast the natives referred to as Bigfoot. "Drasko?"

"Tatiana!" Amara shrieked. "What have you done?"

Blood poured from Dimitri's mouth, and he twitched on the floor. Great Ancients!

"Dimitri!" she cried, lunging for him.

"Get away from him!" Drasko kicked her so hard, she flew against the wall with a crack. Pain ricocheted through her head, making the room spin.

Amara fell on top of Dimitri and ran her hands over his chest.

Please, Ancients, help her save him. What had happened to him and why would her brother kick her?

Dejan returned from the hallway and draped a blanket over her nude body before quickly stepping back as if she was cursed with the plague. He wrapped a robe around himself, tears streaking his face. "Can you save him, Amara?"

Amara didn't answer as she closed her eyes, pressing against Dimitri's chest.

Tatiana sat up, ignoring the spinning in her skull while focusing on Amara's hands, trying to make sense of what was happening.

Drasko's heavy brow hung low. "What in Ancient's name did you do?"

"I-I...." she stammered. "I didn't do anything." She couldn't have harmed her mate. She loved him more than life. "Dejan," she cried, looking to him for help and dismayed when he refused to meet her eyes.

"One minute they were having rough sex," Dejan said with a quavering lip, "and the next she turned into this, this *demon* and tried to stab me. I barely escaped and then she went after Dimitri."

Tatiana's gaze tunneled on Dejan. No. She couldn't have done those things. She heaved a sigh of relief when color returned to Dimitri's cheeks and his chest slowly rose and fell as if he was in a deep slumber.

Amara pulled away from him and sat back on her heels with a groan, her hands and clothes covered in Dimitri's blood.

"She and Dimitri said strange things to each other."

Her gaze snapped to Dejan, her heart crushed by the look of accusation in his eyes.

"What strange things?" Drasko demanded.

"She needed his corpse to feed her offspring."

Tatiana's world came to a slow, grinding halt. No. She couldn't have said that, but why would he lie? And if she didn't stab Dimitri, who had? A scream broke from her when she looked at her bloody hands. No! No! No!

"I didn't do it," she protested, though she feared she was lying to herself.

"Tatiana," Drasko said, "you're covered in his blood."

Her hand flew to her throat when she remembered the sibilant voice inside her head, telling her to murder her mates. "But it wasn't me."

"It was either you or Dejan," Drasko snapped, "and he's not covered in blood."

She gazed helplessly at her brother. "It was neither of us."

"Then who did it?" he boomed, his furry face almost as red as the blood coating her hands.

She slumped against the wall and wiped tears from her cheeks. "The demon."

Raising his fists, Drasko spun around. "Where?"

She fought back nausea. "She's, she's inside me."

Drasko shook his furry head. "If you had a demon, Dr. Johnson and Amara would've cast it out."

She swallowed bile, not liking the judgment she saw in Amara's eyes. "They missed it." She didn't want to acknowledge it, but it had to be true.

"How?" Amara asked.

"This demon isn't possessing me." Gazing at the blood coating her hands, she knew how this demon had seeped into her soul. "It poisoned me."

Drasko scratched the back of his skull. "You're not making any sense."

"The demon is in my blood," Tatiana cried, as a vision of a giant man-eating spider with her face flashed in her mind. "She's transforming me."

"Into what?" Drasko asked.

Swallowing tears, she said, "Something unholy."

DIMITRI WOKE AND BLINKED up at his sister, who looked at him with worry. "Amara, what happened? Why are you upset?"

"You don't remember?" she asked, taking his hand in hers.

Remember what? It felt like he was naked on his back in a pool of water, but that made no sense. He turned his head to the side, blowing a lint ball across the hardwood. What was he doing on the floor? "My mind is a bit fuzzy."

"It's okay." She squeezed his hand. "Just rest."

"Dejan said they were talking funny."

Drasko's blurred figure came into view; he hovered behind Amara in protector form, his furry brows knitted together. "We need to know about the demon inside him."

"Demon?" Sirens went off in his head as the distant memory of a sibilant voice echoed in his brain. "Where's Tatiana and Dejan?"

Drasko crossed his arms over his broad chest, his scowl unwavering. "They're in another room."

Dimitri had the uneasy feeling that Drasko didn't trust him. "Is Tatiana safe?"

Drasko's stony features were unwavering. "For now."

Dimitri shot upright, steeling himself against dizziness. "What does that mean?" The blanket fell from his chest and he saw the crusted blood covering him. "What happened to me?"

"You had an accident, and Tatiana is fine." Amara tucked the blanket around his waist. "Drasko, you're upsetting him."

His heart thudded when he realized he wasn't lying in water, but a dark pool of blood. What kind of accident would cause him to lose so much? He picked up a shard of glass, turning it over in his hand.

"Amara, if he's possessed, too," Drasko continued, "we need to know."

She turned to her mate with stiff movements. "You need to call your fathers."

"I called them when I locked up Tatiana." Drasko's deep rumble rattled the walls. "I'm handling this, Amara."

Dimitri had no desire to get in the middle of their argument. His priority was making sure Tatiana was okay. Why had Drasko locked her up? "I need to see Tatiana." He dropped the shard and again tried to push off from the floor, dismayed by all the slick blood under him.

"No." Drasko pulled Amara away from Dimitri, eliciting lots of swearing and groans from Amara. "I need to know about the demons inside you and my sister."

"What demons?" What the hell was he talking about, and why the fuck wasn't he letting him see Tatiana?

"Quit the bullshit, Dimitri," Drasko snapped. "Tatiana stabbed you in the heart. You would be dead if Amara hadn't saved you."

The sound of Dimitri's pounding heart ricocheted so loudly in his ears, he could scarcely hear himself think. An image of Tatiana pinned on top of him, her eyes glowing red as she sliced open his chest, flashed in his mind. "My mate wouldn't stab me." *You're lying to yourself,* a sibilant voice echoed. A dark seed sprouted in his soul, twisting around his heart like a vine of thorns, planting roots of fear in his gut.

"She did." Kneeling beside him, Drasko flicked a piece of glass across the floor. "Several times."

Grimacing, Amara wrapped her arms around herself. "Dejan said you two had sex so rough, she was bleeding everywhere."

No! "Bleeding?" He barely choked out the word. "Is she okay?"

The look of pity Amara gave him made him want to crawl under the floorboards and never resurface. "I've already healed her."

He hung his head in shame. "I-I don't understand."

"I do," someone said. "You're both possessed by demons. Now to figure out which kind."

Drasko moved aside, revealing a tiny elderly woman with dark, leathery skin, standing in the doorway. He vaguely remembered her name was Nuniq, a strange old woman who lived off the grid with her equally old mates and played with crystals. They had taken the place of the recently deceased tribal elders. What was she doing here? He raised a shaky finger. "You're that medicine woman."

She surged forward, thrusting a gnarled cane in front of her with each step, Tor Thunderfoot in his hulking protector form following closely at her heels. He briefly wondered why she needed a cane when Amara could have healed her infirmity, then realized she'd probably brought it to use as a weapon.

She crinkled puffy eyelids, focused on the blood splatters on his chest. "Were you bitten by a venomous demon during your time in the forest?"

Dimitri's heart stopped, then restarted at an alarming pace. *Don't tell her,* a voice whispered. *Fuck you, demon,* he answered. Clenching his hands, he met her eyes, though he was tempted to look away. "We were bitten by a giant spider with my mom's face."

"Tatiana said she needed his corpse to feed her offspring," Drasko told her.

"Fuck." A chill coursed through him. The memory of her words returned. It had all been so surreal, as if he'd been in a dream when it happened. One minute they were tenderly making love, then a disoriented and drunken feeling had come over him and something else took over his body. He'd fucked her until she bled, and afterward he'd pleaded for his life, knowing she was far stronger, far more lethal. "I remember now."

Nuniq backed up a step, holding her cane in a white-knuckled grip. "This is not good."

"Can you do anything for them?" Tor asked.

"*Hmph.* Me?" Clucking her tongue, the old woman shook her head. "If Dr. Lupescu and Amara can't cast out the jorogumo, I certainly can't."

"Jorogumo?" Amara asked, sharing a wary look with Drasko.

"Spider demon," Nuniq said. "They are tricky beasts and hard to exorcise. They infect their hosts, slowly taking over their bodies until they transform into unholy arachnids."

Fuck. Dimitri blinked hard, praying to the Ancients he was having a nightmare and would wake soon. He swore again when he saw the old woman and Tor still scowling down at him.

He felt like a ten-pound bucket of bear shit for what he was putting his family through. Had he been a better protector, he wouldn't have let Tatiana get bitten by that spider. Now they were possessed by monsters. "H-how do we get rid of them?" He looked at the old woman with pleading eyes, praying she had an answer.

Her leathery face twisted like a balled-up piece of paper. "You need a witch."

A feeling of hopelessness made his chest ache and his breaths come in shallow gasps. "My stepmom is a witch, and she couldn't cast them out."

Clucking her tongue, Nuniq shook her head. "That's because they must be exorcised where they came from. If they escape into the mortal world, they will destroy civilization."

As if the news couldn't get any worse. He couldn't drag Tatiana into hell again, and he certainly wouldn't take his pregnant stepmom. "So you're saying we need to return to the haunted forest to dump these demons?"

Nuniq nodded.

Tor let out a mournful wail and stomped out of the room. Loud cracks, followed by heavy booms, sounded outside; Tor was uprooting trees. Dimitri wished he could shift and join him, but he didn't trust himself not to let the demon take over. It occurred to him that he couldn't feel or hear his wolf. Had the demon muted his shifting power? He ran his hands down his arms and then kicked aside the blanket when he felt something on his leg. Leather amethyst bracelets were chained around his ankles. That explained it. He knew full well Drasko was responsible, but how could he be angry with him? He would've done the same thing had Drasko been in his position. He hoped he'd be able to remove the bracelets before being sent into the forest. He'd need a way to protect Tatiana.

Tor returned from outside, his brown fur dusted with snow, steam pouring from his nostrils. "The Lupescus won't let them take Eilea into the forest."

"Tor's right," Dimitri said. "She's pregnant. My fathers won't let her go, and even if they did, I'm not risking my unborn baby brother's life."

"Amara's not going," Drasko said, shooting Dimitri and Tor a look that would melt steel.

Amara turned up her chin. "I will if it's the only way."

Drasko beat his chest like an ape. "You're not fucking going!"

"Amara is a healer, not a witch," Nuniq interjected. "You need someone with more powerful magic to cast out these demons."

Drasko's shoulders fell, and he wiped a bead of sweat off his brow. He offered Amara an apologetic look as she shot him eye daggers.

"Then who else can do it?" Tor asked.

"Your only other option is to unearth the djinn," Nuniq said, then took a big step back as if she expected Tor to pull the roof down on her head.

"The what?" Dimitri asked.

"Over my dead body!" Tor hollered. "That creature destroyed the Wolf-stalker elders."

Amara gaped. "Annie's fathers-in-law?"

A deep shudder rippled across Tor's fur, knocking the snow off. "The djinn made the alpha crazy and turned the gamma into a Chupacabra that murdered hundreds of humans."

"Great Ancients!" Amara squealed.

The old woman banged her cane on the floor. "She's their only hope."

Dimitri was so frustrated with all the crazy bullshit, it felt as if his head was about to explode. His growing urge to check on Tatiana only fueled his rage. "Can someone please explain what the hell a djinn is?"

"A genie," Nuniq said matter-of-factly.

"A genie?" Amara's expression was a mixture of horror and mirth. "Like in a magic lamp?"

"Only not like the fairytales." Tor puffed up his wide chest, his eyes blazing like twin suns. "This one is evil as sin. She will not do any favors for my daughter and her mates without something in return, and her cure is usually worse than the disease."

Nuniq tapped her forehead. "They must be smarter than the djinn and careful in wording their wishes."

Dimitri gulped back a lump of granite that had wedged in his throat. "And if we aren't?"

Tor gave him a look that made his flesh crawl. "Then your life will be over."

Chapter Two

HANDS BOUND IN FRONT of her, with two amethyst bands around her wrists, Tatiana sat upright in a narrow twin bed meant for a child. It reminded her too much of the cot she'd been chained to while captive to two sadistic demons. She'd been reduced to being a prisoner, entrapped by her family. Her alpha father Tor stood in the corner of the room in protector form, looking at her with such a forlorn expression, she got the feeling he was staring at a ghost. The old medicine woman, Nuniq, stood hunched over in a corner, chanting under her breath and waving a bundle of burning sage. Dimitri sat beside her, a strong hand resting on her arm. Though she hated the pity in his eyes, at least he didn't hate her. He should after what she'd done to him. But he didn't trust her. None of her family did, hence the reason she was chained up.

Memories of the demons Sitri and Balban chaining her while stealing her body flashed through her mind, making it hard to breathe, let alone think. To make matters worse, the pungent smell of burning sage filled her nostrils and made her want to vomit. She glared at Nuniq. Tatiana didn't know this woman very well, because she and her mates preferred to live off-grid, but she definitely preferred the woman's deceased aunt, Raz, to her.

Rip her eyes out, a sibilant voice resonated in her brain.

Shut the fuck up, she answered, knowing it was her unwelcome demonic guest.

She gaped at Dimitri, who had calmly explained the situation as if he was talking about the weather. Her mate confounded her. She'd just stabbed him in the heart, and he wasn't angry or afraid of her.

Releasing a slow breath, she did her best to process all he'd just told her. "Let me get this straight. There is a spider demon inside me, and I have to return to the haunted forest to get it out?"

Dimitri nodded.

"How, when Eilea and Amara healed me?"

"Their magic wouldn't be able to heal you," Nuniq said as she slowly moved forward, leaning over her cane. "It takes dark magic to cast out a jorogumo."

The demon hissed in Tatiana's head, sounding like a cornered serpent. *Jorogumo?* Tatiana shot Dimitri a pleading look. "I don't understand."

"You're turning into a black widow demon, Tatiana." Dimitri's shoulders hunched as if he carried the weight of the world. She'd never seen him look so dejected, not even during their time in the haunted forest.

"It explains why you tried to kill your mate," Nuniq said, eyeing her as if she expected Tatiana to strike her next. "It's common for female jorogumos to kill their mates after mating. Tell me...." The old woman stared at her as if she could see through her. "Do you know this demon's name?"

Don't tell her! the demon shrieked.

Vague memories came back to Tatiana, like the old tape reels her fathers showed her of their grandparents. She remembered calling Dimitri Amon and Dimitri calling her by a strange name.

"Morana!" she blurted. "And his demon is named Amon."

You bitch! Morana's cry made her sound like an injured cat.

"Good, good." Licking her lips, Nuniq straightened. "This will make it easier to cast them into the forest."

"I can't go back there." A deep shiver wracked her. "That place is hell. Literally."

"If you don't cast out the demons, your condition will worsen." The old woman pointed the tip of her cane accusingly at Tatiana. "You will both keep changing until you're spiders, and the protectors of our tribe will be forced to kill you."

Tor threw back his head with a primal roar, the sound of agony reflected in his voice enough to make her heart break all over again. "Nobody's laying a hand on our daughter!"

Nuniq frowned. "I'm sorry, Tor."

Fear pressed heavily on her chest like a dense fog, forcing her to breathe through a wheeze. This couldn't be happening. The one time she'd been stuck in that forest, she and Dimitri had almost capitulated to madness. How could they endure another such trial? "I can't go back there. I can't!"

"Tatiana, look at me." Leaning over her, Dimitri clasped her face in his hands. "We survived the Hoia Baciu before. I'll protect you."

She desperately searched his eyes, dismayed when she saw fear in them. "Who will stop me if I try to kill you there? We won't have Amara to heal you."

"You must take your other mates," Nuniq said.

"I can't put them through that."

"Too bad, because we're going," Dejan said as he came into the room with a platter of food. He set it on the nightstand beside her, grim determination in his eyes.

First of all, no way in hell was he going. Second, did he really think she could eat at a time like this? She fixed him with a hard stare. "No." The forest would destroy her sweet gamma. If the depression didn't eat at his soul, a demon surely would. She and Dimitri had barely escaped with their lives, and they had not returned unharmed.

"I'm not arguing with you." Dejan placed a napkin in her lap and sat beside her. "I've already decided."

Her heart plummeted, and she turned away when he tried to spoon feed her soup. "I can't eat right now, Dejan."

He held his hand under the spoon and it dripped into his palm. "You must keep up your strength if we're to survive the haunted forest."

"This whole plan is madness!" Tor boomed. "Did you not see what the djinn did to the Wolfstalker elders?"

Nuniq shrugged a bony shoulder. "They were fools."

"They are all dead save for one, thanks to her curse, and hundreds of humans were slaughtered."

Great goddess! Tatiana remembered what Annie had told her about the Wolfstalker elders going insane. So this was why? And this crazy old woman wanted them to unearth the same demon who'd destroyed them?

Nuniq's eye twitched as she looked at Tatiana, but this time her face was a blank slate, devoid of emotion. "They will have to make a deal with her."

"Are you mad?" Tor threw up his furry hands, smacking the top of the ceiling. "Who in hell makes deals with a demon?"

The old woman peered at him, seemingly unaffected by his rage. "Tor, she is their only hope."

Tor's bushy brow hung low, nearly obscuring his eyes. "Only Tyr Wolfstalker knows where she's buried, and he will not tell us."

The glint in Nuniq's eyes made Tatiana's flesh crawl. "He must." Her voice was so scratchy, like she was choking on sandpaper. "At the rate your daughter and her mate are changing, they will be full jorogumos by the next full moon, and our tribal protectors will have no choice but to kill them."

"DID YOU ENJOY YOUR soup?" Dejan asked, wiping Tatiana's mouth with a napkin.

She looked at him blankly, processing his words. She hadn't paid much attention to the food after her father took Dimitri out of the room, saying they couldn't be together too long. He didn't trust her not to hurt her mate again. The realization was like a rush of venom to her heart.

When he gave her an expectant look, she finally answered. "I love your cooking, Dejan, but I don't think I'm in a position to enjoy anything right now." She tried to offer him a smile, but the gloom in her soul made it impossible. "I'm sorry."

"It's okay." His frozen smile didn't mask the shadows in his eyes. "I understand."

An uncomfortable ache in her bladder forced her to roll on her side. "I have to pee." How the fuck was she supposed to use the bathroom with bound hands?

Standing, Dejan pulled a key out of his pocket with a trembling hand.

Of course he was afraid of her. She'd tried to kill him. He had a right to fear her. As if she couldn't loathe herself any more, now she had to deal with the guilt of scaring the sweetest gamma in the Amaroki.

"Your dad said I can unlock your cuffs if you need to use the bathroom." His hand shook when he fitted the key into the lock. He paused, looking at her with fear in his eyes. "I'm sorry, but we must leave the door open."

"Are you serious?" She hated the way he flinched at her tone.

He stood there with his hand hovered over the lock, palpable fear radiating off his skin. "And I have to watch."

She should have dropped it. Her gamma was already upset enough, but she couldn't help it. "What if I need to do more than pee?"

A bead of sweat dripped down his brow. "I'm following Tor's orders."

"This is ridiculous," she mumbled, hating herself even more for complaining, knowing that her gamma had no choice but to follow their chieftain.

"Are you ready?" he asked.

She nodded. "I'm sorry. I'll be good," she said, forcing a smile.

He expelled a breath, his shoulders slumping, and unlocked her wrists and ankles. She took a few moments to stretch her arms and legs. Damn those bindings.

When he helped her stand, she was surprised at the weakness in her limbs. She supposed it was a good thing she had little strength to fight, in case Morana took over her body again.

I don't need your strength. I have my own, Morana teased.

She shivered. Her parasite's voice was like poison to her veins. *Fuck off, spider.*

"Are you cold?" Dejan asked and draped a blanket over her shoulders.

"Thanks," she said, pulling it tight around her. She didn't deserve him.

She was shocked when Dejan knocked on their bedroom door and bolts were unlatched on the other side. Wow. Her family really didn't trust her. Her heart plummeted when Drasko greeted them in protector form, holding a gleaming silver axe. At least he had the decency to give her an apologetic look.

Her knees suddenly went weak.

Dejan wrapped an arm around her waist, holding her up against him. "She has to go to the bathroom."

"Okay." Drasko's thick brows knitted together. "You know the rules?"

She gritted her teeth, hating the way her family distrusted her, though she knew she deserved it. "I do."

"Where did my dad take Dimitri?" she whispered to Dejan as they walked down the hall to the guest bathroom.

"Basement," he answered.

So they'd vacated the master bedroom, no doubt because her family couldn't face the horrific aftermath. Or else they were waiting for someone to clean up the blood. She suspected the task would fall to Dejan.

"Does he have a protector at his door, too?" she asked.

He sighed. "Yeah."

"Great Ancients," she breathed. Were her fathers and brothers taking on all the work, or had they enlisted more protectors? She got the feeling her father wanted to keep her demonic possession under wraps. The rest of the tribe wouldn't be pleased to know demons lived among them. "When's Constantine coming home?"

"Within the hour," he said and opened the bathroom door.

"And then we fly to Texas?"

"Yeah." Dejan dragged a hand down his face. "I have to finish packing for everyone."

He looked more haggard than she'd ever seen him, with dark circles framing his eyes, a wan complexion, and frown lines around his mouth.

"I'm sorry I'm putting you through this," she said, willing the threatening tears to recede.

He pressed her hand tight between his large palms. "This isn't your fault."

She refused to answer, because he was wrong. This wouldn't have happened if she hadn't spent the past few months pretending everything was okay, that she didn't have a dark seed blooming within her. She'd known she wasn't right, but she'd lived in denial.

She sat on the toilet, her bones stiff after being tied up. After she finished, she wrinkled her nose at the smell of sweat and blood wafting from her body. "I stink. Am I allowed to take a shower?" She nodded toward the shower/tub with the decorative gray wolf curtain and Alaskan pines.

"Of course." Though he tried to hide it, he was trying not to breathe in too deeply, she reeked that bad.

She wanted to die. "But I have to leave the curtain open, right?"

His face flushed. "I don't mind cleaning the floor."

"Fine," she huffed. It wasn't like he hadn't seen her naked a hundred times before. She should be grateful her father was letting her gamma keep an eye on her and not her brother. That would've been mortifying.

He stood in the corner of the bathroom, looking uncomfortable. Normally when she stripped in front of him, his grabby hands were like magnets drawn to her breasts. Now he looked at her like he was waiting for her to slit his throat.

She turned on the faucet, waiting for the hot water to kick in, and then stripped off her bottoms, flannel pajamas he had probably put on her while she was sleeping. They would need to be washed, along with the rest of her clothes. She left on her striped underwear, deciding those would come off last. No doubt those smelled the worst after her rough sex with Dimitri. She unbuttoned her top and saw a red welt on her stomach about the size of her open hand.

She touched it, then nearly retched at the spongy feeling, like her skin was made of wet noodles. Gross. "What the fuck happened to my stomach?"

"I don't know." He took a hesitant step toward her and parted her shirt.

"It feels weird," she said. "Maybe it's a bruise."

He poked her abdomen with the tip of his finger, then quickly snatched his hand back. "Amara healed you while you were sleeping."

"Maybe she missed a spot," she said, though she knew she was lying to herself. Amara never missed spots. "What is it?" she asked, alarmed when he stepped away from her and pressed his back into the wall.

"It reminds me of the abdomen of a black widow."

Her knees buckled. *This isn't happening. This isn't fucking happening!*

"Maybe you should take a shower later." His gaze flitted to the open door, and she knew he was fighting the urge to run.

Of course, he wanted to run. She was turning into a fucking eight-legged demon!

"No." She spun around and jumped in the tub, grabbing a sponge. "I need to scrub this off." She ran the sponge under the water, not bothering to remove her shirt or underwear, and furiously scrubbed her abdomen, fighting back the bile that rose as her red, raised flesh rippled and bubbled like a cauldron of tomato soup. Tears of frustration ran down her face, and she scrubbed harder. The welt appeared to be growing, looking like a giant cherry birthmark was popping out of her stomach.

Dejan grabbed her wrist. "Tatiana, you can't scrub it off."

"I can!" She shook him off so hard, he stumbled and slammed into the door, causing it to slam shut.

She hadn't meant to hurt him, but she couldn't control herself.

"Tatiana," he said, massaging the shoulder that had taken the brunt of it. "Calm down."

She ignored his pleas, rubbing her abdomen like a madwoman, cursing and crying when the welt expanded even more.

"Tatiana!" Dejan hollered.

Panic numbed her brain, stripping her of all reason. "I can't get it off!" She looked to him with pleading eyes, as if he knew something that would help.

She jumped when the door banged open and splintered and Drasko came in wielding his axe. "Tatiana!" he bellowed, pushing Dejan out of the way as he marched up to her in protector form.

"Don't hurt her," Dejan pleaded, peering around Drasko's wide, hairy ribcage. "She's upset!"

Tatiana dropped the hem of her shirt and the sponge, and gaped at him as he clutched the axe in a white-knuckled grip, determination creasing his brow. "You would swing your axe at me, brother?"

Chest heaving like a wounded animal, he looked at the axe, then at her. "I love you, but if that demon finishes taking over your body, I will have no choice but to be the first line of defense for our tribe."

She swallowed. Of all of her brothers, Drasko was her favorite. After he'd taught her how to fish, they'd spent many memorable days on the water together. Had the time they shared meant nothing?

She looked at the sponge, its bubbles disappearing into the water that pooled at her feet. "I won't let it take over," she murmured softly. "I have too much to live for." At least, she hoped she did.

She barely managed to keep it together when Drasko said to Dejan, "You got this?"

"Yeah, man. I got this."

Cold air flowed in from the hall when Drasko stomped out. She picked up the sponge, refusing to remove her drenched top and underwear, and made quick work of cleaning herself the best she could while also driving back the darkness that threatened to consume her. She didn't dare touch that gross thing on her gut. So far she'd tried to kill Dejan and Dimitri and then her brother had threatened to kill her. Could she be brought any lower?

After scrubbing herself, she rested her palms on the tile wall and cried, her tears blending with the hot water as it washed over her. If only the shower could cleanse her soul of this monster.

Nothing will cleanse me from you. The beast's sibilant laughter echoed in her head. *Not even that djinn is powerful enough to purge my poison from your veins.*

Shut up, she answered. Refusing to let Morana make her lose her cool again, she clenched her hands, digging her nails deep into her palms until the skin broke. She didn't care about the pain. Her physical discomfort was eclipsed by the agony in her soul.

You will not win! she screamed in her head. *You will not destroy me!*

I already have, the beast answered.

Her heartbeat faltered, then threatened to beat out of her chest. Could Morana be right? Tatiana felt like a snowplow was rumbling through her head. Morana wanted her to believe she'd won, perhaps to discourage her from trying to cast her out. She wouldn't let her win. She couldn't!

"Tatiana," Dejan called. "It's time to get out."

She sucked in a sharp breath when he turned off the water. Flinging water and tears from her face, she slowly turned around.

He held out a towel. "Come on, *iubita mea*," he said, his voice tender, his eyes soft, his Romanian accent barely distinguishable.

She practically stumbled out of the tub, falling into his arms with a sob. Wrapping his arms around her, he sat on the toilet with her on his lap and let her cry on his shoulder. She shivered when the cold air made her gooseflesh rise, but she dared not move from his embrace. If he let go, she'd fall into that pit of despair again. His touch was the only thing keeping her tethered to sanity. If she was barely able to hold herself together, how would she endure another trip into the Hoia Baciu?

BY THE TIME DEJAN HELPED Tatiana into dry clothes and back into bed, she was an emotional and physical mess, exhausted from crying and in desperate need of rest. Mostly she wanted to be alone. She appreciated Dejan's support, but she hated the fear and pity she saw in his eyes. Not that she blamed him. As the gamma wolf, he couldn't defend himself if that monster took over her body again. Even if he could, he'd probably rather let Morana win than hurt her. She hoped Constantine came home soon. As a protector, he could defend himself, maybe even restrain her until the possession passed.

She gazed at Dejan through hazy eyes. "When's Constantine expected?"

"He'll be here any minute. Andrei's meeting us in Texas."

"I hope they hurry," she breathed, dismayed when he averted his gaze.

They held hands, the silence stretching between them more aggravating than a thousand banging cymbals. Relief swept through her when she heard truck tires crunching ice outside.

Jumping to his feet, he looked outside. "He's here!" He fell into the chair beside her bed.

It was then she realized how badly Dejan needed Constantine, too. Caught between his demonically possessed mate and brother, he'd no doubt been feeling immense pressure, and she hated herself even more for putting her sweet gamma through hell.

"Tatiana!" Constantine boomed downstairs. "Where is she?"

She thought she heard Amara's muffled voice, followed by Drasko's. What was taking so long? Was Drasko telling her mate that he'd almost had to butcher her with his axe? No, even her brother wasn't that stupid.

"Did anyone tell Constantine what happened?" she asked.

He grimaced. "Just that he needed to get home. They didn't want to tell him all of it until he got here."

Fuck.

It was several minutes before she heard his footsteps on the stairs, slow and heavy, like he was marching to a funeral. She could only imagine the horror he must be feeling at realizing his mate was possessed by a demonic spider.

The door flew open, and her alpha stood there, chest heaving, staring at her as if he was looking into her casket. When he wordlessly fell beside her in bed and took her in his arms, she sobbed in relief.

"I'm so sorry," she cried.

He held her tight, stroking her hair. "You are not to blame, *iubita mea*."

This only made her cry harder. She wasn't one to give in to her tears, but she couldn't control herself. She was on the verge of losing everything, and she had no idea if they'd be able to stop Morana. As she clung to him, digging her fingers into his back, her sobs grew louder.

"Tatiana, look at me." Constantine held her at arm's length, searching her eyes. "We need you to be strong."

"There's a demon inside me!" Her voice was as shrill as nails on a chalkboard. A demon that was already transforming her into a spider. She fought the urge to touch her stomach to see if it had grown.

He squeezed her shoulders so tight, she feared her bones would snap. "We're going to get it out."

She wiped her eyes with the back of her hand. "And if we can't?"

His face was as hard as iron. "We will not fail you, Tatiana."

For the first time since the stabbing, she felt relief, but it was short-lived. Constantine had never been in the forest. He had no idea the horrors that awaited them. Nobody did, until they felt the burn of its shields and the deep, dark depression of the gloom that shrouded their souls. Keeping her eyes focused on her alpha, she nodded, badly wanting to believe him.

Chapter Three

HOLDING TIGHTLY TO Tatiana's hand, Constantine glared at Tor, who was blocking their entrance to the military plane. Standing against the backdrop of a bleak Alaskan winter sky, an icy wind blew Tor's long, peppered hair across his chin as he held the silver axe like a medieval warrior. His mate's father had kept his weapon hidden until now. The moment he'd pulled the axe from his duffle bag, Constantine nearly lost his mind. What did Tor think to accomplish by bringing it? Even if Tatiana sprouted fangs and started spitting poison, Constantine would take the blade to his own heart before letting Tor harm her.

"If you try to use that on Tatiana," he said, "you'll have to get through me first."

"I know." Tor glared at him with glowing, yellow eyes. "And now so does Tatiana's demon."

"Come on, Constantine," Tatiana pleaded, tugging his hand. "It won't come to that."

It didn't matter. The damage had been done. Tatiana was crushed that her father would even consider butchering her. Constantine heard the sorrow in her voice.

With a growl, he shielded her from her father, hovering over her while she ascended the stairs.

Once inside the cabin, Tor motioned to Dimitri, who was already sitting at the front of the plane. "You ride in the back with Drasko."

"Yes, sir." Dimitri got up and trudged to the back.

Constantine flushed with anger at his brother's reaction. Curse the Ancients! He was a mighty protector, yet he cowered like someone who'd been beaten.

Tatiana peered at her father around Constantine's shoulder. "I'm not going to hurt him."

"No, you're not," Tor grumbled, pointing to a seat up front. "Sit."

Constantine seethed. "She's not a fucking dog."

"It's okay, sweetheart." She placed a hand on his arm, blinking up at him with glossy eyes while flashing a pained smile. She sat, curling into herself and staring out the window.

"Dejan and Constantine, you sit with her," Tor said.

"Where else would we be but with our mate?" Constantine asked querulously. He sat next to Tatiana, and Dejan chose the seat opposite him. When Tor dropped down beside Dejan, slipping his axe between the seat and the window, Constantine gripped the armrests and growled.

Drasko went down the aisle toward Dimitri, gripping an axe with white knuckles.

"What the fuck?" Constantine asked. He couldn't believe Tor and Drasko would threaten his mate and brother with axes. So much for family bonds.

Arms crossed, Tor issued Constantine a challenging look, tension radiating off him as thick as stew. Dejan's cheeks flushed, and he fidgeted with his seatbelt.

It was going to be a long flight.

TATIANA DIDN'T SAY much after their plane took off, but her drawn mouth and the panic in her eyes said everything. She was terrified, and Dejan couldn't blame her. Fuck, he was scared, too. Tor and Drasko emphasized the seriousness of the situation by bringing axes on the plane. Would they use them against Tatiana? He prayed they wouldn't have to find out. He looked over at Constantine, whose mouth and eyes were pinched tight, his fists curled into claws while he glared eye daggers at Tor.

Peace, brother, he projected to Constantine. *Your stiffness only fans the flames.*

Constantine turned eye daggers on him, his top lip pulled back in a predatory snarl. *What kind of father would use an axe against his daughter?*

Dejan cast a cursory glance at the weapon poking up beside Tor's armrest, the blade flashing like a warning siren. *I don't think he would.*

Then why bring it?

Maybe the axe is just there to scare the demon.

Constantine grumbled. Dejan wanted to believe his words were true, because if Tor tried to kill Tatiana, he and Constantine would have to fight for their mate—and the demon inside her. Then what? Would Tatiana turn on them if they survived Tor's brute strength? And what about Dimitri and Drasko? If Dimitri won, then Dejan and Constantine would be forced to fend off two demon-possessed wolves. Either way, they were fucked.

He tried to project calming messages to Tatiana, but she didn't respond. Her face remained a blank slate as if she couldn't hear him. Was their bond breaking, and if so, did that mean the demon had fully taken over?

Dejan caught Tatiana eyeing the blade more than once, the fear in her eyes making his heart plummet. He prayed it was enough to keep the demon at bay until they reached the Hoia Baciu.

Then there was the matter of the djinn. What the hell were they supposed to say to her? What if it was the wrong thing?

Tired of everyone glaring at each other, he summoned the nerve to confront his mate's father. "Tor," he said on a rush of air, "we need to know what we're up against. What about the djinn? Why is she evil?"

"I'd rather not talk about her in front of Tatiana." Tor's sternness momentarily softened as he gave his daughter a pitying smile. "I'm sorry, Tat."

"I understand." Feigning indifference, she shrugged. "I need to go to the bathroom." She unbuckled her seatbelt. "I don't think anyone else can fit in there with me either, but you can chop down the door if I take too long."

Tor's lips flattened into a thin line. "Do you think I want it to be this way, daughter?" His eyes flashed yellow. "For Ancients' sake, you stabbed your mate with a piece of glass!"

"Did I?" she asked acerbically, her eyes brimming with tears. "I hardly remember."

Constantine reached for her, but she jerked away from him as if she'd been scalded, then marched to the bathroom.

Tor heaved a long sigh, but then steepled his fingers and cleared his throat. "About sixteen years ago, the Texas Wolfstalker pack was ambushed by drug smugglers. The alpha and their mate were killed and their oldest boy injured."

Dejan nodded. "I've heard this story. Annie told Tatiana all about it."

"Yes, but what you haven't heard," Tor said, "was the curse the remaining Wolfstalkers brought on their pack when they unearthed the djinn."

Icy sludge coursed through Dejan's veins. "How?"

"Humans think genies are benevolent spirits. What they don't know is that djinns are demons trapped by ancient magic inside relics as a means of protecting the world from their evil. The old saying was that they granted wishes to whomever released them from their prisons."

Constantine leaned forward, clutching his armrests. "And did they?"

"Yes and no." Tor grimaced. "You've heard 'be careful what you wish for?' I'm certain it was a response to someone digging up a djinn. These demons always expect something for granting wishes."

"What did she get from the Wolfstalkers?"

"They never revealed what they did for her. I do know that when they dug up the djinn, she told them she couldn't bring back the dead, so they wished for a way to cope with the pain of losing their brother and mate. She made them belligerent, apathetic drunks. Worse, she made the gamma a werewolf-like creature at night. Locals called him Chupacabra."

"How do you know all this?" Constantine asked.

"I forced it out of Tyr Wolfstalker a few years ago," Tor said. "I wanted to ensure what happened to his brothers didn't happen again."

And they were putting Tatiana and Dimitri's lives in this evil bitch's hands?

Constantine raised an eyebrow. "So we have to be careful when asking her for wishes?"

"A demon has the power to cast out other demons. You need her to free them of this spider."

All moisture in Dejan's mouth evaporated, and he had to work hard to swallow. "What do you think she'll expect in return?"

"I don't know, but whatever she asks for, you must pay close attention to her wording, or she could end up stealing your soul."

JEZEBETH WOKE FROM fitful slumber to a strange yet familiar buzzing. Her breath caught in her throat when she saw her crystals were glowing. They hadn't done that in months, not since the day her precious flame had vanished.

She pushed the furs off her legs and rose from the lumpy feather mattress that had served as her bed the past few hundred years. On trembling legs, she took a hesitant step toward the stone hearth, then another, the buzzing growing louder. The crystals were cradled in an old iron cauldron that hung over the hearth, warmed by the flames from the eternal inferno below, a portal into a worse fate than being trapped in a lamp for eternity.

She gawked at the stones that shone with the brilliance of diamonds reflecting sunlight and saw a family of wolf shifters guarding a young woman, a pretty girl with long black hair, high cheekbones, and wide, almond-shaped eyes. Though she'd never met her, she recognized the dark aura that clung to her like a shroud and saw the web of evil a demon had used to ensnare her soul. The girl had been possessed by a jorogumo, and a powerful one at that.

A slow smile cracked Jezebeth's hardened features. The shifters would need her to cast out the beast. Jezebeth would use this opportunity to force their obedience. Though she'd already enacted revenge on the cruel shifters who'd wronged her, she still needed to reclaim what was hers: the rare flame that had been stolen from her bosom. If she discovered it had been extinguished, no god or demon would protect the shifter race from her wrath.

Chapter Four

NO SOONER HAD THEY landed at the military base in Texas than the butterflies in Tatiana's stomach became an angry hornet's nest. She looked out the window. With her wolf-touched vision, she saw Andrei, standing tall in his military uniform, waiting at the edge of the tarmac with her brother Luc, Agent Johnson, the big alpha Tatiana recognized as Magnus Wolfstalker, chieftain of the Texas tribe, and his tracker brother Jax. Both were tall with taupe skin, though Jax was leaner and had buzzed hair, like all trackers. They looked grim. No doubt they would soon fear and mistrust her as everyone else did, if they didn't already.

She followed Constantine off the plane. The moment the door opened and she stepped onto the stairs, she was surprised by the Texas heat. It was early March, and it wasn't sweltering, but it sure was a lot warmer than the weather she'd left behind. The landscape beyond the tarmac was brush and dried grass, all yellows and browns, a stark contrast to her Alaskan reservation home with its tall, snowy pines.

"Tatiana!" Andrei hollered, hurrying toward her.

"Andrei!" Tatiana followed Constantine down the stairs, then took off at a run, ignoring her father and Constantine, who called to her, when Andrei held his arms open. Her tracker mate was probably unaware that she was slowly turning into a demonic spider, but at the moment, she didn't care. She needed to be close to him.

He enfolded her in a fierce hug, spinning her before setting her down and kissing her senseless.

When she finally came up for air she blurted, "I didn't think you'd want to hold me."

"Don't be silly," he murmured, dragging calloused knuckles down her cheek. "I've been dying to hold you for almost three months."

"B-but didn't they tell you?"

Cupping her chin, he looked down at her with an unwavering gaze as thunderclouds darkened his eyes. "That some cursed demon is possessing you? They told me. That doesn't make me want you any less, love you any less. That only makes me want to fight harder for you."

"Oh, Andrei." Overcome with emotion, she buried her face in his chest. "I love you so much."

"We're in this together, baby," he cooed, stroking her back. "I promise we won't let this demon win."

"Thank you." She smiled up at him, momentarily lost in eyes as bright blue as a spring sky. His pale hair was cut so short, it resembled the fuzz on a peach, and his eyes held a confidence she hadn't seen before. He looked too handsome in his cleaned and starched camouflage uniform. Too bad she was a demon, because she would love to take him somewhere private and peel off his clothes. She was dying to hold him while he made love to her. If only there wasn't the risk of her trying to kill him.

They pulled apart when the rest of their family caught up. Her brother Luc gave her an awkward sideways hug before conferring with Tor and Drasko. He didn't even ask if she was okay. Constantine and Dejan hugged Andrei, giving him hard pats on the back and rubbing the fuzz on his head, and she was instantly jealous of their brotherly affection when Luc could hardly look at her. Dimitri tried to hang back, but Andrei refused to let him, forcing him to accept a hug.

Tatiana briefly locked eyes with Dimitri as he released Andrei. The panic and grief reflecting in his eyes made her heart feel like it was imploding. In that moment, as he held her captivated, her family's chatter faded into background noise, and there was no one else but Dimitri. She recognized this feeling as something she'd experienced before she'd stuck him with the glass shard, but this time she was more in control. Or maybe she suspected Morana wouldn't be stupid enough to try anything in front of a bunch of protectors.

I will take his blood and yours by the next full moon, Morana whispered in her mind.

Shut the fuck up. She fought to push Morana to the back of her mind and was relieved when she felt her retreat, like a spider withdrawing into a dark hole.

Dimitri, she projected.

Tatiana, he projected back.

Please be strong, she pleaded, unable to say more for fear of breaking down in front of everyone.

I'm using every ounce of my strength, he answered. *Believe me.*

Is the demon bothering you? she asked, fearing Amon tormented him, too.

I don't want to talk about it. He stared at the tarmac. *How are you holding up?*

Okay, I guess, she lied. Every second of every hour she felt like she was on the precipice of a breakdown, but she wasn't about to tell him that. She had to at least appear strong, even if she didn't feel it. Though she was tempted to press him for more answers, she decided to leave him alone. Acknowledging the demon was hard, much less talking about it.

I will do whatever it takes to save you.

I know. She used all her strength not to fall apart. *Just don't forget to save yourself.*

She wasn't comforted when he looked away.

He knows Amon is winning. Morana's sibilant laughter echoed in her brain. *He will consume him, just as I'm consuming you.*

ANDREI WAS DYING INSIDE. He was having a hard time grasping what Agent Johnson had told him, that his sweet mate had attacked Dimitri, but when he looked into Tatiana's and Dimitri's eyes, he could practically see the dark fog of their demons. They were more haggard and worn than he'd ever seen them, even more so than when they'd first escaped the Hoia Baciu. Their noses were swollen, their pallor gray, and their eye sockets looked like they were receding into their skulls.

He held tightly to Tatiana's arm while escorting her through the hangar and out onto the parking lot, following Magnus Wolfstalker, who'd barely said three words to him since picking him up. He hadn't just been upset. He'd been borderline hostile.

Tor barked orders, forcing Dimitri and Dejan to ride with Drasko, Jax, and Luc in Agent Johnson's large SUV.

The rest crowded into Magnus's truck, Tor sitting up front, his axe laid across his lap. He kept a watchful eye on them in the rearview mirror.

Tatiana seemed focused on her hands, which were fisted in her lap. She'd squeezed between Andrei and Constantine in back.

What the hell is up with the axe? Andrei projected to Constantine.

Don't ask, Constantine grumbled. His gaze shot to Tatiana. *But be ready in case he tries to use it.*

Fuck.

Andrei pulled Tatiana's hand into his lap and refused to let go when she tried to pull away. *I told you, we're in this together.*

Eyes glossy with unshed tears, she nodded. Her hand trembled in his, but she stopped fighting him, slumping in her seat and offering him a wobbly smile.

Magnus put the truck in drive and Tor said, "Thank you for meeting us here, and for your discretion."

"The Thunderfoots saved our Annie when she was a lone wolf," Magnus said, the steely edge to his tone a complete contrast to his declaration. "It's the least we could do."

Tor gazed out the window. "Please tell me you were able to find what we need."

"Our father Tyr refused to tell us, but Jax suspects he knows where it is."

"And that would be...?"

"In a cursed place," Magnus answered solemnly.

When Tatiana gasped, Andrei gave her hand another reassuring squeeze. He didn't know what to say without repeating himself, so he contented himself to be present for her, hoping he could infuse her with some of his strength. Everyone was on edge, not that he blamed them.

The silence in the cab stretched out like a long winter's night on the bleak Alaskan tundra as the chasm in his soul continued to widen.

Finally, Tatiana cleared her throat. "Where's Annie and the baby?" Her exuberance sounded forced.

Magnus shot her a look in the rearview mirror. "You can't go near them."

Andrei bristled, and he and Constantine growled.

"Oh. Of course." She sounded like a deflating balloon. His words had deeply hurt her, but she persevered. "How are they?"

"Fine," he said tersely, back stiff and eyes on the road.

Andrei pressed against her. *He's an ass. Don't let him get to you.*

He's a protector, and I'm cursed. He has a right to treat me like the enemy.

He rubbed her knuckles with the pad of his thumb. *You're not to blame for this.*

I'm a threat to the Amaroki, she said, shoulders sagging. *That's all that matters.*

THE SUN WAS SETTING, lighting the dusky sky in brilliant pinks and golds, when they drove along a narrow dirt road that twisted and descended toward a deep canyon. The truck following was not far behind. Tatiana was tired and hungry, but she didn't complain. Everyone was probably feeling the same way.

As if he could read her mind, Andrei pulled water bottles and granola bars from his backpack. "Want one?" he asked with a wink.

Constantine didn't wait to be asked twice. He snatched two bars and a water bottle from Andrei, ripping into them like a wolf with a bone.

She hesitantly took a granola bar, wondering if her queasy stomach would be able to handle it. "Were you reading my mind?"

"No." He laughed and elbowed her ribs. "Wolf-touched hearing, remember? I can hear your tummy rumbling. Sounds like you've got a pack of protectors in there."

"Thanks." She ate the bar in silence, barely noticing the flavor, which was a shame, because chocolate chip was her favorite.

When they reached the bottom of the canyon, Magnus took off his seatbelt and turned. "We shift and go the rest of the way on foot."

Tatiana thanked Andrei when he helped her out of the truck, her eyes widening when she saw they were near a ledge that overlooked the deep ravine below. How was she supposed to get down that on human legs? She'd have to shift.

She held up her hands, flashing her amethyst wrist bands. "I can't shift with these on."

Tor said, "You and Dimitri will remain in human form. The protectors will carry you."

She refused to argue. She didn't want to shift in front of them anyway. How would her father react if he saw that ugly red thing on her stomach?

Constantine said, "I'll carry Tatiana."

"No. You carry your brother." Tor's tone was unrelenting. "I will carry my daughter."

She pressed a calming hand to Constantine's chest when he growled. She was afraid but put thoughts of her father harming her out of her mind. He'd been her protector for twenty-three years, before she'd bonded with her mates. He wouldn't hurt her now, would he?

Don't trust him, Morana said. *He will toss your body over the side of the cliff without a second thought.*

Magnus, Jax, and Luc had already shifted and were heading down a side of the cliff. Her mates quickly stripped off their clothes and shifted, too. Constantine turned into a large, white protector that looked like the Abominable Snowman. Dejan and Andrei were majestic white wolves with gray ears. Her father and Drasko became mighty protectors with russet fur. She pressed back into Constantine when her father approached.

He offered a hand. "Come, Tatiana." He held his axe in his other hand. "You have nothing to fear."

Nervous laughter erupted from her. "But you obviously do."

"You are my child, and I love you." He stroked the flat end of the blade. "But you have to understand, as an Amaroki chieftain, my duty first and foremost is keeping our tribe safe. This isn't easy for me."

"Let's get this over with," she said, unable to look at him again.

When he tossed her over his shoulder and shuffled along the side of the cliff, she made the mistake of looking down and nearly lost what little food she had in her stomach. The drop-off was sharp. She couldn't see her mates, but she heard them behind her.

She smelled water not long before hearing the roar of the waterfall. It was several more minutes before mist dampened her face and clothes, and the roar was loud enough to diminish all other sounds. They reached the bottom of the canyon, where the waterfall ended in a deep blue/green lake that branched off into another stream farther along. When her father set her down on a ledge above a deep pool, her head felt like it was full of marbles, but she didn't complain. Her mates were here, Constantine as a protector, Dejan and Andrei still as wolves, and poor Dimitri, his hands in restraints. Why was he the only one tied up when she was obviously the most dangerous?

Constantine quickly pulled her to his side and draped a big, hairy arm around her shoulders. "You okay?"

"I will be. Just need to get my balance." She had no words to express how grateful she was to Constantine for his caring and consideration, even though she was demon-tainted. He'd showed her more devotion and understanding than her flesh and blood.

"It's beautiful here," she said, wiping moisture off her brow. "What is this place?" she asked nobody in particular, though Magnus was looking directly at her.

"Not far from where our mother and father were murdered by demons." He gave her an accusatory look, as if she was somehow connected to the drug runners who'd shot his family. "You should probably wait here while Jax and I search for the lamp."

Was the genie behind the waterfall?

"No," Tor said, "we're going with you."

"Suit yourself. Hope you're good swimmers." He and Jax dove into the water, splashing them all, and swam toward the waterfall, Magnus as a big, brown protector and Jax as a wolf with copper-colored fur.

Tor pointed at Dimitri and then at Tatiana. "You stay here. Drasko and Luc will watch you. Constantine comes with me."

Constantine shot Drasko an accusatory look. "Tatiana goes where I go."

Drasko stomped a big foot. "As if I'd hurt my own sister."

Constantine said nothing as he glared at Drasko's axe.

"Fine," Tor growled. "Stay here. I will follow Magnus."

Constantine rubbed his furry chin. "So you and Magnus are going to negotiate with this demon?"

Tor stomped over to Constantine, lips pulled back in a feral snarl. "Do not doubt your chieftain."

"Father!" Tatiana scolded, pushing between them. "My life is on the line. I think I should go, too."

Tor let out a string of curse words before dragging a hand down his furry face. "You and Constantine can go, but do not make a deal with the bitch without consulting with me first."

She quickly said goodbye to Andrei and Dejan, then cautiously approached Dimitri, hating how her father and Drasko hovered behind her. She could practically feel the phantom hacking of their axes through her spine.

She reached for him slowly, and they entwined their pinky fingers.

"Be safe," he whispered.

She swallowed back her sorrow. "You, too."

When he brushed his lips across her forehead, it took all of her willpower not to break down.

"You ready?" Constantine asked.

Her heart leapt into her throat. She wasn't much of a swimmer. "Not really." But she didn't want to make her family wait. She slipped off her shoes and jeans, but left the rest of her clothes on. Nobody questioned her modesty. She feared that thing on her stomach was spreading.

When Constantine tugged her hand, she had no choice but to follow, screaming when they soared through the air and she broke through the surface with an ungraceful smack. The water was colder and blacker than she'd expected. She shot up above the surface with a gasp. Constantine had already surfaced and was shaking moisture from his hair while treading water.

"You okay?" he asked.

Repressing a shiver, she nodded.

She heard a distinct *thunk*, then her hairy protector father swam past them toward the waterfall that splashed into the aquamarine water, causing foamy bubbles to rise to the surface. Were they planning to go through it?

Tatiana followed reluctantly. What if they couldn't find the djinn? Or worse, what if she refused to help them?

"The current is strong," Magnus called to them as he floated precariously close to the foam. "It's easier to dive deep beneath it and then swim back up."

She held her breath as Magnus and Jax dove under the surface, then slowly released it when their heads bobbed up behind the roaring curtain of water.

Tor swam toward them, the head of his axe slapping the water with each stroke. "Our turn."

Tatiana accidentally swallowed water. It had a strong mineral taste.

Constantine held out a hand to her. "Let me take you, *iubita mea.*"

"I can take her," Tor said.

She wrapped her arms around Constantine, warily eyeing her father.

Tor stopped, frowning. "I would not hurt you, daughter."

She vehemently shook her head and clung even tighter to Constantine. What had he been expecting? That axe he carried practically had her name and face carved into the handle.

When they reached the waterfall, the boom of the rushing water was so powerful, she felt as if her skull was being filled with concrete.

"Take a big breath," Constantine yelled, his deep protector voice barely carrying over the din.

She clung to his wide, hairy neck, then sucked in a scream when he dove. The current was stronger than she imagined, pounding her bones like she was being pulverized by a giant meat tenderizer. She clung tightly to Constantine while he dove deep beneath the falls, praying he wouldn't let go as the water beat down on their backs. The sound of rushing water filled her ears like a thousand hurricanes were swirling around in her brain. Clutching tightly to his neck, she dared not open her eyes for fear of what she might see.

They swam so deep the sound abated, and she panicked that she'd run out of breath before they surfaced.

I need air! she projected to him.

Almost there. Hang on!

The roar of the water grew louder as he bolted up like a torpedo. The current bounced off her backside, burning her skin like the onslaught of an avalanche. Just when she thought they'd almost reached the surface, there was a loud crunch, and they were knocked back. She lost hold of his neck and flailed against the relentless current. Her eyes flew open, and she stared into an inky black abyss, and swallowed water while screaming for help. Her heart beat hard, and her lungs burned so badly, she feared her chest was on the verge of splitting open.

She let the water take her, thinking perhaps it was for the best if she died. Then strong arms hauled her to the surface and deposited her on a rocky shore. The waterfall thrummed loudly behind her. She vomited water, then heaved so hard her head spun. She didn't know whether to be grateful or perturbed to see her father's silhouette hovering over her. Her eyes slowly adjusted to the dim light.

Still in protector form, his matted fur dripped water on her face. "You okay, *iubita mea?*" he asked loudly above the din, sounding like a bear waking up from slumber. He smoothed a wet lock of hair off her forehead.

She flinched when he set the silver axe on the ground beside him.

He still wants to kill you, Morana hissed. *Next time he will let you drown.*

She didn't have the strength to answer.

She thought she heard Constantine cry her name, but she was too sick and dizzy to respond.

"I'm sorry." He wedged in beside her father. A gash on his head was bleeding into his white fur. "I hit my head on something."

When he gave Tor a side-eyed glare, her limbs went numb with fear. Had her father struck Constantine with his axe?

"You swam into the ledge." Magnus scowled down at them, crossing furry arms over a wide chest. "I watched you hit it."

She blinked at her alpha. "It's not your fault," she rasped. Even the act of speaking was torture. Her lungs were still burning.

Constantine pulled her onto his lap, and she wiped blood off his brow. "You need medical attention."

"It's nothing."

It was not nothing, but they didn't have first-aid kits, so it would have to wait.

They were inside a wide cavern with dark, moss-covered walls and rocky ground. Between them and the opening was a high mound of oblong, gray stones that reminded her of a hill of skulls.

She squinted and looked more closely. *Were* they skulls?

Whimpering like a wounded animal, Jax paced, his tail tucked between his legs, water dripping from his wet fur. Why was he so upset? She didn't see any blood, and he wasn't limping.

"What is this place?" Constantine asked.

"It's where our father Sami discarded his human kills," Magnus said.

The breath expelled from her lungs as she tightened her grip on Constantine. "Great Ancients."

"You think the djinn is here?" Tor asked.

Magnus said, "We began to suspect it after Tyr begged us not to come here again."

Tor held up a silencing hand. "Listen. Do you hear that?"

A distant buzzing sound emanated from the ground beneath her. She and Constantine rapidly stood, gaping as if it was made of lava.

Tor pointed at the pile of human remains. "It's coming from under the skulls. Stand back."

Fuck. Before her legs gave way, she sank back down onto her knees, too overcome with fear and shock to stand.

Tor and the other alphas threw the skulls into the water. They splashed with hard *plunks*, disappearing into a black, watery graveyard. Her stomach churned as she wondered how many of them had family mourning their disappearance, not to mention none of them would receive a proper burial. She prayed that those humans were able to pass on to their version of heaven and find peace.

After several minutes they made a wide dent in the skulls. Jax scurried under a pile and reappeared with what looked like a rusty gravy boat in his mouth. Tor snatched it from him, and Constantine took it from Tor.

"How do we summon her?" he asked.

Magnus rubbed his chin. "If the ancient stories are correct, you rub it." He gave Constantine a dark look. "Are you sure you want to do this?"

"Magnus, we don't have a choice." Tor jutted a finger toward the waterfall. "If you and your brother want to leave, we won't hold it against you."

"No, we'll stay." Magnus grunted, kicking up pebbles like a bull preparing to charge. "I want to see the bitch who destroyed our family."

Constantine cradled the lamp against his chest like a father protecting a newborn. "Now's not the time for vengeance."

"I know." Magnus's hooded eyes narrowed. "I will not harm her—yet."

"Constantine, listen." Still clutching that damned axe, Tor laid his other hand on Constantine's shoulder. "Do not make a wish until you confer with me, understood?"

"You've told me this at least three times already," Constantine snapped.

The chasm between her family was widening, and she didn't know how they could ever repair it.

Tatiana's world came to a grinding halt as she watched Constantine rub the lamp, and it shot out of his hands like a rocket, crashing to the ground with a loud *clank*, smoke pouring from the spout. Coughing, they fanned the acrid smell away.

A woman with taupe skin, long, thick black hair plaited on top of her head, and large tapered emerald eyes materialized in front of them. A skimpy top barely covered her breasts, and a low-cut skirt clung to curvaceous hips, leaving little to the imagination. She was as beautiful as a goddess, and judging by the gleam in her eyes, as seductive as a siren.

She batted impossibly thick lashes at Constantine. "Thank you for freeing me from that infernal prison." She bowed low before him, giving him an eyeful of generous cleavage. "I am Jezebeth, an ancient and wise spirit guide."

Clenching his hands, Magnus stood beside Constantine. "You are a djinn, a deceptive demon."

Nostrils flaring, she licked full lips. "You smell like a Wolfstalker. You must be Raine. Your fathers told me all about you."

"Wrong," Magnus growled.

Her eyes widened. "You can't be Magnus, unless you found a witch skilled enough to grow back a hand."

His gaze faltered for a heartbeat before he looked at her like a lion ready to pounce on his prey.

"You did?" Squealing, she clasped her hands together. "Well done!" When he didn't answer, she plastered on a contrite expression, her bottom lip turning down in a pout. "To what do I owe the honor, Magnus?"

Magnus waved a fist in the air. "You fucking bi—"

"Magnus, enough!" Tor roared and pushed Magnus behind him.

Magnus reminded her of a volcano on the verge of exploding, but he remained behind Tor and stayed silent.

"Ohh," Jezebeth cooed, turning her eyes on Tor. "What a mighty protector you are. You must be the Alaskan chieftain."

How much did this djinn know about the Amaroki? The elder Wolfstalkers either had big mouths or the genie had tricked them into revealing shifter secrets. Either way, it didn't bode well for them that she knew so much about their race.

She floated over to Tor like a balloon tethered to a string, the tips of her slippered feet pointing back toward the lamp. A thin wisp of that reminded Tatiana of the smoke trails left behind airplanes stretched from her feet to the lamp. It was then Tatiana realized this genie was attached to her lamp like a dog on a leash.

"How do you know so much about our race?" Tor thundered.

"The Wolfstalkers told me everything," she teased in a sing-song voice. "Didn't you know we were very, very close?"

Magnus and Jax let out howls that echoed across the cavern. Tatiana had to cover her ears until they faded.

"We are in need of your assistance," Tor said.

She touched her temple. "Don't tell me you need me to free your she-wolf of her demon?" She looked at Tatiana for the first time, flashing a fanged grin that made her flesh crawl.

"Y-you know?" Tor stammered.

"I can see her dark aura." Linking her hands in front of her, she smiled at Tatiana like a mother doting on her child. "Why don't you use the witch who grew back Magnus's hand?"

Tor cleared his throat. "She was a healer, not a witch."

"I see." She gave Tatiana a long, thoughtful look. "That demon isn't just possessing you, she's poisoning you, changing your composition from the inside out. Soon your bones will break and reform, you'll sprout hair all over your face and back, and your teeth will drip a deadly venom."

Tatiana didn't know if the look of pity Jezebeth gave her was sincere or not, but it didn't matter. The djinn was right. She was changing. Her growing, fleshy red abdomen was proof. She willed herself not to vomit.

No use fighting it. The djinn won't help you. Give in now, and I will make the transition painless. Morana's words were like piercing daggers.

She gritted her teeth. *You're not taking me without a fight, demon bitch.*

"She's talking to you now, isn't she?"

Tatiana's gaze shot to Jezebeth. She thought about lying, but something in the way she looked at her, almost as if she was looking into her soul, told Tatiana the trickster genie would know.

Not trusting herself to speak, she nodded.

"She gains power when you are most vulnerable, when you are not in control of your body."

"When I'm sleeping?" Tatiana asked.

"No." She grinned and glanced at Constantine. "When you are fucking."

Heat fanned her chest and face. It made sense. She'd stabbed Dimitri after sex, after the beast had begun to take over. Unable to stand the amusement in Jezebeth's eyes, she looked down.

Constantine knelt beside her and kissed her forehead.

Thank you, she projected. She was unworthy of his affection, but she cherished it, for however long she'd have it.

Tor cleared his throat. "We have resurrected you to do one thing," he said, "and one thing only. Expel the demons from my daughter and her mate."

Jezebeth looked at him like a petulant child who'd just been scolded for stealing candy. "No."

The hair on the back of Constantine's nape stood on end. "No?"

She folded her arms, pushing her breasts up until they practically fell out of the skimpy top. "Not unless you agree to my request first."

"Don't bargain with her," Magnus said hastily.

"Hmm." Jezebeth looked lost in contemplation. "I'm afraid you wolves don't have a choice, since I'm the only one who can extract the demons."

Magnus stomped so hard, the walls shook, and debris fell on their heads. "You must find another way."

"The demons will have taken over by the next full moon." She turned to Magnus, her smile fading. "Besides, it's not them I wish to bargain with, it's you."

His jaw dropped. "What do you want from me?"

Flames rose around the djinn's feet, and her skin turned crimson. "To right the wrong done by your fathers." Her voice was deep and menacing.

"You deceptive bitch!" Magnus waved a fist at her. "You destroyed my fathers!"

Her face morphed from crimson to purple, and her eyes shifted from green to fiery red. "What I did to your fathers was payback for the pain they inflicted on me, the pain I still suffer because of their cruelty." Her voice cracked and she bit down on her hand.

Tatiana wasn't sure if this was an act or if the djinn was truly hurting. What could they have done to her?

Magnus wasn't buying it. "You turned Sami into a monster and Vidar into a raging drunk. You ruined their lives. You ruined *all* our lives!"

Her features transformed into something horrific, reminding Tatiana of a decaying corpse. "Those curses I would've gladly lifted had they returned what they took from me."

Nostrils flaring, Magnus stormed up to her. "They took nothing from you."

She let out an unholy wail, her face drooping like a melting ball of wax. The entire room shook, and skulls rolled into the water. "They. Took. Everything!"

Chest heaving, Magnus actually had the courage to turn his back on her. "She's a deceiver," he said to Tor. "I will not bargain with her. She will curse me like she cursed my fathers."

Jax howled his agreement.

Constantine stood, glaring at Magnus. "Then my mate and brother are doomed."

"I'm sorry." Magnus's shoulders fell. "It cannot be helped."

Morana's laughter resonated in Tatiana's skull. "No!" she cried, gripping her hair by the roots, feeling as if the gates of hell had opened and were about to swallow her whole.

Constantine moved toward her. "Jezebeth, what did they take from you?"

"Constantine," Magnus warned, "get away from her. Don't be fooled by her tears. Demons have no feelings."

"Jezebeth." Constantine ignored Magnus's warning. "Please tell us."

She floated above Constantine so he had to look up at her. "For thousands of years I've lived a bleak existence, trapped in this prison." She motioned toward the lamp. "But I'd gladly trade a thousand years of boredom for the past fifteen years of agony. They took from me my heart, my soul."

"Demons have no hearts!" Magnus roared.

She turned up her chin, a queen sneering at a peasant. "Once I would've agreed with you, but that all changed the day I birthed my daughter."

Tatiana gasped. Magnus swore. Jax howled.

Constantine and Tor shared wide-eyed looks.

"You have a child?" Tor asked.

"I did until Vidar and Sami took her from me." Her eyes welled with tears. "She was perfect in every way, and they called her an abomination!" Crying out, she buried her face in her hands, shoulders shaking while she sobbed profusely.

Well, holy fuck. Were the Wolfstalker elders the fathers? Had they bred a demon wolf shifter?

The look of horror in Tor's eyes reflected how Tatiana felt. "You mated with the Wolfstalkers?"

Magnus snorted. "More like she seduced them."

"I didn't seduce them," she snapped. "I granted their wish by transforming into the image of their dead mate." She flashed a seductive smile, smoothing a hand down her hip. "I couldn't help it they wanted to bed me after that."

Tor remained surprisingly calm. "Where is the child?"

"I don't know." She wiped her tear-stained cheeks. "She was an infant when they took her."

"What was her name?" Tor asked.

Her eyes lit with a mother's pride. "Phoenix. Born of the ashes to a cursed mother, yet her flame burned brightly."

Magnus charged her until she backed up against the pile of skulls. "What do you want from me?"

She squared her shoulders, looking defiant. "Find Phoenix and bring her to me. First you will swear a blood oath you will not let any harm come to her. Then you must raise her, provide for her, and teach her the ways of the Amaroki."

"And if I can't find her?" Magnus asked. No doubt he wasn't thrilled to learn he had to take care of a half-demon sister.

Her skin turned ashen as the ugly corpse demon appeared again. "Then your friends will turn into spider demons."

"What if he can't find her in time?" Tatiana asked. "The demons will take over by the next full moon." If she truly had developed a heart, then surely she would show Tatiana some sympathy.

"I know all about your trackers," she snapped, giving Tatiana a cool glare. "You can find her in a few days."

"We will find Phoenix and vow no harm will come to her." Constantine splayed his hands. "But before we give her back to you, you must cast these demons out of my mate and brother."

She wagged her finger at him. "Do you honestly expect me to trust you wolves after you stole my daughter? You will save my child first, or there is no deal."

"We're wasting time," Tor grumbled. "We need to find the girl."

Jezebeth blocked Tor. "You must take me with you."

"No!" Magnus yelled.

"I don't trust you not to harm her." She turned on him with a snarl. "Take me with you or we're finished talking."

"If you deceive us, I will make your pathetic life even more miserable," Magnus promised. "I'll follow you into the pit of hell if need be. I will rip out your heart and make you watch me eat it!"

Her eyes narrowed to glowing, red slits. "And if you deceive me, the curse I place on your souls will pale in comparison to the curses I inflicted on your fathers."

Chapter Five

TOR FOLLOWED MAGNUS and Jax into the smoky bar, irritated with Jezebeth for refusing to heal his daughter first, angry with Tyr Wolfstalker for making them hunt him down, and furious with himself for his handling of the whole thing. Tatiana was going to be mentally scarred after this, if she wasn't already, and she'd never forgive him for his role in keeping the Amaroki safe. What else was he to do? He was the chieftain, and the demon in her head was a threat to society.

He doubted he'd have the strength to bring the axe down on his daughter, but the demon didn't need to know that.

Drasko and Luc fanned out behind him, stalking through the room like lions following their prey through the reeds.

He smelled Tyr before he saw him. Tyr was the drunkest patron at the bar, practically hanging off his stool and banging on the counter for another drink.

The bartender, a pretty Hispanic woman with shoulder-length purple-frosted hair, scowled at Tyr while putting glasses on the shelves.

"Hey!" he hollered, banging the glass so hard, Tor was surprised it didn't shatter. "Didn't you fucking hear me?"

When the bartender curled her fingers around a can of mace, Tor stepped up and held out a staying hand. "Sorry about him. I'll handle it." He tossed a twenty on the bar. "And he'll have coffee. So will I."

He sat next to Tyr, and Drasko and Luc stood behind them, boxing in the drunk. Tyr had a scar on his temple that Tor didn't recognize and another on his chin, and he wondered if he'd gotten those during his service as an Army tracker. Shifters healed faster than humans, which meant these scars had to have been deep. Tor had heard from Agent Johnson that he'd had to put Tyr on leave for fighting with the other trackers.

Tyr sulked into an empty beer mug. "What the fuck do you want?"

Tor fought the urge to slam Tyr's head against the bar. He was bone tired and in no mood to argue. "Where is she?"

Tyr reached for a bowl of peanuts, the vein above his brow twitching though he feigned disinterest. "Who?"

"Don't play dumb. It won't end well for you."

Grinning, Tyr shoved a fistful of peanuts into his mouth.

Reaching over Tyr's shoulder, Magnus snatched the bowl of peanuts from his beta father's hand. "The demon spawn you and our fathers sired with that djinn."

Tyr spit out a mouthful of peanuts, coughing and gagging. "First of all, I didn't fuck the demon bitch, my brothers did. Second, the demon spawn is dead."

"You're lying," Magnus snapped, his eyes shifting to blinding gold. "Where is she?"

When the bartender set down a steaming cup of coffee, Tyr swallowed several mouthfuls, avoiding eye contact with everyone. He set down the cup with a trembling hand. "Listen to me." He slapped his chest with a snarl. "She's been hidden for her own good. For the benefit of all."

Tor stood, hands on the back of the stool, sorely tempted to smash it over Tyr's head. "Your *brothers'* demon lover will curse us if I don't bring her back, and she'll let Tatiana and Dimitri die."

Tyr dragged a hand down his face. "Fuck."

"Where is she?" Tor pressed. "Where is Phoenix?"

He let out a resigned sigh, shoulders caving inward. "The only place she'd be safe from the world, and the world would be safe from her."

"No more fucking riddles." Barely able to contain his rage, Tor worked to unclench his teeth as his protector clawed to break free and smash his face in. "You will tell us where to find her."

"Very well," Tyr said, "but don't say I didn't warn you." He scribbled an address on the back of a napkin, handing it to Tor.

Disgusted, Tor snatched the napkin and turned his back on him, marching out of the smoky hellhole with long strides.

As soon as the door closed behind him, Tor breathed in the fresh, warm air, wishing he could purge the stinky ashtray smell from his clothes.

"Wait!" Tyr called as soon as they reached the truck. He pulled a faded photograph out of his wallet and slapped it in Tor's hands.

It was a picture of a beautiful, smiling girl with tawny skin and black pigtails who couldn't have been more than thirteen, linking arms with an old, stooped nun. The latter held a rope tied to a donkey. His chest tightened when he recognized Jezebeth's features. "She looks just like her mother."

Tyr nodded. "You'd better pray she doesn't act like her, too."

TATIANA SAT ON THE Coyotechaser's porch beside Constantine and watched the sun set. She was glad he was in human form and not a mighty protector; that he felt comfortable enough to be human around her meant he didn't fear her. Watching her father carry an axe was torture enough. Dejan and Andrei were inside, cleaning up the kitchen after they'd eaten takeout tacos in silence. They were also packing food for tomorrow, since they weren't sure when or if they'd find any on their journey.

Though her mates had sworn off alcohol, Constantine was drinking vodka, and she wasn't about to scold him as he nursed the bottle. Andrei and Dejan had snuck vodka in their sodas during dinner. They probably thought she hadn't noticed, but she was watching them closely, praying they wouldn't become addicted again after their battle with the substance.

Her heart ached for Dimitri. He was sleeping in the barn tonight with her father, Drasko, and Luc after her father had forced them to separate after supper. They also had Jezebeth with them. Tatiana imagined the djinn was probably tormenting them, possibly seducing them. The hair on the back of her neck stood on end when she thought of Jezebeth trying to tempt Dimitri. He had hardly spoken to her during supper, and she was afraid the chasm between them would only widen. Though he'd said he didn't blame her for stabbing him, she couldn't help but wonder if he resented her. Or maybe Amon was getting to him. She hoped he'd stay strong, and if they survived their ordeal, their love would recover.

"You okay?" Constantine murmured in her ear, wrapping an arm around her.

She relished his warm, possessive grip, wanting him to carry her into the bedroom and make love to her, but she didn't trust Morana not to start trouble. "I've got a lot on my mind," she said hoarsely, resting her head on his shoulder. Had Amara been with them, she would've healed Tatiana's sore throat. It still burned from nearly drowning under the waterfall.

He tenderly brushed his lips across her temple. "I know you do, *iubita mea.* I'm here for you."

Her heart swelled. How did she deserve such a loyal and loving alpha? She planted a kiss on his cheek and adjusted the bandage on his head, thankful the blood had stopped flowing. A quick peak under his bandage, revealed wolf-kind healed faster than humans. Already the gash had started scabbing over. "You're the best protector a wolf girl could ask for."

When he turned her hand over and gently planted a kiss on her palm, she jerked free, cursing her libido when moisture soaked her panties.

"Not now, Constantine."

He arched a brow, flashing a devious grin. "Why not?"

She rolled her eyes. "Uhh, because I have a demon inside me who takes over when I'm having sex."

He nuzzled her neck, purring like a cat. "I'm not afraid of a demon."

You should be, Morana said.

Tatiana loathed that voice in her head so much, she wanted to scream, but she kept her composure. If she lost her cool, the demon would win.

Constantine nibbled her ear. "We've got the whole house to ourselves. I won't let the demon hurt us."

The Coyotechasers were on a beach vacation, so Tatiana and the rest of her mates were alone. Even though the Coyotechaser's mate, Ilona, was also her mates' kind aunt, she was relieved they were gone. She doubted they would've allowed Dimitri and her to stay here and endanger their children.

Children are delicious, Morana taunted.

That's what some demon will be saying about you soon enough, she said. *I hear grilled spider is a devil's favorite snack.*

Her demon shrieked and then went quiet. Good. She couldn't wait to rid herself of this parasite.

She stiffened when the sliding barn door creaked open and Magnus and her father, both in human form, headed toward the house. She hoped they weren't planning a visit. She was in no mood to deal with their dark moods. They'd both been angrier than bears waking too soon from hibernation since leaving the waterfall. Her father still carried the axe, which was beginning to look like an extension of himself. Was he enjoying torturing her? Because that's all she felt when she saw it: pure torture. The worst part was her demon didn't seem upset, so if his purpose was scaring the spider, he was failing miserably.

"What if she's lying and won't help us?" Magnus grumbled as he trailed Tor. "It would be like a djinn to deceive us."

"She will, because she fears for the safety of your sister."

"My sister?" Magnus halted, looking as if he'd just accidentally swallowed a bug. "That demon spawn is *not* my sister."

Well, damn. Tatiana didn't even know this girl, and already she felt sorry for her. Maybe she was an evil trickster like her mother, but he didn't know that yet. He'd probably be anything but brotherly when they finally found her.

Tor turned to face Magnus. "I'm tired and need rest. I'm not going to argue with you, and I need to talk to my daughter and her mates."

He left Magnus stewing on the gravel sidewalk and came up the stairs, feet dragging as if they were weighted with bricks. Whatever he had to say, he was obviously not looking forward to it.

Constantine released her and stood. "What is it?"

She got up, too, and grabbed Constantine's hand, feeling the tension radiating off him in waves.

"We leave tomorrow at dawn," Tor said, his gaze fixed on Constantine and not even sparing a glance in her direction. "We're flying in a military helicopter to Mexico."

"Is that where she is?" Constantine asked.

"Yes. Tyr told us."

"Okay." Constantine tugged her toward the door. "We need to get to sleep."

When Tor cleared his throat, intuition told her there was about to be trouble.

"You and your brothers will take turns keeping watch." He pulled a set of black handcuffs from his pocket and dangled them in front of him. "Tatiana must be bound, and this must be within your reach."

Tatiana's world spun when he thrust his axe forward with the other hand.

Constantine's eyes shifted to brilliant white, and he let out a roar that shook the porch. "You fucking dare!"

Her heart practically leapt into her throat. She didn't want her mate and father fighting over her. The screen door slammed, and she glanced over her shoulder at Dejan and Andrei.

Help, please, she projected to them. *I don't want a fight.*

There won't be, Andrei said.

Dejan didn't answer as he stood behind Constantine. Hadn't he heard her? Or was he ignoring her?

Tor remained surprisingly calm. "You have no idea the power a fully turned jorogumo wields or the death and destruction that will follow in her path if you let her escape."

Tatiana swallowed bile. Great Ancients, he spoke as if she was already a demon.

It won't be long, Morana teased.

"We will not let her escape," Constantine said stiffly.

Tor thrust the axe at him. "Take it."

Constantine stepped back, his nose and chin lengthening. "No, you take it, and shove it up your ass!"

Constantine, please, she projected to him. *Don't fight with my father. Just take it.*

No, Tatiana. His refusal was like a gong in her ears.

"At least bind me," she said aloud, holding her hands out.

Constantine jerked her arms back. "No!"

"A full jorogumo can break bindings," Tor said.

She shot him a glare. "So why do I have to wear the cuffs?"

"That's the first line of defense." Tor's voice sounded hollow. "The axe is the second."

Constantine let out a howl. When her other mates joined him, her heart felt as if it had shattered.

Nostrils flaring, the look he gave Tor reminded her of a caged animal. "She's not supposed to turn until the next full moon."

"We can't take chances." When Tor looked at Tatiana, there was no mistaking the pity in his eyes. It was as if she was already dead.

Her mouth suddenly felt more parched than the Texas desert, and she had to work hard to breathe, much less speak. She didn't want to admit it, but her father was right. The demon inside her was too unpredictable.

She pulled Constantine's hand to her chest. "Look at me. Let's save our strength for the bigger fights ahead."

His face fell. "It's not right."

"I love you." She took the cuffs from her father and handed them to Constantine. "It's okay."

He shoved them in his pocket, then snatched the axe from Tor. "Aren't you worried your daughter will never forgive you?"

Tor shrugged. "I don't think I'll forgive myself." He gave Tatiana one last woeful look and joined Magnus on the walkway, plodding back to the barn as if he was walking behind a funeral procession.

That's when Tatiana realized he didn't think she'd survive.

You won't. The spider laughed.

TATIANA TWISTED IN bed, trying to shake out a cramp in her side. The handcuffs were digging into her wrists. Constantine was in the shower across the hall. Knowing he was so close and also naked, probably lathering up his big cock and bulging muscles, did little to ease her discomfort. She hadn't had sex with him since he'd left for his shift in the oil fields. What she wouldn't give to make love to him. It had been even longer with Andrei, who'd been at basic training for what felt like years. He'd been the first to take a shower. His scent had hit her hard when he'd first come out of the bathroom. Trackers were so virile and clever, and incredibly feral in bed. She heard him in the kitchen, getting a drink of water, and wished she was there with him, imagining him laying her across the table and fucking her hard and fast.

Do it! Morana squealed. *Let them fuck us and then take their blood.*

She chose not to respond to Morana. Engaging her only emboldened her to say more disgusting things.

Despite her discomfort, her eyelids grew heavy as mental and physical exhaustion threatened to overwhelm her. At some point she may have drifted off to sleep for a few minutes, but the sound of Constantine coughing into his hand startled her awake. There were two silhouettes in her doorway, and she recognized her tall and broad-shouldered alpha and her beta, a few inches shorter with wiry, lean muscles that had become even more pronounced since his time at basic training. If she hadn't been a wolf shifter, their feral eyes glowing white in the darkness would've been unnerving. Instead, her libido involuntarily sprang to life.

Andrei greedily inhaled her scent.

Busted.

They both sprang on her bed, their eyes glowing even brighter, their bare chests glistening and their erections bulging under their sweatpants. They smelled so damn alluring, like fresh soap and an earthy spice that was all their own.

Fuck. Fuck. Fuck.

No matter how badly she wanted them, they couldn't have sex. She didn't trust Morana to behave.

She briefly wondered where Dejan was, then remembered the look of horror in his eyes when she'd attacked Dimitri, and the unease he demonstrated around her after that. "Where's Dejan?" she asked, instantly regretting her question. He was afraid of her, and she suspected he was repulsed by Morana, too.

Andrei briefly averted his eyes. "He took the first sleeping shift."

Her heart clenched. No doubt they'd asked him to join them, and he'd refused. She doubted he was asleep at all. "Oh, okay."

Andrei twirled a lock of her hair around his finger. "You look kind of cute in handcuffs."

"Seriously?"

"You know," he said to Constantine with a wink, "we can make this fun."

He'd lost his mind. She arched back against the overstuffed pillows. "No."

Andrei flashed an exaggerated pout. "Why?"

"Yeah, why," she said, annoyed with him for thinking this was a game, and annoyed with herself when her stupid body melted like butter when he laid a hand on her thigh. "You know I have a demon inside me."

Constantine leaned into her, his breath a whisper of heat in her ear. "That doesn't make us love you any less... want you any less."

Her pussy swelled and ached. "Constantine," she said without conviction, "stop."

"Don't fight us, *iubita mea*." Nostrils flaring, Andrei's hand traveled up her leg, stopping at the juncture between her thighs. "I smell your heat."

She wanted to let them have their way with her, feel them deep inside, filling her with their seed. "Of course I want you, but, but—"

"But what?" they begged, looking at her with wide, luminous eyes like her mom's little dogs begging for table scraps.

Damn. They were so cute. Double damn. This was so hard. Unable to look into their handsome faces another moment, she hung her head. "I'm ashamed."

Constantine cupped her chin, forcing her to meet his gaze. "For something not your fault?"

She swallowed back the sorrow that threatened to close off her throat. "I could hurt you."

"I won't let you."

When Andrei moved his hand higher, cupping her mound and flicking her sensitive bud through her underwear, she nearly came undone. She let out a groan when he circled her swollen clit, soaking the thin fabric of her panties.

"Come on, *iubita mea*," he whispered, dropping delicate kisses across her inner thigh. "Let us love you."

Slave to her passion, she widened her legs, then lifted her hips so Andrei could slide off her underwear.

When Constantine reached for her nightgown, she bucked against him, making slapping motions with her bound hands. "Leave it on!"

Constantine frowned down at her. "I want to kiss your breasts."

"No! Please, I beg you."

When tears welled up in her eyes, he backed off. "Okay."

She motioned to the white glare coming from the hall. "And turn out the light."

"*Iubita mea*, it's us." Constantine dragged his knuckles down her arm. "We've seen your body before."

She couldn't help the lone tear that slipped down her face. "Please don't make me say it again."

Andrei wiped her cheek and gave Constantine a warning look. "We won't."

She hated that they were probably communicating telepathically about her and leaving her out of the conversation. They obviously didn't know about the red growth on her stomach. Was it because Dejan had been kind enough to keep her secret, or was he terrified of acknowledging the truth, that she was turning into a spider demon?

So consumed was she in dark thoughts, she hadn't noticed that they'd shut the bedroom door and then closed the curtains. Good. She preferred the darkness, just in case her nightgown slipped. Not that it mattered too much. They'd see her blemish of shame with their wolf-touched eyes.

This was a bad idea. A very bad idea.

She struggled to sit up with bound hands. "Guys, maybe we should wait until we get back from the forest."

"Why, *iubita mea*? You need this." Constantine stroked his thick erection. "*We* need this."

She hated denying them. He was right that she needed it, too. Maybe a few good orgasms would ease the tension that was coiled around her neck like a noose. She suspected a majority of her back pain came from stress and not her bindings.

She froze when Constantine produced a gleaming silver key. "No," she said on a strained whisper. "I need to stay bound."

He grinned wolfishly. "You will. Trust me." He nibbled her ear, turning her into jelly once more.

He removed her cuffs and chained her right wrist to the bedpost. Then Andrei pulled out a length of rope and they tied her other hand to the other bedpost. So these two had already planned their seduction? Naughty wolves. The thought that they'd planned it meant they'd probably asked Dejan to join them. As much as she wanted to focus on their kinky foreplay, she was momentarily distracted, wondering Dejan's excuse for refusing her.

Arms stretched from the bedposts, the kink in her back magically straightened, and she was able to enjoy watching her mates remove their sweats, revealing long, thick erections. Her mouth watered at the sight. She wanted to suck them.

When Andrei knelt beside her, his cock jutting next to her chin, she turned her head and licked the clear liquid off the tip. He sucked in sharply, then eased the tip into her mouth, cupping the back of her head as she swirled her tongue around his cockhead. At this angle, there was only so much she could take and she regretted not having hands to lather up his balls, but his groans of delight told her he was pleased. Her pussy flooded with each flick of her tongue as she tried to take him deeper.

When Constantine crawled between her legs and dug into her thighs with thick fingers, she braced herself for invasion.

"Relax," he purred, licking her clit with one long, languid stroke of his tongue.

"Oh!" she cried, nearly levitating off the bed as he continued licking, flattening his tongue up the length of her ribbon and then swirling the tip around her tender pearl.

So consumed was she that she lost focus on Andrei, pausing while he continued to drive the tip of his erection into her mouth. A few more strokes, and she was seeing stars, her orgasm piercing her like a blade as she flooded his mouth with each contraction. He laughed against her quivering skin, licking up her juices before climbing the length of her body.

Andrei was kind enough to sit back on his heels while Constantine seated himself between her legs. Had she the use of her hands, she would've stroked Andrei's cock, but she enjoyed watching him slowly pump his hand up and down his glistening shaft.

Constantine was not gentle when he thrust deep inside her. She forced herself to relax to accommodate his girth. He gripped her ass and lifted her off the bed, her bindings digging into her wrists while he pumped into her harder, faster, a look akin to pain etched on his face. He came hard and quickly, the look in his eyes one of agonized bliss as he withdrew.

Constantine was usually more gentle in their lovemaking, allowing her several orgasms while he took time savoring her. This felt like nothing more than a need for release. Depression darkened her mood. He was vulnerable during sex, and he was afraid of her.

After cleaning them up, he kissed her forehead. "Thank you, *iubita mea.*"

Choked with emotion, she didn't respond. Andrei crawled between her legs.

Constantine was right. It was his job as protector to be on guard and keep his family safe, even from her.

Andrei didn't seem to be in a hurry as he stroked her swollen bud, making her libido spring back to life and coaxing more moisture out of her. He took her lips in a tender kiss, balancing himself on one hand and stroking her with the other. He trailed hot kisses down her neck and over the fabric covering her breasts, somehow knowing to stop there and stay away from her stomach. Hungry for his kisses, she strained for his mouth again, sighing when he accommodated her. The head of his thick cock replaced his thumb, circling her clit before he eased into her while never breaking the kiss.

She wanted to cling to him while he fucked her, feel the warmth of his skin seep into her hands. There were so many things she wanted to tell him while their tongues sparred in a timeless dance of passion, like how grateful she was to him for making love to her with abandon, for not being repulsed by her touch. She let him love her, taking her to that pinnacle with each thrust. Her tight sheath swelled, cradling his thick cock in a loving embrace as he thrust faster and deeper, panting into her mouth. As her euphoria grew, she felt her last thread of restraint snap, and she surrendered to orgasmic bliss, pleasure consuming her as her pussy throbbed against him. He bathed her with his seed and murmured words of love into her ear.

He doesn't love you! He chained you and raped you! Morana howled. *Kill them. Kill them all now before they slit your throat!*

Something inside Tatiana snapped. She bucked the wolf man off her. A burst of energy surged through her and her restraints broke.

A giant, hairy beast landed on top of her, flattening her. The bed broke and crashed to the floor. Thrashing and flailing, she fought her captor as a screech for help tore from her lungs, a primal call designed to drive others of her race to her aid.

Sink your fangs into him!

She tried, but the beast's hairy paw was wrapped around her throat, squeezing and squeezing until her vision tunneled and her world went dark.

TOR AWAKENED WITH A start when an unholy screech rent the air.

"What the fuck was that?" Drasko asked.

His gaze shot to Luc, who was standing by the barn door, all color drained from his face.

"I don't know, but it doesn't bode well. We need to shift." Slipping off the cot, he threw off his shorts and became a protector, vaguely aware of his sons shifting, too.

Dimitri's eyes shot open. They were bloodshot and glowing red like hell's fiery embers.

Well, fuck.

Dimitri sprang out of bed with such height, he hit the rafters before dropping down on all fours, scrambling around the floor like a spider.

Tor and Drasko launched on Dimitri with angry growls.

"Ancients, he's stronger than two protectors!" Tor focused on pinning his arms, difficult to do while he thrashed. Thank the Ancients Dimitri still wore the amethyst bands. Tor couldn't imagine restraining him if he'd been able to shift into a protector. Choking on straw and dust, Tor kept losing his grip. Dimitri's human bones felt like they were made of liquid.

Drasko tried to capture Dimitri's legs and wasn't having much luck.

Luc ran circles around them, barking and snarling.

"Morana, I'm coming!" Dimitri wailed.

"Morana?" Tor repeated.

Dimitri squirmed out from under them as if he was made of jelly and knocked over the kerosene lamp, which set the hay on fire. Tor grabbed the horse trough and dumped it over the flames, then turned the trough upright and used it to contain the smell of acrid smoke.

The horses became restless in their stalls, stomping and whinnying.

Luc blocked the door in wolf form, snarling at Dimitri and pushing him back.

"Watch out!" Tor called.

But it was too late. Dimitri's leg shot out like a rubber band and knocked Luc against the wall.

Luc hit it with a *thud* and collapsed, whimpering.

Drasko leaped on Dimitri and wrapped his hands around his neck.

Dimitri let out an ear-piercing shriek. What the fuck?

"Don't kill him!" Tor warned.

Dimitri's head lolled to one side as he slumped to the ground. Drasko got up and ran to Luc while Tor went to Dimitri.

"Brother!" Drasko cried, cradling Luc in his arms.

Dimitri was knocked out cold. The handcuffs hung loosely on his wrists, the broken chains snapped as if made of cheap plastic.

Tor dragged a hand down his face after falling on his ass into the dirt.

Luc moaned in pain, his right shoulder sagging much lower than his left as he cradled his ribs with one arm.

Drasko slipped his phone out of his pocket. "Hakon!" he barked. "Luc's hurt. Get Amara down here *now*!" Without waiting for an answer, he ended the call, then dialed 911 and asked for an ambulance.

"I-I'm okay," Luc said, then coughed blood all over Drasko's shirt.

Chest heaving, Tor rose on shaky legs, glaring at Dimitri. He let out a primal roar and pounded his chest. "Fucking demons, you will not win! Do you hear me? You will not win!"

A soft, feminine chuckle resonated through the barn. Tor's attention shot to the rusty lamp sitting on top of a hay bale. He'd almost forgotten about the djinn. "You won't win, either, bitch," he spoke through gritted teeth, rage pounding a loud drum in his ears. "I'll cast you into the lake of fire myself if you don't save my daughter and her mate."

The djinn's shriek was his vindication, though his relief was short-lived. He got the feeling the screech they'd heard earlier had come from Tatiana.

Chapter Six

TATIANA GLARED AT THE strange creature's reflection in the mirror. She'd woken up to find her Native American skin an alarming shade of deathly gray. Her eye sockets were sunken and framed by dark circles. Even worse were the thick, black hairy spikes that had appeared up and down her arms and back. Yes, her back! She looked like a fucking porcupine corpse! Her stomach protruded like she was pregnant, the red bubbly mark expanding like a giant boil. She was fucking hideous.

She jumped at a knock on the door.

"Tatiana," Constantine called, "we have to go."

She quickly slipped into the long, flannel shirt and stretchy gray sweatpants she'd found at the back of the Coyotechasers' closet. Constantine knocked louder. "Hang on!" She was alarmed at how hoarse her voice sounded. Well, fuck. Add eighty-year-old chain-smoker voice to the list of changes.

She tied her thick hair up in a bun, then quickly removed it when black hairy spikes poked out behind her collar. After fanning her hair around her neck, she opened the door. "I'm ready," she said, unable to meet his eyes.

He pinched the edge of her sleeve. "It's going to be hotter there than it is here."

She backed away from him. "I don't care."

He followed, reaching for her shirt again. "You're going to sweat."

"Leave it!" she practically screamed, violently shaking him off.

Pain flared in his eyes. "Tatiana, I'm so sorry. I had no choice but to knock you out."

She heaved a frustrated breath. That's what he thought this was about? "I don't blame you for that." Shame washed over her, and she was unable to look at him again.

"Last night was my fault," he continued. "I shouldn't have asked for sex. The djinn warned us that's when you were most vulnerable. I don't know what came over me."

"Morana knew what she was doing." She spared him a quick glance before looking back down at her boots. "She released pheromones to seduce us. That's why weren't thinking clearly."

She fought the urge to pull away when he grabbed her hand.

"Morana?"

"The demon," she answered flatly, hating the notion of even acknowledging the evil bitch.

"Oh, right. Guess she's a horny demon, huh?"

Ugh. This was nowhere near being funny.

"That's not why she did it." Her voice rose in pitch with each word. "Every time I lose myself to her, I change."

He visibly swallowed. "Is that the reason for these clothes?"

"Yes." Wrapping her arms around herself, she fought a wave of insecurity and embarrassment. "She's running out of time, and she's trying to take over sooner than the next full moon."

He forced her to look into his eyes, which revealed so much tenderness, it made her heart weep. "We won't give her any more chances, okay?"

"Okay."

When he took her in his arms, she was unable to hold back her tears any longer.

Ancients, please, I don't want to lose my mates!

DEJAN HAD BEEN EVEN more terrified of Tatiana when he set her breakfast down on the kitchen table, refusing to look at her. She thanked him for the breakfast tacos and got a nod of acknowledgement before he returned to the kitchen.

Though she was in no mood to eat, she couldn't deny she was famished. She ate quickly, washing it down with lukewarm coffee, before joining Constantine and Andrei on the porch.

"How are you doing?" Andrei asked.

She shrugged. "So-so. You?"

"Worried about my mate."

She simply nodded, then looked away, afraid to trust herself to speak. The sun had barely risen over the horizon, pink and orange rays fanning across the desert landscape like ribbons of colorful smoke. This place was beautiful in its own way, but she preferred the Alaskan pines to brush and dirt. She hoped she'd be able to return home when this was finished.

A black pinprick far down the dirt road materialized into Agent Johnson's SUV. She imagined her conveyance to be the chariot of death, coming to take her across the veil.

He parked in front of the porch and got out. Tor emerged from the barn, Dimitri sandwiched between him and Drasko. She bristled when she noticed chains binding Dimitri's ankles that rattled with each tight step. What the hell? Why was he in chains? Had his demon done something? There was a new layer of tension in the air, so thick she could almost touch it. Her father had probably heard about her demonic possession last night. She had no idea what had happened after she'd blacked out. Dimitri stood behind her father, head down, while Tor talked to the agent. Drasko stood behind Dimitri, staring bullet holes through his back.

Johnson dragged a hand over his shaved head and talked to Tor in hushed whispers. When everyone turned their eyes on her, she cringed under the weight of their attention. Drasko opened the back truck door, and Dimitri pulled himself up and onto the seat, dragging his bound legs behind him.

Why is he chained up like a dog? she projected to Constantine.

Just be thankful it's not you, he answered tersely. *I already had to fight your dad on it.*

What?

There's something you should know. Constantine regarded her from hooded eyes. *Dimitri lost his cool last night, too.*

Is he okay?

He's okay now. He injured Luc.

Fuck! Is he okay?

He's in the hospital in stable condition. Amara is flying down. She should be here in a few hours.

Tatiana felt sick to her stomach. *So he's not going to die?*

No. Constantine placed a comforting hand on her shoulder. *He has a punctured lung and a few broken ribs, but he'll be fine.*

A million questions raced through her mind, and they all centered on one smiling, smug face—Jezebeth. She clenched her fists until nails broke skin. *Why did he lose his cool? Did that fucking djinn seduce him?*

Nothing like that. Constantine released her shoulder. *He was responding to your scream.*

She sucked in a sharp breath. *I screamed?*

If that's what you call it. You sounded like a fucking injured dragon.

Great Ancients, she wanted to slide through the cracks in the porch and hide for eternity!

Tor stomped up to them, a bulging backpack slung across his shoulder. Tatiana had a feeling the djinn's lamp was inside it. She was sorely tempted to yank it out and demand the genie expel those demons immediately.

Tor said to Constantine, "You two ready?"

"Yeah."

Tor stomped back to the truck. Obviously he was pissed at them about last night. Why the fuck had she let Morana use sex to manipulate her?

That's because I'm in control. Morana chuckled.

Not for long.

Andrei stepped onto the porch, looking wary. He reached for her as if she was the coil burner on their old stove, and he was trying to determine if she was still hot. Finally he latched onto her wrist, then slid his hand down to thread his fingers through hers. "You doing okay?"

"I guess. You?"

"I'll be doing much better when that demon is out of you."

She grimaced, hating the strain between them and fearing their bond would never return to normal. "Me, too."

THE TENSION IN THE cab of the truck was as thick as a ten-foot snow drift as they drove down the dusty road toward the base. She sat in back, squeezed between Constantine and Andrei, while her father was up-front with Agent Johnson. Dimitri and Dejan rode ahead of them in Magnus's truck. She felt the chasm between her and her mates widening and not just physically. There was a chasm in her soul, as if their blood bond was breaking.

Magnus and his brother were waiting for them on the base beside an armored vehicle with bars on the windows.

Is that prison van for me? she asked Constantine.

Nu. He shook his head. *It's for Dimitri.*

Her heart plummeted. *But why?*

"Tatiana," he said aloud. "It's obvious after last night that you and Dimitri need to be far away from each other."

When Tor turned to her, she arched back, wishing she could sink beneath the leather upholstery and never come out. She'd thought she and Constantine were having a private conversation. Why did he have to answer her aloud? Maybe their bond *was* breaking.

She stiffened when Constantine's elbow brushed against her. "Where are they taking him?"

"Someplace where he will be kept safe," Tor answered.

"You mean where the world will be safe from him," she snapped.

"They're doing the right thing." Constantine took her hand.

She jerked away from him. Soldiers guarded the truck. Each carried very big guns. What if they got scared? Would they shoot Dimitri? "You're sending him with a bunch of humans?"

"Drasko and Dejan will be with him," Tor answered.

A blade twisted inside her heart when she thought about Dejan leaving her. She wondered if Dejan had volunteered to follow Dimitri because he was frightened of her. The thought was too depressing to consider.

Forcing a confidence she didn't feel, she turned up her chin. She wouldn't let them see how badly she was hurting. "Can I at least say goodbye to them?"

"Make it quick," Tor grumbled.

Yanking off her seatbelt, she nudged Constantine, giving him an impatient look while he opened the door and let her out. Warm air hit her face, and the morning sun pierced her eyes. She ignored Constantine when he called to her to wait.

Dejan and Drasko's images blurred behind Dimitri as her attention tunneled on her second alpha and the haunted expression in his eyes. His clothes were disheveled, his hair a mess, and his eyes had heavy, dark circles as if he hadn't slept in a week. His wrists and ankles were chained, like he was a hardened criminal. She ran to him, the sound of her shoes pounding the pavement ricocheting through her brain. She felt as if she was living in a waking dream when she reached him, taking those last few steps slowly, breath hitched as she looked into his eyes.

"Dimitri," she breathed.

He jutted a foot forward, his chains rattling with the movement. "Tatiana."

She flung herself against him, wrapping her arms around his neck and letting out a blubbery breath. "I'm scared."

He kissed the top of her head, his lips searing her scalp and branding her as his. "This demon can take my body, but he can't take away my love for you."

She searched his face for any sign of hope. "Don't let him take either."

He lifted his bound hands. When the tip of his sleeve pulled back from his thick wrist, she saw a black, hairy spike. Great Ancients! His spider demon was turning him, too.

Eyes bulging, he quickly lowered his hands. "I'll fight these demons to my last dying breath. Promise me you'll do the same."

"I will." Cupping his cheeks, she looked deeply into his eyes, once a bright blue, now swirling with wisps of gray smoke. The voices and activity around them faded into background noise as she pressed against him. "I love you." She didn't care if his eyes turned gray or black spikes sprang from his flesh. His wolf's heart still beat strong, and it belonged to her.

"I love you." He paused. "More than the stars, more than the sun, and more than my soul."

"Oh, Dimitri!" Clutching his collar like a lifeline, her lips sought his, and they met for an explosive, passionate kiss.

When Constantine finally pulled her away, she felt as if he was separating her soul from her body. "No!" She kicked and screamed, flailing in his arms.

"We have to go, Tatiana," he said, his voice as hard and unforgiving as iron. "Time is not on our side."

Dimitri reached out to her, his bindings only letting him lift his arms so far. "Be strong. We will be together again." He cast a wary look at the human guards flanking him. "If not in this lifetime, then another."

She glared at the guards, then at Dejan and Drasko, who had the decency to look away. "If anyone harms you,"—she stuck a thumb in her chest—"they will have to face me."

He smiled. "I'll let them know."

As Constantine pulled her toward a helicopter on the other side of the runway, she realized she hadn't said anything to Dejan, and he hadn't so much as said goodbye to her. He gazed at her as if he was looking at a ghost.

When they reached the big, imposing black helicopter, Magnus looked her over. "I still think it's a bad idea she comes with us."

Constantine pulled her close.

At least he still cared enough about her to be protective.

"I'm not letting my daughter out of my sight," Tor declared, pushing past Magnus.

"Then let my brother and me go alone," Magnus said. Jax, who was standing as stiff as a board in a camo military uniform, nodded.

"And risk you letting your temper drive your sister away?" Tor snorted. "I don't think so."

"She's not our sister," Magnus and Jax said simultaneously, the force behind their denial making Tatiana jerk back.

"You just proved my point." Tor snickered.

She took her father's hand, and he helped her into the helicopter, then rushed to sit beside Andrei, who was already planted against the back wall on a narrow bench seat. As family came aboard, she realized this was going to be one hell of an awkward reunion. Then again, it couldn't be any more tense than what they were going through at the moment. Ancients save them. Even if they defeated these demons, they still had to survive the experience.

Chapter Seven

THE NOON-DAY SUN WAS beating down on them by the time they landed. After they disembarked in a small pasture somewhere in the Mexican mountains, the helicopter took off, flying away swiftly, hovering sideways through the air like a giant bug. As she scanned the foreign terrain, she hoped their ride would be back soon. The air was thick, yet refreshing and clean. The steep mountain slopes were covered in bright green grass that contrasted nicely against the pale blue sky. It was as pretty as a postcard, and not at all what she'd envisioned Mexico to look like.

An old man wearing a wide-brimmed straw hat was leading a slope-backed donkey down a windy, dirt road. He stopped to stare at them as they followed Agent Johnson across a field to the tower of what looked like an old mission. There were cracks in its sand-colored walls and ivy growing up the sides.

Johnson turned to Tor. "This is it."

"Something smells off." Tor heaved his backpack off his shoulder.

Tatiana heard a *clank* when it hit the ground. So the djinn was inside. Tatiana didn't like the idea of taking the demon with them. What if this was all an elaborate trick, and she was trying to get them killed?

You should get rid of the lamp now and the genie with it, Morana warned. *Throw it down the mountain.*

Tatiana looked to her right. There was a steep drop-off into a narrow canyon at the end of the field. She'd seen it from the helicopter. They'd never find the lamp if she threw it down there. A dark feeling passed over her and she rubbed her hands together at the temptation.

She abruptly recognized that feeling. The demon spider was trying to take over. Straightening her shoulders, she issued a command in her head, imagining she was screaming at the top of her lungs. *Shut the fuck up, spider. You just want her gone, so she can't banish you to hell.*

The spider's screech confirmed her suspicions.

They moved toward the charred shell of a burned building. One wall had completely caved in and the other three looked ready to crumble at the slightest wind. Several other smaller buildings had also burned. What had happened here?

Johnson waved down the old man. "Donde esta el orfanato?"

Remembering what she'd learned from high school Spanish, Tatiana translated it automatically in her head: *Where is the orphanage?*

The old man shrugged and hurried away, pulling his braying donkey behind him.

Tor nodded toward Constantine and Andrei. "Stay here with Tatiana." He and Johnson fanned out in one direction. Magnus and Jax in the other.

Tatiana sat on the edge of a decaying brick wall, waiting for them to return. Her nose wrinkled at a strange, subtle stench on the breeze. There was something off here, something that marred an otherwise picturesque landscape.

Her father and the others returned wearing grim expressions.

"Tyr said there was an orphanage here, but we can't find anything but an abandoned church and a burned building."

Magnus rubbed his chin, his irises elongating and his voice dropping to a protector's rumble. "Maybe the demon spawn burned it down."

Tatiana flinched as if the insult had been meant for her. Why did he hate the sister he'd never met?

"You don't know that," Tor said.

"Demon spawn?" Tatiana said coolly. "I thought her name was Phoenix."

She refused to back down when Magnus and Jax gave her quelling looks.

Constantine wrapped a possessive arm around her shoulders, pulling her against his side while issuing the brothers a challenging look.

"We're wasting time here!" Tor gazed at the old man, who stared at them from behind a crumbling wall of the burned building, his protesting donkey loudly giving away their location.

"You there!" Magnus said, advancing toward the wall in a few long strides.

"Magnus," Tor said, hurrying after him. "Let me handle this."

Constantine tugged on Tatiana's hand and they followed everyone toward the building.

"Do you speak English?" Magnus asked the old man.

The man nodded. "A little."

"What happened here?" Magnus asked gruffly. When the old man said nothing, Magnus's lengthening eyes shifted to a brilliant gold and he snatched him by the collar.

"*Mierda, es el diablo*!" Trembling in Magnus's grip, he made the sign of the cross.

"Let him go!" Tor commanded, grabbing Magnus's arm.

Magnus released him with a curse before stomping away.

Tor helped him sit on the edge of crumbling stairs that led nowhere. "Come now, we won't hurt you." He dropped his voice to a soothing burr. "What do you know about the orphanage that was here?"

Tatiana rarely saw this soft side of her father but it reminded her of when she was a child. He'd been gentle and affectionate with her then. Had their relationship been forever soured by what was happening to her?

Removing his hat, the old man cradled it against his chest like a shield. "It burned," he said with a thick accent.

Tor leaned closer. "Who did it?"

His eyes darted to each of them. "Some say it was *la diablesa*."

Tor pulled a tattered picture from his pocket and showed it to the old man. "Her?"

The girl had to be Phoenix, and Tatiana briefly wondered where he'd gotten the photo. She had dark honey skin, long, shimmery black hair in pigtails, large almond eyes, and a wide, pretty mouth. She held a stuffed wolf and was linking arms with an old nun who held the reins of what looked like the very donkey the old man had.

The old man backed away from the photo, making the sign of the cross. "La diablesa!"

"Demon girl!" Magnus boomed. "I knew she was an abomination."

Tor spun toward him and spoke in a low, menacing voice. "Control your temper."

But the old man had taken that opportunity to slip away and was scurrying down the road amazingly fast for someone his age. He yanked the donkey's rope so hard, it looked ready to snap, and swore at it in Spanish when it brayed its disapproval. He finally gave up, leaving the donkey to graze while zipping up the hill without him.

"Hey! I found this." Andrei bounded over, the tattered remains of what might have been a stuffed wolf toy in his hand. It was missing an eye and several patches of fur.

Jax snatched it from him and buried his face in it. "This has her scent."

"You sure?" Tor asked.

"I'm sure." He handed the toy to Magnus.

Magnus smelled it, made a face, and tossed it to Tor. "It's her. I know Wolf-stalker blood."

"So you're acknowledging she's a relative," Tatiana blurted, unable to contain the acid in her tone. "You're making progress."

Magnus didn't even spare her a glance. No doubt he felt her opinions insignificant. She instantly regretted her words when Tor gave her a dark look, but she couldn't help herself. She felt offended on behalf of this shifter she'd never met. The girl couldn't help it if she was part demon. Tatiana wanted to laugh at the irony, for she, too, was part demon, even though her demon side was a parasitic bitch.

"We can track her now," Andrei said, taking the toy from Magnus.

Jax shook his head. "We should wait for Luc."

Andrei stiffened. "There isn't time."

Tatiana wanted them to wait for Luc, too. Her brother was the best tracker in the Amaroki, but they needed to find the girl now.

"Okay," Tor said to Andrei and Jax, "you two follow her scent."

"They will need a protector." Magnus puffed up his chest. "My brother isn't going without me."

Tor's upper lip twitched. "All right, but when you find her, do not engage." He pointed an accusatory finger at Magnus. "You will wait for me."

Magnus threw up his hands defensively. "I wouldn't dream of confronting the demon spawn without you there."

"Let's go," Andrei said. "We're wasting daylight." He hugged Tatiana tightly.

She looked into his eyes, which were brighter than Dimitri's smoky color. "Please be safe," she begged, clinging to him.

"I will be," he said, kissing her quickly. "My brother and my girl are depending on me."

Her heart imploded when he pulled away. Andrei, Jax, and Magnus shifted into wolves, becoming smaller and smaller the farther they traveled away from her and Constantine. By the time they disappeared over the side of the mountain, she felt as if she was in a waking dream as life slowly stripped away her last threads of sanity.

DEJAN LAID IN THE COT across from Dimitri, bored out of his mind, throwing a ball in the air and catching it. He wished he had something to get his mind off his worries, but electronics were forbidden in the cell, and Dimitri refused to play cards.

Dimitri stared at a crack in the ceiling above his head. He'd been calm and so quiet Dejan wondered if there was anything left of his brother at all or if the demon had completely taken over.

"How long do you think they'll take?" he asked.

"I don't know," Dimitri answered tersely. "You know, you don't have to go into the forest with us."

He shot upright, losing hold of the ball, which fell to the floor and rolled under Dimitri's cot. "What?"

Dimitri didn't even spare him a glance as he continued to stare at the ceiling. "If you're scared, you don't have to go."

Dejan bristled. He'd never said he was scared. "I go where my pack goes."

Other than the subtle movement of grinding his teeth, Dimitri remained motionless, eyes as hard as twin stones. "We need strong wolves."

Jumping to his feet, Dejan stomped over to his brother's cot, bearing down on him with a scowl. "You think I'm not strong?"

Dimitri finally looked at him, sparing him a fleeting glance. "You won't even look at our mate anymore."

"Ancients, Dimitri!" Heat raced into his chest and face like a steaming geyser as he shook a fist at his brother. "She tried to kill us!"

"No." Dimitri's chains rattled as he sat up and rotated his neck. "The demon named Morana did that. You need to learn to distinguish between the two."

His shoulders slumped. "How? I don't know if there's anything left of Tatiana." Saying the words aloud made their situation too real. The thought of losing his sweet mate was so painful, he could barely contemplate it. And if they lost her, Dimitri was sure to follow.

"Take. It. Back."

He looked into Dimitri's eyes and took a big step back when he saw twin flashes of red. The chains binding Dimitri's legs also tethered him to the wall. Would his demon be strong enough to break them?

"Take back what?" He took another step back. "That monsters are taking over my mate and brother?"

"You're staying behind," Dimitri said in a voice that didn't sound like a wolf or protector. No, it was more like an injured cat.

He stood his ground, knowing he wasn't talking to Dimitri anymore but the beast that dared to steal his brother. "I love my mate and my brother, and I'm fighting for them."

When another alien growl erupted from Dimitri, gooseflesh rose and fell on Dejan's arms. "I don't need you fighting for me."

Dejan arched a brow. "Is that Dimitri talking or the demon?"

"You fucking cunt!" Dimitri howled and lunged for him, jerking to a stop just short of Dejan when he ran out of chain.

Dejan fell back to his cot, snatched the axe from beside the bed, and raised it with a trembling hand. Would he have the courage to fight his brother?

He flinched when Dimitri feigned an attack.

"That's what I thought." He let out a low chuckle. "Tatiana sees through your cowardice. She knows you don't love her."

"She knows I do." He said it with less conviction than he'd intended.

Dimitri's lips pulled back in a feral snarl. "You didn't even say goodbye to her."

He was tired of fighting this demon. He knocked on the door for the guards to let him out. "I'm getting some fresh air," he said to the demon in Dimitri's shell. "Tell my brother I said goodbye."

After he was let out, he practically flew down the hall, then took the stairs two at a time, anxious to get the fuck away, but no matter how far he walked, he couldn't dismiss what the demon had said. He should've kissed Tatiana good-bye, but the mere thought of it left a sour taste in his mouth. He found a small stone garden and sat on a bench, desperately wishing he could chase away his memories or take up drinking. What if Dimitri was right? What if his rejection of Tatiana had broken their bond? But no, he'd felt the threads unraveling after she'd stabbed Dimitri, and his suspicions were confirmed after their flight. He'd sent several telepathic messages to her, and she hadn't answered any of them. He could no longer feel her presence. Even her scent had changed. Whoever was speaking for Tatiana wasn't his mate. He just prayed he could get her back once they reached the Hoia Baciu.

TATIANA CAME OUT OF the bathroom and was shocked by her father's loud snores. Though he was in human form, he sounded like a protector. His feet dangled over the end of the bed, and the hotel's bright, floral-print blanket was pulled up to his neck. How was she was supposed to sleep in the same room as him?

Constantine sat in a chair by the window, seemingly unfazed by the racket, his attention focused on his phone. After cinching her robe tightly around the waist, she tugged on the sleeves, wishing they were longer. She'd tried to yank the thick, black fibers out of her arms, but that had been a mistake. Not only had it hurt like hell, but she'd opened gaping holes, blood dripping down her arms. Bandages had slowed the flow but hadn't stopped the bleeding completely, and she had a hard time wrapping them with only one hand. She'd thought about asking Constantine for help, but she was too ashamed of her hideous transformation.

The room had two double beds, one of which was being occupied by the snoring bear, and a small bathroom. Tor and Constantine were supposed to take turns watching her, which meant her alpha had to stay up half the night, waiting for his turn to sleep. No way was she making him stay up alone.

Tor's backpack was on top of the dresser. She thought she heard a woman's sigh coming from inside it and was sorely tempted to have a word with the djinn, though she had no idea what she'd say.

Take the lamp outside and burn it, Morana said. *Or better yet, throw it in the ocean.*

Nope, she answered her demon, then did her best to ignore the spider's keening groans.

She curled up in the chair on the opposite side of the table from Constantine. An uncomfortable silence stretched between them, and she gazed out the window, which overlooked a lush jungle. They were in a small fishing village at the southeastern tip of Mexico, waiting for word from Andrei and the others. They had traveled to the ocean because her father said trackers were heading this way. She hoped the trackers wouldn't need to go much farther, because they were close to the Guatemalan border; Johnson had warned them there were dangerous drug cartels. She listened to the sounds of strange animals and birds. This place was unlike anywhere she'd been before. She'd only ever been to Alaska, Romania, and recently Texas. She'd love to go outside and explore.

Hey, want to take a walk? Constantine asked telepathically.

I would love to. Tor was snoring so soundly, he was in danger of inhaling every speck of dust and mosquito within a ten mile radius. *But my father.*

Won't know. Constantine smiled. *I can't hear myself think with all that noise.*

She slipped into her shoes and they stepped outside, where she was hit with the warm, humid jungle air. She heaved a breath of relief. It felt good to be out of that stuffy room.

He took her hand, and they walked downstairs and through a beautiful courtyard in the center of the complex. It had all kinds of large, leafy plants, colorful flowers, and tall, tropical trees. She suddenly realized how much she enjoyed seeing a different part of the world, even if she was currently being occupied by a demonic spider.

Have you heard anything from Andrei? she asked, thankful they still had that mind connection.

Not yet.

What about Dimitri and Dejan?

Constantine looked guilty. *Dejan called while you were in the shower.*

Her heart stuttered. *Oh?* Dejan had said something about her, or maybe he hadn't said anything at all. Maybe he no longer cared for her, and Constantine felt guilty for his brother's indifference.

He took her to a garden that had a pond-shaped pool in the center. The water reflected colorful lantern lights hung from crisscrossing wires strung across the space. She dipped a toe in the water. It was warm. If she hadn't been covered in hideous demon pubes, she'd probably strip off her robe and hop in.

She sat on the edge of a lounge chair and looked longingly into the pool. Maybe after this was all over, she and her mates could take a real honeymoon someplace tropical like Mexico. Maybe a seaside resort with an infinity pool and the sound of ocean waves splashing the shore. This lush town was beautiful, but too many bad memories would be associated with it.

Yes, after they were healed, she would insist on a romantic honeymoon. Maybe she and Dejan could reconnect, and he'd actually learn to love her again.

She looked at her alpha as he sat on the lounge across from her, his knees brushing hers. *You gonna tell me about Dimitri and Dejan?*

Dimitri is getting restless. Constantine's audible sigh resonated in her brain as he dragged his hands down his jeans.

Do they still have him chained up like a dog? She was unable to keep the venomous tone out of her thoughts. She'd been so angry when she'd seen Dimitri's bound wrists and ankles.

It's for his safety. He's a danger to himself and others.

She snorted. *So am I.*

He leaned toward her. *But I can handle you, iubita mea.*

Moisture soaked her panties. She badly wanted him to handle her, maybe tie her up again with handcuffs.

If Dimitri breaks his bindings and turns into a demonic protector, they're all fucked.

His sobering thought interrupted her wicked fantasy, and she felt guilty for thinking of sex at a time like this. *I just want to find this girl so we can get these demons out.*

Is the demon bothering you?

She hated the look of pity in his eyes. *She bothers me every minute of every day.*

I'm sorry. He held out his arms.

Though she didn't want his pity, she couldn't say no to his love. She'd come to depend on it too much. She crawled into his lap, resting her head on his broad chest.

They sat like that for several minutes, listening to the monkeys in the trees. They apparently had a lot to say and even sounded distressed. Her wolf instinct told her they didn't welcome her presence. They sensed her demon but were too frightened to do anything other than protest.

The monkeys don't want me here. We should go.

He kissed her cheek. *They'll get over it. I'm not ready to let you go.*

She wished all their troubles would melt away. Pressing a hand to his chest, she cherished his steady heartbeat. *I cannot tell you how grateful I am that you're my mate. Despite what I am, what I am becoming, you love me and keep me safe.*

I'm your protector, he said. *It's what I do.*

She was lucky to have such a dependable, selfless mate. *No, your job is to protect me, not love me even when I'm possessed by a disgusting demon.*

You can't help that you're possessed. You still have a wolf's heart.

"Tell that to Dejan," she blurted aloud, instantly regretting her words.

Constantine brushed a strand of hair out of her eyes. "He's scared."

"We're all scared." That still didn't excuse the way he'd been treating her.

Deep creases marred Constantine's brow. "Your demon tried to kill him. That's gotta leave an impression on a guy."

She appreciated her alpha's honesty, knowing it probably hadn't been easy to bring up that ugly incident. "That's just it. My demon did it, but I don't think Dejan can tell the difference."

"He will once we expel the demon."

"In the meantime, I'm a leper." She jerked when Constantine ran his hands down her arms. He was trying to offer her comfort, but she was afraid he'd feel the spikes under her robe.

He let go and rested his hands at her waist. "Do you want me to talk to him?"

She twitched, afraid he'd move to the growing tumor on her stomach. "No. That will only make things worse."

He threw up his hands in surrender. "What can I do?"

Just don't stop loving me, she projected.

Never. I will go to hell and vanquish every last demon before I let one of them come between us.

Oh, Constantine, she cried and flung her arms around his neck, her lips seeking his.

The kiss they shared was more magical than a cascade of falling stars, and she never wanted it to end. His tongue sought hers as he groaned into her mouth. Digging his fingers into her scalp, he deepened the kiss while toying with one of her nipples. When the damn of desire threatened to burst, she reluctantly pulled back.

"Constantine," she said between heaving breaths. "We can't."

He looked shocked. "I'm so sorry, iubita mea." He released her as if he was holding a hot poker. "I don't know what came over me."

"I do." Rage made her shake. "This demon releases pheromones to tempt us. She's putting us both under a spell."

His eyes widened with alarm. "We can't let her win."

"I know." She winced when one of her spikes poked through the robe, standing out against the white cotton with all the audacity of a glaring strobe light. "I can't risk another change."

Chapter Eight

DRAGGING HIS TAIL, Andrei whimpered. He was scared, exhausted, and hungry. He'd thought three months of basic training had prepared him for such a long excursion, but he realized he still had a lot to learn. Luckily Jax was a sergeant with his own squadron and had done several reconnaissance missions already.

The farther south they traveled, the hotter and more humid the jungle air became—not the best climate for a Romanian wolf's thick fur. There were many strange sounds in the jungle, and a lot of itchy plants, slithering serpents, and odd bugs, some as big as his face.

They had been following the girl's scent for nearly two days. They should've found her by now, but they kept running into dead ends, fooled by strange scents, and then backtracking and picking up new scents. He was starting to feel like they were chasing their tails.

To make matters worse, Magnus and Jax's moods became more foul with each passing hour, and they snapped at him for every little misstep.

Jax's ears pricked and so did Magnus's. Andrei scented the air, smelling something strong, powerful and quite odd, unlike anything he'd ever scented before.

He backed up when Jax whined, wishing he could speak telepathically to all wolves. Magnus yelped and ducked behind a tree, his brother following. Andrei wasn't as surefooted, and he didn't move fast enough. The fur on the back of his neck stood on end when a large, scaly head rose from behind a thick bush.

What the fuck? Was it some kind of Anaconda? Whatever kind of snake it was, it was twice the size of a protector. He'd had no idea snakes got that big.

The head rose until it towered at least twenty feet above him, the canopy of leaves raining down on its scales. Its long neck arched back like a cobra preparing to strike. A parasol opened around his jowls, clacking like a rattlesnake, and then two large wings expanded from its back.

No. Fucking. Way.

One word popped into his mind: dragon!

He jumped behind a tree as the beast released a stream of fire. The tree caught fire, and he dove behind another and another as the whole forest went up in flames. He had no idea where Magnus and Jax were, but when he heard a wolf howl in pain, he feared the dragon had found them.

When he heard a low, dark growl above him, he raced through the bush, not caring that sticks and leaves cut his face and sides. Magnus and Jax caught up to him, and the three of them ran for several miles, until they nearly slammed into Luc Thunderfoot blocking their path in his human form. Wearing shorts and a heavy pack slung across his back, he scowled at them.

Andrei shifted, took the blanket Luc held out to him, and wrapped it around his waist. "Hurry. There's a dragon chasing us."

Luc scrunched his brows. "What the fuck have you been smoking?"

Magnus and Jax shifted, too.

"It's true," Magnus said, clutching his chest. "He burned Jax."

All eyes shot to Jax, who didn't have a mark on his nude body.

Luc arched a brow. "Where are the burns?"

"All over." He looked at his arms and over his shoulder.

Andrei scratched the back of his head. "I heard your cry of pain."

"It burned like hell!" Jax practically screamed, spinning like a dog chasing his tail. He had a few scratches from the brush but nothing else.

Luc grabbed Jax's shoulder, forcing him to stop spinning. "Did you guys eat any of the plants?"

"No!" all three of them said in unison.

"We only ate the rations the chopper dropped last night," Magnus said, "and we drank from a few streams."

"Luc," Andrei said, waving to the path they had cut behind them. "There was a fucking dragon. He lit up the whole forest."

Luc threw off his shorts, shifted, and loped into the forest.

"What the fuck, Luc!" Andrei called, then dropped the blanket, shifted, and chased after him. Magnus and Jax followed.

Luc slowed when they reached the clearing where they'd first encountered the dragon. Andrei knew the beast was near. He still smelled his sulfuric breath. Dropping his tail, he trailed Luc, not making a sound.

The trees that had been on fire were no longer smoking. In fact, they were still bright green, without so much as a trace of soot.

He shared confused looks with Magnus and Jax, then froze when a deep rumble shook the ground. The dragon rose to full height, and just like before, its parasol and wings expanded.

Luc tilted his head, then straightened and barked so loudly, the sound echoed through the forest, making a flurry of colorful birds squawk and fly away. The dragon looked down at Luc with a frozen expression and then burst into a million tiny fragments that fluttered in the wind.

Luc shifted into human form, held out a hand, and captured one. Andrei shifted as Luc opened his hand and a butterfly flew out of it, fluttering into the treetops.

"What the fuck was that?" Magnus asked after he shifted into a human.

"That," Luc said, eyes narrowing, "was an illusion."

"I didn't know such magic was possible," Jax said, shooing away the butterflies that swarmed him.

"I didn't either." Luc thoughtfully rubbed his chin. "But that illusion was created to drive us away. I have a feeling the demon girl was behind it."

TATIANA WOKE UP WITH a start, looked around for Constantine, then noticed the empty space beside her. Throwing off her covers, she went to the bathroom and heard the shower running. She sniffed at the door, recognizing Constantine's scent. He was in the shower, and her father wasn't in the room. After checking out the mini fridge, she hoped he'd gone to fetch them breakfast. Her stomach rumbled almost as loud as a protector. She drew back the curtain, letting sunlight spill into the room. Her attention shot to Tor's backpack, and she remembered he had military food rations.

She started to open it but thought better of it when she realized the djinn was inside. The backpack lurched, and she heard a muffled scream from inside.

She looked over her shoulder, even though she knew she was the only person in the room. The bag shook again, the scream growing louder. Curiosity won out, and she unzipped the bag, pulled out the lamp, and rubbed it like Constantine had. The top popped open and she dropped it like it was a flaming firework. The beautiful dark-skinned woman with the almond-shaped eyes poured out of the tip.

"Thank you." The djinn turned up her nose. "Smelled like moldy socks in there."

Tatiana gaped at the woman like a fool, not knowing what to say. What was her name again? Jezebeth?

The djinn placed a hand on one curvaceous hip. "Why do you look at me like that?"

There were many things she wanted to ask her, but one burning question was paramount. "Do you really have a daughter, or are my mate and friends risking their lives for nothing?"

Jezebeth's eyes widened, then narrowed. "Yes, I have a daughter."

Crossing her arms, Tatiana impatiently tapped her foot. She could play the bitch game, too. "How do you know she still lives?"

Jezebeth smiled, revealing two very sharp canines. "Because I've seen her."

"Where?"

"I have powerful crystals that let me see things."

White hot rage shot through her veins like liquid fire. "Then why can't you tell us where she is?" Was this all a game to her? What kind of fucked up mother sent a search party on a wild chase when she knew exactly where to find her daughter?

"I haven't been able to see her for months." The djinn's plump lower lip hung down. "She disappeared, and she's using magic to conceal her location."

A low growl rose from Tatiana's throat, which was strange because the amethyst bracelets suppressed her shifter. She didn't want to ruminate on where that growl had come from. Besides, she had bigger issues at the moment. "That would've been helpful for my family to know."

"They are wolves," she said flippantly. "They can scent her."

Stomping over to the deceptive djinn, she pointed at her protruding chest. "You just said she's using magic to conceal her location."

"I know how powerful an Amaroki's nose is." Jezebeth laughed, tapping the tip of her nose. "They can smell through magic."

Tatiana's suspicions grew, along with her ire. "How do you know?"

"My dear." She tossed her thick, black braid over her shoulder. "Who do you think created your race?"

Now she knew the bitch was lying. She curled her hands into claws, repressing the urge to scratch her eyes out. "Our Ancients," she said.

The bitch looked at Tatiana with a smug smile. "And who do you think created *them*?"

Tatiana had to work hard to unclench her jaw. "You lie."

"Do I?" Jezebeth laughed. "What does your instinct tell you?"

"My instinct tells me to put you back inside the moldy backpack."

Ignoring the djinn's protests, she shoved the lid back on the lamp, delighted when Jezebeth was sucked back into the relic, screaming. She stuffed the lamp inside the backpack and covered it with her father's crusty underwear. She felt satisfaction when she heard the djinn's horrified gasp, but she had more pressing concerns, mainly that instinct told her Jezebeth hadn't been lying. She was indeed the creator of the shifter race.

TATIANA AND CONSTANTINE had just finished their third round of spades when she smelled a change in the air.

Constantine scented it, too, because he jumped to his feet with a smile. "I smell Andrei."

"So do I," she squealed, flying off the bed.

She ran into Constantine's backside when someone pounded on the door and he abruptly stopped.

"Where is she?" Magnus Wolfstalker yelled in an angry baritone on the other side of the door as the banging continued. "Where is that demon whore?"

Constantine impatiently threw open the door. Magnus wore a pair of shorts, a three-day beard, and carried a huge grudge.

"Where's my brother?" Constantine asked as Magnus pushed past him.

"He's coming." He snatched the backpack off the dresser and dumped the contents on the floor.

Her father joined them from the bathroom, zipping up his jeans. "What's wrong?"

A wisp of smoke materialized at the tip of the lamp, then formed into the image of Jezebeth, who was smiling as if she hadn't a care in the world.

"What's wrong?" Magnus screamed. "She didn't tell us her demon spawn can summon fucking dragons!"

Tatiana flinched. Demon spawn? Dragons?

"It was an illusion," Luc said from the doorway.

"Luc!" Tatiana went to her brother, then stopped when she realized he may not want to hug her.

When he held out his arms, she gave him a big hug, relieved to see he was okay and he still cared for her. She brushed a clump of dirt off his brow. "You okay?"

He grinned. "Just another day at the office."

She couldn't help but laugh at his casual attitude. He acted like tracking a demon through the Mexican jungle and facing down a dragon was no different than a stroll through a theme park. No wonder he was the best tracker in the Amaroki.

"Well?" Magnus asked. "What do you have to say for yourself."

"I had no idea she had such powers," she answered calmly. Too calmly.

"Don't lie," Tatiana said. "You told me you'd seen her." She turned to Tor. "She's been watching her through magic crystals."

"I also told you I haven't seen her in many months." A look akin to pride shone in her eyes. "I knew she had the gift of illusion, but her powers must have grown since she disappeared."

"Where is she?" Tor demanded.

Her smile faded. "Don't you think I'd tell you if I knew? She's using powerful magic to conceal her location. I can't see her in my crystals anymore."

"I know where she is," Luc said.

Magnus turned to him. "Where?"

"Not far from where we encountered the dragon," he said, leaning against the wall. "She's using it to guard her location."

Jezebeth clasped her hands to her heart. "Oh, my clever girl!" Her eyes narrowed on Luc. "Then why didn't you get her?"

Luc pushed off the wall, folding his arms while glaring up at her. "Because we have to cross the border into Guatemala."

"We're not going into Guatemala," Magnus said. "That's a good way to get shot."

"You don't get my daughter," Jezebeth said, haughtily turning up her nose, "and I don't expel your friends' demons."

Luc sighed. "I'll go."

"No, not you!" Jezebeth boomed in a surprisingly dark voice, the ugly demon making an appearance. "Magnus goes. The deal was made with him. He must right the wrongs done by his fathers."

Magnus's eyes hardened. "I should toss you in the ocean." And before anyone could stop him, he picked the lamp up off the floor.

Jezebeth screamed and disappeared back into the spout.

Constantine and Luc blocked the door when Magnus tried to leave. It pained her to see them fight, knowing they were essentially fighting for her very soul. For Dimitri's soul. She wanted to be angry with Magnus for his outburst, but the djinn had destroyed his fathers and his childhood. She remembered the stories from Annie about the monsters his fathers had turned into. And what if he was right? What if this was all a game to Jezebeth, and she had no intention of helping them? Then Tatiana was doomed, just like Magnus's fathers.

"Magnus!" Tor commanded, holding out his hand. "Give me the lamp."

"She's a deceiver," Magnus spat, shoving the lamp at Tor. "She will not follow through with her promise."

"I will," Jezebeth cried from inside the lamp. "But you'd rather leave your sister to languish. I was hoping you were a better man, but you're *just* like your fathers." She let out a wail so powerful, it shook the room.

Tatiana didn't know if the djinn was faking her tantrum or not, but she was getting tired of her outbursts.

Magnus released a slow breath. "Jax and I will find this demon. The rest of you stay here."

"'This demon,'" Jezebeth's accusatory voice echoed through the room. "You mean your sister?"

Magnus let out a protector's roar. "Your demon spawn is no sister to me!"

Tatiana moved closer to Constantine, afraid the humans staying at the hotel had heard Magnus and thought a lion or bear was nearby.

"We're coming, too," Tor said.

"Why?" Magnus snapped. "You don't trust us?"

"My daughter's life hangs in the balance."

"So you'll take her across the Guatemalan border, where there are known drug cartels?" Magnus asked.

Tatiana was in agreement with him for once. She was by no means a coward, but the axe resting against the wall by Tor's bed reminded her why she didn't want to go with him.

"You let me worry about my daughter," Tor snapped, his gaze darting to the axe, too.

Well, fuck.

Bile projected into her throat. *Are you okay with this, Constantine?*

No. His eyes elongated into slits that flashed silver. *But we don't have a choice. We must stick together.*

Nausea twisted her gut. *Okay.*

But in reality, she wasn't okay going with her father, because wherever he went, he was sure to carry that axe, and she had a sinking feeling Morana would cause more trouble.

Andrei stumbled into the room, carrying several bottles of water and a big sandwich. Dark circles cupped his eyes, and he was covered with deep cuts and bruises.

"Tatiana," he breathed. "You're okay."

"Oh, Andrei!" She went to his side.

She started to hug him, but his eyes rolled back in his head, and he collapsed on the floor at Luc's feet. Luc and Constantine placed him on her bed.

"We need a healer!" she cried, wishing Amara were nearby.

Luc checked Andrei's pulse. "He's dehydrated. I'll call Johnson to get him airlifted to Texas. Amara is still there with Hakon."

All eyes turned to Jax when he entered the room, looking not much better than Andrei.

"Make that two airlifts," Luc grumbled.

Well, fuck. They were about to travel to a dangerous foreign country, and they were down two trackers. What could possibly go wrong?

Chapter Nine

TATIANA HELD TIGHTLY to Constantine's hand as the helicopter took them into Guatemala under the cover of darkness. She was so frightened, she barely kept from puking. They were going to be dropped off at the edge of a jungle and left to fend for themselves.

The contents of her gut lurched into her throat when the helicopter abruptly dropped, then hovered over a field. She could barely hear Luc over the noise from the rotor blades as he helped her get unbuckled and ushered her to a rope ladder. With Constantine telling her not to look down, she made the descent, eyes focused on Tor above. Luc was the last to descend, sliding down the ladder like a spider on a thread, then the helicopter departed quickly, disappearing into the night sky like a phantom.

She swatted a mosquito that landed on her neck, cursing the humid heat and bugs that buzzed around her head, and cursing again when a bug landed on her tongue.

Constantine knelt in front of her. "Hop on my back. It's muddy here."

"Are you sure?" she asked, then jumped when something slithered over her foot. "Okay," she eagerly agreed and climbed on his back. "Where are we going?"

"We're following Luc," he said. "He has a contact dropping off a car."

They walked across the field, a shallow stream, and then alongside a narrow, muddy road for over an hour. Not once did Constantine complain about carrying her.

"How much longer?" she asked Luc when he turned to check on them.

"Our ride shouldn't be far from here."

She cringed when there was a popping sound somewhere in the distance. "Is that gunfire?"

"It's far away," Luc said. "Relax, sister. I take these risks all the time when I'm tracking."

She was thankful she had three protectors with them. "What exactly is the American government making you do?"

He tapped his shaved head with a grin. "That's classified."

By the time they reached an older white European van parked along the side of the road, she heaved a sigh of relief. She climbed in back with Constantine, Magnus sat up front, and her father jumped in the driver's seat.

"Where's Luc?" she asked.

"He's following us," Tor said.

She didn't see any sign of him. When a wolf howled, Tor started the engine and drove down the road, headlights turned off. Struck by the severity of the situation, she leaned into Constantine, a chill wracking her despite the warmth in the van.

She froze at the sound of Luc's distressed howl. They'd only made it a few miles when Tor slowed, swearing. A blockade blocked the road—a convoy of several trucks and men dressed in ragged clothes, carrying big guns. At least a dozen swarmed their van like bees to a hive. They were so fucked.

"Bandidos," Magnus said quietly. "Prepare yourselves."

"Everyone quiet," Tor said. "Let Magnus do the talking."

"Tatiana," Constantine said, "if things get ugly, shift and run to Luc."

"No fucking way am I leaving y—"

"Quiet!" her father hissed and stopped the van.

She shielded her eyes when bright lights were shined inside the van.

Her father rolled down the window with one hand, then slipped it down out of sight. She heard the clank of the axe. That weapon was no defense against all those big guns, even if he shifted into protector form.

A man with a bushy beard, who reeked of smoke, leaned in the window. *"Donde van?"* Where are you going?

Magnus leaned forward. *"Somos Americanos, vamos a visitor un familiar."* We are Americans going to visit a relative.

"Visiting family? All the way down here?" Bushy Beard asked, switching to perfect English.

"Yes," Tor said.

"I think you're headed the wrong direction, Americano." He straightened, chuckling. "There's nothing out this way but bandidos." His men burst into laughter.

Fuck. Fuck. Fuck.

Magnus leaned across Tor, flashing a hundred dollar bill. "If you send us in the right direction, we'll be on our way. We think we made a wrong turn."

Bushy Beard snatched the money, a wicked grin splitting his face. "I think you did."

"We'll turn back," Tor said, putting the van in gear.

"Too late now!" He kicked the door. "Get out. *Vamanos*!"

Tor slammed the van into reverse. A huge truck slammed into their rear end, and she lurched forward, a sharp pain shooting up her neck.

"We need to do something," Magnus said.

"Not yet." Tor jerked off his seatbelt. "They outnumber us."

Constantine's hands were at her wrist, removing the amethyst bracelet. His eyes were feral white. "Remember what I said." He removed the other bracelet.

Her wolf howled beneath her skin, clawing to break free. At least the demon hadn't taken that from her. She noted also how Morana had been unexpectedly quiet. Was she as scared as Tatiana?

She wasn't leaving her family. She'd stay and fight with them, bringing down as many bandidos as she could. Her life was nothing without Constantine.

"Empty your pockets!" Bushy Beard clapped his hands like he was ordering school children to get in line.

Tor handed over his wallet. The man slipped the money in his pocket before examining the ID. "Thunderfoot." He smirked. "You tribal?"

"Yes," Tor answered gruffly, his voice deepening.

He was having a difficult time restraining his protector. Any moment Tor would shift and start popping heads. Then what? They'd shoot him full of holes. How many would the protectors be able to take down before they were killed?

Behind her, men worked on disabling their van. They made quick work of the tires before popping the back hatch and going through the cab.

"Victor!" one of the men said, handing Bushy Beard Tor's axe and backpack.

Victor took the axe and turned it over in his hands. "What's this for, Americano?"

"Protection," Tor grumbled.

"Doesn't work against guns." Victor chuckled.

Tor turned bright red.

She thought she heard noise from the bushes beside the road, turned, and spied a pair of glowing, yellow eyes. Luc. She hoped he wouldn't get himself killed trying to save them.

Victor tossed the axe to someone and dumped the backpack on the ground. The lamp rolled out. "What the fuck is this?"

"An old family heirloom," Magnus said. "It's junk."

"I can see that." Victor picked it up and took off the lid. The inside was empty. Either the djinn had escaped, or she was using magic to conceal herself. He threw the lamp over his shoulder, and it landed in the ditch.

Victor dropped Tor's wallet. The tattered picture of Phoenix landed on his muddied boot. "Un momento." He let out a sharp whistle, then waved to his men. He snatched the picture off the ground and shoved it in Tor's face. "Why do you have a picture of *Diosa de las Flores?*"

"Who?" Magnus blurted.

Tatiana wracked her brain to come up with a translation. *Goddess of the Flowers?*

Tor elbowed Magnus in the ribs. "She's our relative. The one we came to see."

"You came to see *her?*" Victor's jaw dropped.

Hushed whispers rose from the bandidos, who backed away from him as if he carried the plague.

"*Si.*" Magnus crossed his arms. "She's my sister."

"*Lo siento!*" He apologized, then dropped the picture and held up his hands as if Magnus was pointing a gun at him. He let out another sharp whistle. "Put their fucking shit down!" he snapped at his men and smiled at Magnus. "Why didn't you say you were visiting *La Diosa?*"

"Why didn't you ask?" Tor grumbled.

"*Mierda!*"

Tatiana recognized the term for *Oh shit.*

He slapped his forehead and pointed at what was left of their borrowed van. "My men already stripped it." He rattled off a bunch of Spanish, and they began putting the van back together. "It will take them some time to fix it."

One of the men picked up Tor's backpack and even retrieved the mud-covered lamp from the ditch. When Tor reached for it, Victor snatched it away.

"You get your things back after we see La Diosa." He rubbed his beard. "The goddess never mentioned a brother, but don't worry." Victor offered an oily smile. "I'll take you to her."

What the fuck is happening? she projected to Constantine.

I don't know, but go with it.

THEY FOLLOWED VICTOR and a dozen of his armed men around a bend and through a large compound where men were loading boxes into the backs of trucks. They walked between rows of buildings to another gate that led to a lush, tropical garden. Constantine had never seen anything like it, but if he were to die, he suspected Amaroki afterlife, Valhol, would look similar. The garden was a virtual paradise, overflowing with colorful flowers and tropical birds. In the center was a tall fountain with water that shimmered with a lavender glow. The fountain poured into a stream that bisected the lush grass and disappeared into a copse of colorful trees covered in thousands of monarch butterflies.

His nose was assailed by sweet lavender, and he was overwhelmed by a feeling of calm. He smiled at Tatiana. Her eyes looked even more sunken, and her skin was gray as a corpse, but somehow he knew everything was going to be okay.

"Are we in heaven?" she asked, eyes glazed.

"It's an illusion," Tor said. His usual scowl had been replaced with a soft smile.

"A powerful one," he said, if it brought about a change in Tor's mood.

"It's no illusion." Victor threw open his arms. "This is Paraiso, home of our La Diosa." Something occurred to him, and his hand dropped to his gun. "Didn't she tell you?"

Instinct told Constantine to lie. "We had no idea it would be this grand."

That seemed to appease Victor, whose smile widened. "It is shocking, but as you know, La Diosa is capable of anything."

Victor walked them through another set of gates. Blinding light shone through their high, golden arches, making him think of a portal to heaven. The soothing feeling diminished as the lavender scent faded. He wondered if something in the garden had bewitched him. They came to a bridge lined with ivy and flowers. On the other side of it was a castle that looked like it had been taken from a little girl's fairy tale. It had pink turrets and purple trellises, and wide terraces overlooked verdant fields.

Tatiana clapped her hands. "It looks like my doll castle!"

"La Diosa made it like that." Victor snapped his fingers, implying it had taken her only seconds, then blinked hard.

"Remarkable," Tatiana said.

"Let us hope she's as benevolent as she is powerful," Magnus mumbled.

Constantine shot him a side-eyed look. "Just don't piss her off."

He snorted but said nothing, which wasn't reassuring. What if his sister held grudges, like her mother? If Constantine didn't know better, he would've thought Phoenix had even stronger powers than Jezebeth.

After they crossed the bridge, Victor called up to one of the towers, and a massive door was raised just high enough for them to duck under. Two armed guards led them through another large door and then into a courtyard. Tatiana slipped on the slick marble floors, and Constantine reached out to steady her. The inside was as grand as the outside, with shimmering chandeliers, opulent vases—some as tall as Constantine—and ivory statues of the same pretty young woman holding musical instruments, flower bouquets, or baskets of fruit.

They came upon what could only have been described as a throne room. A girl on the cusp of adulthood, with flawless, dark honey skin and long, sleek black hair dyed pink at the tips, sat on a dais covered with a mountain of pillows, stroking the mane of a fluffy rabbit with white fur. She had to be Phoenix.

Three young women with serene smiles sat beside her, sharing a bowl of strawberries and leaves with another white rabbit.

Glistening, billowing skirts fanning around her ankles, she stood and frowned at her man. "Victor, you know I don't like guns in Paraiso." Her English was flawless, and her voice, touched with a light Spanish accent, was as soft and lilting as her appearance.

"I'm sorry, Mi Diosa." He bowed low. "I carry it for your protection." Victor's men also had guns. That didn't bode well for Constantine's party.

He waved at the shifters. "Look who I've brought to see you."

She handed her rabbit to one of the girls. "I do not know these people."

Victor thumbed toward Magnus. "This man claims to be your brother."

She walked down the stairs, her movements so graceful, it was as if she floated on air. "Who are you?"

"Magnus Wolfstalker," he answered, not bothering to bow, "and these are my cousins." He paused and corrected himself. "Your cousins."

Constantine felt like a flower wilting under a heat lamp when she turned her attention on him.

Putting a hand on her hip, she gave them looks of mistrust. "I have never heard of a brother or cousins."

Magnus splayed a hand across his heart. "Our fathers never told you about me?"

Constantine fought the urge to roll his eyes at his false indignation. If Constantine wasn't buying Magnus's act, he doubted this cautious girl would either.

"Fathers?" She tilted her head like a dog confused by a strange sound. "I had one father, and I have only seen him once. He called me an abomination and wanted to kill me." The accusatory look she gave Magnus spoke volumes. She had good reason not to trust him.

Victor pushed ahead of them. "We found this among their possessions, Mi Diosa." He pulled out the axe and placed it at her feet.

She looked at Magnus with panic. "Is that why you're here? Did my father send you to kill me?"

Victor's men fanned out around them, weapons ready. Tor let out warning growls, and the men backed up.

Magnus held out his hands defensively. "Your mother sent us."

"I don't have a mother!" Phoenix's face turned an alarming shade of red, her pretty features morphing into something horrifying, like a ghoul with melting skin, reminding Constantine that she was the daughter of a demon.

"You do," Tor said. "You were taken from her by your fathers when you were a baby. We promised her we'd find you."

"Why do you keep saying fathers?" She picked up and swung the axe as if it weighed no more than a bag of feathers. "How could I have had more than one?"

"Children of our species have more than one father," Tor said.

"Our species?" she snapped, then pointed the axe toward him with surprising strength. "What are you?"

"Similar to you," he said. "You've hit puberty already. I'm sure you've experienced the change."

She didn't say anything. Possibly she was shocked to meet others like her.

Victor's men spoke in hushed whispers, their hands trembling on their guns. One wrong move, and they were sure to fire.

"Why did you bring a weapon?" Her voice held more bewilderment than accusation. Good. Maybe she was finally warming up to them.

"It was for our protection," Tor said, his voice as smooth as glass. "We have not come to harm you."

"Who is my mother?" She morphed back into a pretty young woman. "Why didn't she come with you?"

"She *is* with us," Tor said.

She glanced at Tatiana. "That girl doesn't look old enough to be my mother."

Constantine pulled Tatiana to his side. He could feel bumps under the thick fabric of her shirt and knew that's why she wore long layers in the heat. The demon was changing her body. He hadn't said anything to her, but he was alarmed.

"She's here." Tor nodded at Victor. "He has her."

"Where is she, Victor?" the girl snapped.

"He lies." Victor aimed his gun at Tor's chest. "There are no others."

"She's in the backpack, in the lamp," Tor said. "Where did you put it?"

Victor looked at Tor as if he was crazy, and his men whispered to each other.

Phoenix gaped at Tor. "You expect me to believe my mother is in a lamp."

"She's a djinn," Tor answered solemnly. "Considering the magic you've created, it shouldn't be that hard to believe."

Phoenix scrunched her brows. "A what?"

"A genie."

She stared at him a long moment, then she laughed. The girls behind her shared nervous looks and giggled behind their hands.

"I am not the child of a genie. I am an ancient goddess, reborn of magic." She swept a hand across the room.

"You are *not* a goddess," Magnus's eyes flashed yellow. "You are what happens when a demon mates with wolf shifters."

Tor took a step back toward Tatiana.

Constantine shook his head and stepped back, taking Tatiana with him. Magnus and his big, fucking mouth.

Her face fell, then she wiped all expression off her face. "Victor, this is not my family. You've brought me a pack of locos."

Victor looked like she'd just kicked his puppy. "Lo siento."

"I speak the truth," Magnus boomed.

We have to do something, Tatiana projected to him.

I know.

"What do you wish me to do with them?" Victor asked.

She plopped down on her dais. "Send them away."

"No!" Constantine flashed his protector eyes when one of the men reached for him. "Phoenix, listen to us."

She jerked back as if she'd been slapped. "How did you know my name?"

"Your mother told us," Tor continued. "We didn't know you existed until a few days ago, after we found your mother. She asked us to find you and bring you back with us."

The bandidos swore, puffing up their chests like roosters. They weren't going to part with their goddess without a fight.

"You expect me to leave here?" Her lips twisted. "My people will never let me go."

They wouldn't let her go? She was trapped, and maybe she needed someone to save her.

"Phoenix, we need you," Tatiana blurted, clasping her hands in supplication. "If you don't come with us, my mate and I will die."

A horrific expression marred her smooth brow. "What's wrong with you?"

"I'm ill, and only your mother has the power to heal me." Tatiana's pallor turned an even more sickly shade of gray. "But she won't unless we bring you back."

The sound of rapid gunfire made him push Tatiana to the ground, his protector breaking free with a roar. Tor and Magnus shifted, too. Three of them circled Tatiana, growling at Victor, who turned his weapon from the ceiling to them with trembling hands as plaster from above rained down on their heads.

His men made the sign of the cross. One man's hands were trembling so badly, he accidentally fired into a friend's arm. When that friend hit the ground, the man dropped his weapon and ran, screaming "El diablos!"

Chest heaving, Magnus turned to Phoenix, whose face was almost as pale as her rabbit's fur. "If we wanted to kill you, we wouldn't need an axe."

"Tell your men to lower their weapons," Tor said to Victor. "Your bullets can't penetrate our flesh."

Constantine pounded his chest like an ape. It was a lie, but they didn't need to know that.

"Mi Diosa isn't leaving!" Victor waved his men forward. "*Encierrenlos en una celda.*"

He told them to put us in a cell, Tatiana projected to him.

The men crept toward them like they were walking on black ice.

"Nobody's locking us up!" Magnus boomed.

The tension in the room was electrifying. They didn't stand a chance against a dozen heavily armed men.

"Wait, Victor," Phoenix cried. "You know I don't like violence."

"No waiting, Mi Diosa," he said firmly, waving his gun like a flame thrower. "They've come to kill you."

Tor lurched forward roaring, and suddenly the entire room went black, and not the usual darkness, where Constantine could make out shapes and shadows with his wolf-touched eyes. This blackness was complete, a deep, dark chasm that felt as if it was sucking out his soul. All sound was muted, as well, which made it twice as bad.

Tatiana, he cried. *Where are you?*

I'm here. Where are we? What is happening?

The blackness slowly faded, and there was a faint, red glow in the distance. He breathed a sigh of relief when he saw her on the floor beside him. He pulled her into his arms as Magnus and Tor came into view.

"Where are we?" Magnus asked.

The red glow became the soft flame of a flickering wall sconce. Another appeared, and another, revealing the inside of what could only be described as a medieval prison cell with three cave-like, black walls and one wall of rusty, iron bars.

Tor frowned. "The last order Victor gave was to put us in cells. Looks like they managed that somehow."

Magnus curled his hands into fists. "I think Phoenix is behind this."

"She did it to protect us," Tatiana said, pulling free of Constantine.

"Protect us?" he snorted. "By locking us up?"

Her eyes shone in an admirable act of defiance. "You heard her say she didn't like violence."

"Yet she burned down an orphanage." Magnus pointed out.

"We don't know that's what happened," she snapped, offended.

"Don't forget she's half-demon," Magnus mumbled.

"So am I!" Her anger passed as quickly as it had come, and she placed a hand on her chest. "But I have a wolf's heart, and don't you forget it. Don't *any* of you forget it." She dropped onto a wooden bench hanging from the wall.

Knowing that bench wouldn't hold the weight of a protector, Constantine sat on the floor beside her legs, clasping her small hand in his big, furry one. "Now what?"

Tor bent one of the cell door bars with ease and then snapped it like a toothpick. "Now we kick some bandido ass."

LUC THUNDERFOOT SLIPPED soundlessly through the tall grass and circled the camp once more, preparing to strike. Thank the Ancients Andrei and Jax had arrived with backup. Those bandits wouldn't know what hit them. He let out a low howl, a signal to the others. When he was answered by the same, followed by another and another, he shifted into human form and took the lighter out of his pack. He lit the fuse, watching the spark race across the ground like a fiery serpent toward the encampment's propane storage tank.

Shifting back into wolf form, he sprinted away, diving into a ravine moments before the west side of the camp exploded into an inferno, sending debris flying everywhere.

Panicked shouts rose as men raced around the camp like angry hornets while Luc crept back behind the trees and prepared for battle.

TATIANA HELD CONSTANTINE'S hand, swearing when she slipped again on the slippery moss-covered rocks. She hated having to traverse this unfamiliar cavern on human legs, when four wolf legs would've glided over the uneven terrain with ease.

"This sucks," she complained in a low voice.

Constantine squeezed her hand. *I already said I'd carry you.*

And I already said you need both hands in case we're attacked.

"Father," she called to Tor in a heated whisper. "It would be much easier if I could shift."

He stopped unexpectedly, and she accidentally ran into his big, hairy backside. "Listen to me." He loomed over her like a tree about to snap under the weight of heavy snow. "You do not shift unless there is no other choice. We don't know what that demon will do with your wolf. Understand?"

She gritted her teeth. "Yes, Father." Though she was angry he didn't trust her, he wasn't to blame. It was Morana who was causing all the trouble.

Me? Morana said indignantly. *He's the one who wanted to axe you.*

No, he didn't. I'm not falling for your mind games.

They continued on, the only sounds their labored breathing and the slow and steady drip of water trickling down the stone walls into pools that lined the sides of the rough path. They stopped when they reached a set of stone steps, rising from the rubble and winding up into the darkness.

"Where do you think that goes?" she asked.

Magnus reached the steps first, squinting up and then waving them forward. "I hope these lead to the castle."

A wolf howled in the distance.

Tor held up a silencing hand. "Listen. Did you hear that?"

"It's Luc," she said with a mixture of relief and fear warming and then chilling her veins. What if he got hurt or killed trying to save them?

Two more wolves howled, one after the other. "Jax and Andrei!"

Constantine dragged her toward the stairs.

There was a loud boom above them, and Tatiana tumbled into Constantine. He shielded her when debris fell on their heads, pinging off Constantine's backside.

Once the earth settled, they raced up the steps, chests heaving, braced for battle.

Chapter Ten

THEY SURFACED INSIDE a massive tent. The roof and walls were nothing more than black tarps held up by wooden poles. Huge barrels smelling like ammonia and gasoline were at one end, and crates full of fragrant leaves were at the other.

"Where are we?" Tatiana held her nose.

"This is where they make cocaine," Tor said. "Try not to breathe too much of the fumes."

"Cocaine," she gasped. "Phoenix is part of this?"

"You forget she's a demon," Magnus said, kicking a crate of leaves onto the floor.

The *pata-pata-pata* of gunfire whizzed over their heads. They ducked behind a crate. She heard agonizing screams outside, followed by silence.

Tatiana shook so violently, she could hardly breathe. *You don't think those were wolves?* she projected to Magnus.

No, he answered grimly, *they were humans.*

She sighed in relief. Maybe she would feel bad for them later, but now she was focused on survival.

"You stay here," Tor whispered to them. "I'm going to check it out."

He shifted into a wolf with russet-colored fur and slunk away like a phantom.

Every second he was gone, she strained to hear anything, but all was silent. The thought of Tor being shot full of holes filled her with dread. By the time Tor returned as a mighty protector, her nerves were so shot, only the adrenaline fueled by terror kept her heart pumping.

"Come on," he said with a fanged grin. "Coast is clear."

Her knees buckled, and she was flat on her ass, thanking Constantine when he held out a furry hand. She refused his offer to carry her, though. She had to get through this on her own two feet. They'd face even greater dangers in the Hoia Baciu.

They were in a hillside garden, the morning sun filtering in through the thick trees along one edge. At the bottom of the hill was the back of the fairy-tale castle. Smoke rose from the other side of the wall, and she wondered if that was the result of the explosion they'd felt underground.

"What are these plants?" she asked Tor and picked a leaf off a stem.

"Coco leaves. Used to make cocaine."

She dropped the leaf and wiped her fingers on her pants.

"You're not going to get high from touching the plant," Constantine said, laughing.

"I know that," she lied. Truthfully she knew nothing. She licked her parched lips. "So Phoenix lives on a cocaine farm?"

"More like she runs it," Magnus said.

She didn't want to believe him, but it was looking more and more like that was the case. What the fuck had this girl gotten herself into, and how the hell were they going to get her out?

Luc was at the bottom of the hill, barking orders to several armed shifters. Some wore skimpy shorts like him and were covered in mud. Some were completely naked. She averted her eyes, knowing Constantine wouldn't like her looking at other naked men. A few dead humans were lying in the ditches beside the plants. The rest were huddled together, hands behind their backs while shifters bound them.

She looked around for Andrei, worried when she didn't see him. She could've sworn she'd heard his howl earlier.

When they reached Luc, Tor patted him on the back. "Nice work, son."

"It was nothing."

But it wasn't nothing to her. She'd never been more proud of her brother.

A sharp whistle made her turn. Andrei bounded up to them, naked as a babe, his junk bouncing like three coyotes wrestling in a hammock.

She threw herself in his arms. "Andrei!" she cried, then pulled back to run her hands over his chest. "Are you okay?"

"Sure." He smiled at Luc. "Thanks to your brother's leadership. The humans didn't know what hit them."

Constantine slapped him on the back. "Brother, you're healed."

"Yep," he said. "They took us to Amara and then we came straight back."

She wrapped her arms around his waist. "I'm glad you're okay."

"You don't need to worry about me."

She reached for Constantine, and they shared a three-way hug, foreheads pressed together until she caught her breath and her heart rate slowed.

"We survived this, Tatiana," Constantine said. "We can get through anything."

"Even the Hoia Baciu?"

"We'll be ready," Andrei said.

They're wrong, Morana whispered in her ear. *My power over your body will only strengthen in the dark forest.*

You won't be around long. You don't scare me, spider, so you can fuck off now, or you can fuck off when we get to the Hoia Baciu. Either way, you're leaving.

The spider's hiss was her only response, before she faded away, no doubt crawling into some dark hole in Tatiana's mind. No matter. She'd squish that arachnid soon enough.

The three of them joined Luc and Tor. She thanked Luc when he handed them water bottles and meat sticks. She hadn't realized it until that moment, but she was famished.

"We captured the ringleader," Luc said. "We were about to make him talk."

Tatiana and her mates ate and drank and followed Luc to an old pickup truck.

Victor was sitting on the tailgate, bloody from his nose dripping down his beard and onto his shirt. He scowled at Tor. "Get away from me, you fucking, *demonio*!"

Tor let out a growl so terrifying, even Tatiana's knees wobbled. He raised his fists as if he was about to flatten the human into a pancake. "Where is the lamp?"

Craning his neck, Victor spat on Tor's chest. "Fuck you, diablo!"

"Wrong answer," Tor said and grabbed the man's head.

When the human let out an agonizing scream, Tatiana looked away, not wanting to see his brains splatter like a bug against a windshield.

"*Por favor! Por favor!*" he cried. "I will show you!"

Tor released him and stepped back. "Take us to that lamp *now*."

"And don't try anything funny, bandido." Luc stuck a gun in the man's face. "Or I'll let him pop off your head." He flashed a wolfish grin. "After he rips off your *cajones*."

Tor hauled a whimpering Victor up by the arm like a ragdoll and gave him a hard shove forward.

"You're in charge until I return," Luc said to Jax. "If we're not back in twenty, send a search party for us."

"Yes, sir," Jax answered.

When Magnus stepped forward, Luc held up a hand. "Stay with your brother. We may need a protector on the other side if things go south."

Luc took them around the side of the walled compound and through a familiar gate.

"Stay focused," Tor said. "There's something in the air here that makes you lose your inhibitions."

"Whatever that means," Tatiana blurted, then slapped a hand over her mouth.

They all burst into laughter.

She recognized that lavender smell, so powerful she wanted to drown in it. Had it been that intense before? No. This time it was much stronger.

They wandered through the garden, admiring the flowers and letting the butterflies land on their outstretched arms.

Suddenly remembering they had a very important mission, she pulled Constantine toward the exit. "We have to be somewhere."

"Where?"

She didn't remember. "I don't know, but we need to go right away." She whistled to the others, and they staggered toward her like drunks.

They stumbled through the gate, bumping into each other like pins in a bowling alley. She swore at Tor when he stepped on her with his big, furry foot.

The sound of a gun locking and loading was her only warning before she realized Victor was aiming the long barrel of his weapon at them. Constantine fell on top of her, and Tor charged the human, twitching and jerking with each bullet that pierced his chest. He fell on top of Victor, tearing the gun from his hands, yanking his head off, then tossing it into the river. Tor sank to his knees, clutching his chest, and fell on his side with a groan, blood frothing from his mouth.

"Father!" she cried, pushing Constantine off her.

Luc was kneeling by his side first. "Hang on, Father. I'll go for help." He jumped to his feet and sped back through the gate, holding his nose.

She slowly moved toward him, her insides feeling like ice, then fell to her knees, barely aware of Constantine and Andrei behind her. Her father was filled with holes, and there was no Amara here to save him.

His features were screwed up in pain, and the color had drained from his ruddy cheeks. "Tatiana," he rasped, holding out his hand.

When his large, furry hand engulfed her smaller one, she was unable to hold back her tears, grief and despair overwhelming her. "Yes, Father."

"The axe was to scare the demon." He managed a weak smile that didn't mask the sadness in his eyes. "I'd never hurt you."

She kissed his hand, sobbing. She wanted to beg him not to die, to hold on, but when blood flowed from his lips, she knew he was out of time.

"Help me!" she cried to Constantine. "He can't die like this!"

He went behind Tor and lifted him. Tor's blood seeped into his white fur.

"Tatiana," Constantine said with great sadness. "There's too much blood."

"I know." She rubbed warmth into her father's cold hand. "He can't die alone on the ground."

"I understand." Constantine frowned, holding up her father as blood dripped down his chin.

She was vaguely aware of Andrei rubbing her back. Though she knew full well he could feel the quills through her sweatshirt, she didn't care anymore. All that mattered was her father. She kissed his furry brow. "I love you," she said, unable to contain the rising tide of depression that threatened to pull her under, drowning her in despair and regret. She knew without a doubt he had taken those bullets to save her, despite the demon living inside her, despite the way she'd refused to show him an ounce of understanding while he was making the hardest decisions of his life.

He opened his mouth to speak but went limp in Constantine's arms. He didn't need to tell her he loved her. She knew it because he'd died protecting her.

When Luc returned with a first-aid kit and a few other trackers, she shook her head at him, her vision blurring from tears. He cried out and collapsed beside Tor, picking up his other hand and kissing it, then reached for Tatiana.

They formed a triangle, holding their father's lifeless hands and holding each other. Tor shifted, becoming a man once more. A tracker threw a blanket over his nude body, which was riddled with so many holes, his organs were exposed.

Tatiana's wolf took over, releasing a mournful howl. Luc and her mates joined her, and they howled at the sky until her lungs ached.

She was shocked to see Phoenix standing behind Luc, pale, shimmering robes billowing behind her as if she'd just descended from the clouds.

"What happened here?" she asked.

Tatiana was too choked up to answer. She still wasn't sure how she felt about Phoenix or the role she'd played in Tor's death; Phoenix had locked them in the cell beneath the ground.

"Your man killed my mate's father," Constantine said.

"Oh." She clasped her hands to her heart, peered at something beyond Tatiana's shoulder, and recognized Victor's decapitated body. "Your father killed him?" she said to Tatiana.

She wiped her eyes with her sleeve. "After *your* man shot him full of holes."

Her mouth formed a perfect *O*. "And his men?"

"Dead or captured," Constantine said.

A single tear slid down her cheek. "Then I am free."

Free? Had she been their captive? She'd thought Phoenix was their ruler.

She offered Tatiana a hesitant smile. "Do you mind?" she said and knelt beside Luc to place a hand on Tor's forehead. "He is still warm. I might be able to save him if his spirit hasn't passed."

Luc sat back on his heels. "You're a healer? Like my Amara?"

"Well." She shrugged. "I don't know Amara, but I am many things."

"Please save him!" Tatiana cried.

"I will try my best." Placing a hand over Tor's heart, she closed her eyes, her face a mask of serenity.

Tatiana held tightly to Luc's hand, hoping, praying that Phoenix could save him. Constantine and Andrei drew closer, pressing around her protectively. Time seemed to drag, stretching like frost spreading from a slow breath in the dead of an Alaskan winter.

Phoenix pulled down the blanket and placed both hands on Tor's chest. They began to glow, softly at first, and then with a steady, thrumming pulse. Tatiana sucked in a hiss when bullets *plunked* on the ground beside him, each of his wounds healed, and color returned to his gray skin.

When Tor let out a gasp and then sucked in air, she cried out, unable to stop the flow of happy tears. Despite the demon inside her, and all the trauma from the past few days, she was smiling. Her father would live to see another day, and that's all that mattered.

Tor looked at Phoenix first, then Luc. "I was at the edge of Valhol. The Ancients were waiting for me. W-what happened?"

Luc released Tatiana's hand and wiped away tears. "She brought you back, Father," he said, gesturing to Phoenix. "She has healing powers, like Amara."

Tor shuddered. "Thank you."

"I am glad I could help."

Tor gazed at Tatiana. "I tried to tell you I loved you, daughter, but the words wouldn't come out."

She fell on top of him and kissed his blood-stained cheek. "That's okay. I already knew that."

PHOENIX SAT ON THE marble stairs beneath her throne, hesitantly looking around the room as if she was waiting for the boogie man to pop out from behind the heavy embroidered curtains. The three young attendants had been sent home, wherever that was, though the two white rabbits remained, alternating between licking each other's heads and eating hay out of a box. Constantine and Andrei were nearby. Her alpha stood by the windows in human form, keeping an eye on the activity outside. Andrei sat on a rug beside her, and she knelt beside the pile of cushions they'd fashioned into a bed for Tor, who was also in human form.

Tatiana rubbed his arm. Despite the heat flowing through the open doors, he still felt cold. She could tell by the heavy circles under his eyes that he was exhausted and hoped he would get some rest.

"Where is my brother?" Phoenix asked, nervously toying with her fingers.

"Magnus is with the others," she said. "They have a lot of cleanup to do. Do you want me to send for him?"

Phoenix turned ashen. "Not really."

"He's married to my cousin." Tatiana forced enthusiasm into her voice. "He's not bad once you get to know him." She had no idea if Magnus intended to continue being a jerk, though she hoped not. Phoenix was nothing like her genie mother. She deserved to have siblings that treated her with kindness.

Phoenix smiled at Tor. "Are you comfortable now?"

"Very," he said and yawned, his eyes heavy, "but I should be helping the others."

She patted his shoulder like she was comforting a child. "Healing magic takes great strength, especially when you've died."

Ordinarily, her father would've been furious with anyone for forcing him to rest, but Phoenix was an exception. Tatiana understood why he'd mellowed. Something in that throne room made her feel like she was back in the soothing lavender garden. Tatiana wondered if it was the same magic. Luckily, it wasn't as strong, just mild enough to take off their edge.

"What is it that makes me feel so relaxed?" she asked Phoenix.

"My soothing magic," Phoenix answered. "It's not as strong as it was in the garden. Sorry about that. I meant to calm everyone. I had no idea Victor would shoot your father."

"It all worked out," Tatiana said with a wink, rubbing her father's hand.

After her father had finally given in to sleep, she sat back on her heels and rubbed her sore shoulder. She didn't remember pulling the muscle, but it hurt now. Andrei had offered to massage it earlier, but she'd refused. She didn't want her mates touching her there, or anywhere, given the state of her skin. She wiped sweat off her forehead. It was hot, and her heavy clothes made it worse. What she wouldn't give for her old body back, so she could switch to a tank top and shorts or return to the Mexican coast and take a dip in one of the pools. But now was not the time to mourn the loss of her body. She had too much to be thankful for, starting with her father's miraculous recovery.

"I can't thank you enough for bringing him back to us," she said to Phoenix for at least the tenth time. "Your magic is absolutely amazing."

Phoenix shrugged off her compliment. "You and your father love each other?" There was a watery edge to her voice, and she suspected Phoenix longed for a father's love, too. That made her appreciate Tor and her three other fathers all the more. They might have been strict at times, but they'd spoiled and adored her. She couldn't imagine having grown up without them.

Her heart ached for Phoenix. "Yes, we do. I'm so thankful we still have him."

"You're very lucky." There was a flash of defiance in her eyes. "If you'd stayed in that cell, he wouldn't have been shot. I sent you there for your protection."

Constantine joined them. "Why there?" he asked.

Her grin was sheepish. "It was the first place I thought of."

Tatiana laughed. "Next time, please think of a beach."

Phoenix shook her head. "My teleportation wouldn't take you that far."

Interesting. Tatiana's five-year-old nephew, Hrod, had just learned to teleport several miles away. Her brothers had had to fly him to Romania so her mates' stepmother Eilea could put a spell on him and his younger brothers to mute their magic. She wondered if Eilea could help Phoenix develop her magic. It was already powerful if she had been able to create a dragon illusion.

Constantine said, "How did you come to be Victor's hostage?"

She turned her gaze to her hands, fisted in her lap. "I had a special bond with the nuns at the orphanage. One of them in particular, Sister Mary, was like a mother to me. She taught me English, and settled for nothing but perfection." Her eyes were alight with what Tatiana hoped were happy memories. "One day she collapsed. Liver disease. She had months to live." She held up her hands, looking at them as if they were foreign objects. "I'd felt my power while growing up, but it was never very strong until I reached puberty. I was afraid at first, but I couldn't let Sister Mary die. I crawled into her bed one night and said I'd had a bad dream. I saved her while she slept and never told a soul."

Her heart expanded at the girl's beautiful story. And Magnus said she was an abomination? She was more saint than demon.

"And nobody suspected you?" Constantine asked.

"I think they suspected it was me that saved her, but they didn't say anything." She grinned. "They called it a miracle from God. Two weeks later, Mr. Martinez fell from the ladder while fixing a leak and broke his back. He was paralyzed. Mr. Martinez did so much for our orphanage, I couldn't let him suffer. The nuns declared me a saint. Next thing I knew, people from neighboring villages were coming to me to heal them." She frowned. "Word kept spreading."

"And that's when Victor found you?"

She shook her head. "Victor's boss, Omar. He and his men came after me, slaughtering everyone who stood in their way." Her face hardened. "Including Mr. Martinez."

"We spoke to an old man from your village," she said, recalling his donkey and the picture her father had taken from him. "He called you La Diabla."

"I showed my true powers when Omar tried to take me. I fought back, setting the town on fire in an effort to save them. In the end, they wanted me to go. They thought I was the devil." She heaved a shaky breath. "I guess they were right."

"What happened to Omar?" Constantine asked.

She dragged a shaky hand through her hair, her Spanish accent growing thicker as she told her story. "He wanted me to cure his child's cancer, which I did. Then he made more demands. He told me to slaughter his enemies, who were rival drug cartels. I refused. There was a revolt. Victor killed Omar and took over." A rabbit jumped in her lap, and she stroked its long, silky ears. "He tried to kill Omar's entire family, even babies. I convinced him to let them go. They fled to Mexico, and Victor assumed control. I had hoped things would be different, but he was a tyrant just like Omar, refusing to let me return to the orphanage, refusing to let me leave here at all."

Listening to Phoenix and observing her gentleness with the rabbit told Tatiana all she needed to know about the girl. She was indeed a treasure. Though she may have been part demon, there was no doubt she had a wolf's heart. Thank the Ancients, for she could have easily used her powerful magic for evil. The Amaroki needed to ensure Phoenix remained kind. Perhaps that was why Phoenix's fathers had taken her from Jezebeth and placed her with nuns. Tatiana could not imagine what Phoenix would've become had Jezebeth raised her.

A shame, Morana said. *So much power gone to waste.*

Tatiana cringed at hearing Morana's voice. She'd thought the demon had finally decided to leave her alone. Wishful thinking.

She moved over beside Phoenix and settled a hand on her wrist, pleased when she didn't pull away. "I'm so sorry about what happened to you, but I'm very glad we found you."

"I have to admit I was skeptical at first. I thought you were only more humans trying to take advantage of my power."

Andrei cleared his throat. "Is that why you put up that dragon at the border?"

She looked at him as if seeing him for the first time. "Oh, you saw that?"

"It scared the shit out of me."

"I did that for Victor. It was the only way he'd let Omar's family leave alive. There are several surrounding the compound."

Andrei smiled. "You might want to take them down now."

Her answering smile was subtle. "I wouldn't think giant ape-men would be scared of a little dragon."

Andrei laughed. "I'm just a wolf shifter, and the ape-men prefer to be called protectors."

"So you can't turn into a protector?"

"No," he said. "Only the alphas in our tribe."

She turned to Tatiana. "And what about you?"

"I can turn into a wolf," Tatiana answered, "like all Amaroki women. Like you can, too, I assume."

"I can. It was the shock of my life when I hit puberty. What are Amaroki?"

"You have a lot to learn about our race," Constantine said.

"I'm part of your race?" Her eyes brightened with apprehension. "The one who claims to be my brother said I'm a demon."

"Your mom is a demon," Tatiana corrected. "Your fathers were wolves, which makes you an Amaroki, too."

"Were?" She blanched. "Are they all dead?"

"All but one," she said.

"I'm sorry, but also I'm relieved. The only father I met wanted me dead."

"Do you remember his name?" Constantine asked.

"It was Vidar. He came to see me when I was ten."

Her heart ached for the girl. She knew the same crushing feeling of believing her father wanted her dead, though Tor had only been trying to scare her demon.

"Do you know why?" Constantine asked.

She shook her head. "The nuns brought me to the courtyard to meet him. I sensed his dark aura the minute I stepped outside. He said he wanted to take me home with him, and I refused. I told him he was cursed."

Annie had said Vidar had been a belligerent drunk. "I bet he didn't handle that news well."

Rocking back and forth, she wrapped her arms around herself. "No," she said. "His eyes turned yellow, and he told the nuns they should've killed me, said he'd do it for them if they didn't want blood on their hands. They told him to leave and never come back."

"Great Ancients," Tatiana breathed. "He was the second alpha, and he died a few years ago. Magnus killed him in a battle. Vidar had gone mad. He tried to kill Magnus's mate, my cousin Annie."

Phoenix looked away. "No offense, but after that experience with my father, I hope you understand why I was apprehensive when you first arrived and why I'm not excited to meet my mother."

"She said she's been mourning your loss ever since your fathers took you," Tatiana said in an effort to cheer her up, though she thought Phoenix would be equally disappointed in her mother when she learned her fathers had most likely been apathetic toward her because of her mother's curse.

Jezebeth might have loved her daughter, but she had an evil side that was impossible to ignore. She'd not only cursed the Wolfstalkers, she'd condemned hundreds of humans to a gruesome death by turning Sami into a Chupacabra. Phoenix would one day learn the truth. Magnus wouldn't waste time telling her. Then what? Would Phoenix reject her mother? The poor girl would be alone in the world without any parents to love her, and Magnus would continue to blame her for her mother's sins. They couldn't allow that to happen.

TATIANA AND PHOENIX had fun playing with the rabbits and getting acquainted. Phoenix talked a lot about the nuns and even quoted Biblical scripture. Clearly her religious upbringing had had a strong influence on her, which was why Tatiana didn't bring up the Ancients. She knew it would take time for Phoenix to adjust to this new way of life, and she didn't want to overwhelm her. The bandits were nowhere to be seen, and there were several trackers loading trucks with crates while Agent Johnson dealt with the Guatemalan authorities.

Her father slept for a good two hours and finally woke for a meal of smoked meats, cheese, crackers, and pickled vegetables. Tatiana was famished, eating seconds and then thirds. They sat around a dining table on a terrace overlooking verdant fields she realized were plants used for making cocaine. Tor sat at the head of the table, Constantine and Andrei next to him, and Tatiana and Phoenix across from them. They shared light, pleasant conversation, though Phoenix rarely spoke as she daintily picked at her food. She mostly observed everyone else, and Tatiana knew it would take time for her to get accustomed to other wolves.

The warm sun beat down on her, and she breathed in the fragrant air. Even though the most harrowing part of their journey still awaited them, hanging over her like a black cloud, she was grateful for this day and for getting a second chance with Tor.

"Found it, Father." Luc trotted up the terrace's curved staircase carrying Tor's backpack. It was covered in crusted dirt.

"Nice job, son," Tor said and took it from him.

Luc helped himself to a piece of bread and a chunk of ham. "The son of a bitch buried it, but it was easy to find your scent," he said between bites.

"Of course." Tatiana laughed. "It had his crusty underwear."

"They weren't crusty," Tor protested, eyes twinkling.

"That's a matter of opinion," she teased, happy she could joke with him again.

Tor removed the rusty old lamp from the pack and set it on the table. "Well, Phoenix, are you ready to meet your mother?"

She blanched. "She's in there?"

"As a djinn, she's attached to her lamp."

"There's nothing to be nervous about." Tatiana gave Phoenix's hand a reassuring squeeze. "She adores you."

Phoenix frowned. "She doesn't even know me."

"She does," Tatiana said. "She's been watching you through her magic crystals."

Phoenix gasped. "What?"

Tor picked up the lamp and rubbed it three times. "We'll let her explain it."

Jezebeth escaped with a flourish of smoke and sparkles, tossing her long black hair over her shoulders. "It's about time you wolves freed me from that prison cell."

Tor pointed at the lamp. "You went in there on your own."

"Yes, but I can't come back out until you rub the damn lamp, and you sure took your time doing it."

"Forgive us, but we were being shot at." He gestured. "Jezebeth, Phoenix is here."

Jezebeth spun around, her hands morphing into wisps of smoke as she threw them in the air. "My darling child!" she squealed, leaning over Phoenix's chair. "Is it you? After the most wretched fifteen years of my life, has my baby girl returned to me?"

Eyes bulging, Phoenix leaned back. "Hi."

"Come, let me look at you." She motioned for Phoenix to stand.

Phoenix got to her feet, her face turning ten shades of red.

"My," Jezebeth cooed. "What a beautiful young woman you have become." She winked at Tor. "Isn't my child exquisite?"

Tor smiled. "She's certainly beautiful."

"I recognize you." Phoenix tilted her head. "I've dreamt about you many times."

"Those were no dreams. That was the only way I could visit you." Tears welled up in her eyes, dripping over impossibly long lashes. "Even though I haven't been able to hold you in fifteen years, I have always been with you, daughter."

Phoenix looked at Jezebeth's feet, which were tethered to the lamp. "Oh!"

Floating down to her, Jezebeth dabbed her eyes. "I've longed for the day I can hold you once more." She held out her arms. "May I?"

Phoenix silently nodded.

Jezebeth put her arms around the girl. Phoenix looked pained.

Tor rose, making some noise. "We'll leave you two alone."

Phoenix broke the embrace, alarmed. "Please don't go," she said and she stepped away from the genie.

Jezebeth's expression fell, but she quickly plastered on another smile. "You must leave here, darling, and be with your own kind. You're not safe here."

"Where will I go?" Phoenix asked, gazing at Tor instead of her mother.

"With your brothers and Annie," he said.

Tatiana interjected. "You'll love Annie. She's super sweet, and she grew up a lone wolf, too."

"Oh, okay." She nervously toyed with the end of her silk belt. "Are you sure they want me?"

Eyes lighting up like fireworks, Jezebeth hovered above her daughter. "How could they not want such a treasure?"

"And where will you be?" Phoenix asked.

"Wherever you are, my dear."

Tatiana grimaced, then quickly hid it. She didn't remember that as part of the bargain. How would Magnus react to having the djinn living with him? She already knew he wasn't fond of his sister.

Her father was right. This djinn was tricky.

Chapter Eleven

DEJAN WOKE WITH A START, chest heaving, eyes burning from crying. A dark fog hung over him, as he was unable to shake the memories from a horrible dream.

Sitting up, he rubbed his eyes with shaking hands. Ever since Tatiana stabbed Dimitri, he'd had the same recurring nightmare. He was lying in bed, Tatiana by his side, when suddenly she rolled on top of him, sprouting eight legs and long fangs that dripped venom. Before he could stop her, she sank her fangs into his throat, draining his blood like a vampire. His wolf went silent, unable to help him as he tried to fight her, but she pinned him down with powerful legs, cackling and hissing while his lifeblood slowly seeped away.

The dream left him so traumatized each morning, he could hardly function the rest of the day, and when night came, he fought sleep, terrified she'd visit again.

He wondered, not for the first time, how he would ever be able to reconcile with his mate. Just the sight of her brought back all the emotions engendered by the nightmare, as well as those connected with her trying to kill him and Dimitri. His brother's blood splattered across the walls and on the floor—! How was he supposed to get over that?

TOR STOOD BY AS MAGNUS paced the garden in protector form. He'd shifted into the big beast as soon as Tor had broken the news about Phoenix. He'd suspected Magnus wouldn't take the news well, and he cursed himself a fool for ever thinking this was a good idea.

"You expect me to take a djinn into my home?" Magnus roared. "You go too far!"

He was right to be angry. Tor would've been uprooting trees if he'd been put in the same position, but Tor didn't see an alternative. "How do you think Phoenix will react when you dump her mother under that pile of skulls?"

Magnus bore down on Tor. "She won't have a choice."

Tor could've easily shifted, but he didn't want to escalate an already tense situation. "That child has more power in her little finger than all the Amaroki put together. Thank the Ancients, she is compassionate and kind." He paused. "Don't let your prejudice and hatred turn her against us."

"You expect not one, but two demons to live in the same house as my infant?"

Tor repressed a grimace. Good point, and the more he thought about it, the more he realized his plan was insane.

"Why don't you take them, Tor?" Magnus said. "You've got plenty of room in Alaska."

There was just one problem. To do that Magnus had to break his deal with Jezebeth. Would the demon use that as an excuse to curse him? "Jezebeth specifically asked for you to take in Phoenix."

Tor swore he saw new red veins popping out of Magnus's eyes.

Magnus stomped the ground so hard, it shook. "I should have never made a deal with her."

A feeling of hopelessness washed over him. This wouldn't work. There was too much bad blood between Jezebeth and the Wolfstalkers. Cursing their misfortunes, he said, "We can discuss your sister's living arrangements after my family and I return from Romania. I'd rather focus on one demonic battle at a time."

JAX WAS SITTING ON the side of an Olympic swimming pool with a dozen other trackers, feet dangling in the water, when Magnus found him. He couldn't fault them for goofing off, pushing each other into the water and stunt diving off the board. They'd earned the reprieve.

Several statues of Phoenix were planted in the manicured bushes lining the area. These people believed her to be a goddess. He sure as hell hoped she didn't expect to be treated like one at his house. If she was going to live with him, she'd have chores like his brothers.

Walking behind a row of tall hedges, he let out a sharp whistle, waving at Jax.

Jax saw him and walked over, his bare feet crunching the grass. "What is it?"

Magnus gave his brother a dark look. "The djinn whore expects to live with us, along with Phoenix."

"So she can put more curses on our family, our children?" He let out a menacing growl. "No fucking way."

Magnus was hoping for exactly this reaction. It would make it easier for Jax to go along with his plan. "There is a good chance Tor will take them both to live with him."

"Jezebeth said you must be the one to take Phoenix," Jax pointed out. "I wouldn't put it past the spiteful bitch to curse you if you go back on your word."

"Even if I allowed them to live with us, what kind of influence will she be on Phoenix?" A dozen different scenarios, all of them ending badly, ran though his mind. "The girl has all the powers of a goddess." Even though she wasn't one.

Jax turned as cold and unyielding as a block of ice. "Her mother will poison her mind. Imagine that kind of power in the hands of an evil shifter."

Magnus's spine stiffened, his veins slowing to icy sludge. "The world would not be safe."

"What can we do?"

Magnus's plan was dangerous but appealing. "Discard the lamp somewhere it can't be found."

"What if Phoenix finds her?" Jax asked, his voice rising to a feverish pitch. "We don't know the extent of her powers."

Magnus mentally prepared himself for what he was about to say, knowing his brother would think he'd gone mad. Even he was starting to doubt his sanity. "Then she must be put where not even Phoenix can find her." He paused, releasing a slow breath while gathering the nerve to continue. "In the Hoia Baciu."

"Do you think Tor will leave her there?"

His brother still hadn't caught on. He tensed, waiting for understanding to dawn. "He's not going into the forest. Only Constantine's pack is."

"That's right." He looked thoughtful. "Older wolves become disorientated in that haunted place. Will Constantine discard the djinn if we asked?"

"Tatiana won't let him." She was a she-wolf and had a soft heart. She wouldn't let Magnus do anything that would hurt Phoenix.

"Damn. Then what do we do?"

Magnus felt a darkness permeate his soul at the very thought of his crazy scheme. But he had no choice. How else would he ensure the safety of his family? "There is only one thing to be done. I must go into the forest with them."

Jax's eyes bulged. "You could be killed or worse."

"I could, but it's a chance I must take. The fate of wolf and humankind depends on it."

LUC HAD SOMEHOW SECURED a small tour bus, and there was plenty of room for them all. Their seats faced each other, so Magnus was forced to watch Tatiana and Phoenix holding hands, acting like secret best friends as they laughed together and whispered in each other's ears. Seeing his sister bond with another shifter should have put him at ease, but Magnus was still worried about the girl's future. If she turned out to be evil like her mother, Magnus would have to cut her down. He couldn't imagine what havoc an untethered evil like Jezebeth could unleash on the world.

He saw no sign of the djinn, but judging by the way Tor kept his backpack close, he knew she was inside it. He didn't like the way he held protectively onto the backpack, his knuckles whitening as he dug his fingers into the fabric. Had the Alaska chieftain forgotten the harm she had caused the Wolfstalkers? He wanted to believe Tor was being protective of the djinn because he needed her to cast out Tatiana's demon, and not that these wolves were growing too attached to the tricky bitch.

"Magnus, do you mind if we take Phoenix to Romania?" Tor asked. "She wants to accompany us."

He glanced at Jax. *This is my chance, brother.*

Then take it, but I still don't like it.

Neither do I.

He wiped sweaty palms on his military-issue sweats. "I made a vow to Jeze-beth that I'd look after my sister."

"I know," Tor said, "But the girl doesn't want to part from her mother."

Magnus's gaze shot to Phoenix, who clutched Tatiana's hand, a wide, hope-ful look in her eyes. For the span of a heartbeat, he felt guilty, knowing he was going to break her heart. Banishing Jezebeth was the best thing for Phoenix in the long run. That evil woman would poison the child's mind. "They will have to part when Constantine takes the djinn into the forest."

"Of course." Tor patted his backpack when it buzzed and shook on his knees. "She will stay with the Lupescus and me. Jezebeth will not hold you to your vow until we return."

"I will go with you to Romania."

Tor shook his head. "You have already done so much for us, Magnus."

"Phoenix is my sister, my responsibility." He dropped his voice, leaving no room for argument. "I'm going to Romania."

"Very well," Tor said. "We can always use more protectors in case Atan Albescu's pack causes trouble." He glanced at Tatiana, who looked like a walk-ing corpse, with her gray skin and limp hair. "We can't afford to waste time. When we get back to Texas, say goodbye to your family. Then we must go."

Magnus's heart rate slowed to a slow steady thud as realization dawned. He was going to risk not only his life but his soul, but if it meant Jezebeth couldn't harm his family again, it would be worth it. "I'll be ready."

Chapter Twelve

TATIANA DIDN'T KNOW how she felt about Magnus coming along. She'd hoped to get rid of him after they left Texas, but he insisted on accompanying them to Romania. Why? Instinct told her it wasn't to keep an eye on Phoenix. He had yet to show her any brotherly affection. In fact, he had yet to do anything other than brood. She felt guilty for not wanting him around. He was Annie's mate, and she adored Annie. Plus, Jezebeth had put his family through hell. He had a reason to be broody. She did her best to put her fear and mistrust out of her mind. Annie's mate wouldn't cause her family problems. At least she sure as hell hoped so.

Her group sat close to the front of the plane. She was between Phoenix and Constantine, and Tor and Andrei faced them. Phoenix's two bunnies were in a big crate on the floor beside Tor, munching on hay and not showing the slightest fear that they were surrounded by wolves. Phoenix occasionally fed them banana and cilantro through the bars, talking sweetly to them when they took her offering. After observing Phoenix with her rabbits, it was hard for Tatiana to reconcile that she was half demon. She might have looked like her mother, but there was no denying she had a wolf's heart.

Magnus sat by himself in the row across the aisle from theirs, stealing glances at Phoenix, who never looked in his direction while she talked to her rabbits through their cage bars. Tatiana reminded herself to ask Constantine to switch seats with Phoenix once the plane had leveled off. Phoenix hadn't wanted to sit by the window, but perhaps she'd change her mind after ten minutes of being next to her big, grumpy brother.

Agent Johnson, along with two other agents who worked with the Amaroki, had the first two rows to themselves. Ignoring the captain's intercom request to wait until they reached cruising altitude, they had their paperwork and laptops laid out on trays in front of them.

Everyone else sat in back with Dimitri. Dejan had barely spoken to her after they were reunited. Though he'd said he was relieved they'd survived Guatemala, that was the extent of the conversation. She hoped it was just because the thought of going into the dark forest filled him with dread.

She worried about him and their bond more and more. What if their ties had been completely severed? What if he didn't want to restore the bond because he hadn't forgiven her for attacking Dimitri? She could tell her skin had turned more gray since she'd last seen him. Her eyes had hollowed out even more and those hairs on her arms and back had grown thicker. Maybe he was too repulsed by her to love her.

Tatiana held Phoenix's hand when the plane took off. All color drained from her face and she shut her eyes, whispering the same prayer over and over. "Our father who art in heaven, hallowed be thy name...."

Tatiana didn't understand it. Who was this father? Why was he doing art in heaven? Was he a painter or sculptor? This had to be something Phoenix had learned from the nuns. She'd had no idea the Christian religion centered around art. Then again, she'd seen images of beautiful chapels, so it kind of made sense.

Morana's wicked laughter echoed in her head. *It's old English, you idiot.*

I didn't ask you, she snapped. *So fuck off.*

"How high does this plane go?" Phoenix asked.

Her gaze shot back to Phoenix, then to her father, because she had no clue.

"Not too high," Tor said. "Six to seven miles up."

Phoenix's eyes bulged. "That seems awfully high."

They jumped at the sound of a muffled scream coming from behind Tor's legs. Pulling his backpack out from under the seat, Tor set it on his lap and unzipped it. "Have you ever flown on a plane before, Phoenix?"

"No." She pulled her legs to her chest, making herself smaller. She probably still felt strange having a genie for a mother.

He set the lamp on the empty seat between him and Andrei. "There's nothing to be nervous about."

"The Amaroki fly this route all the time to see our Romanian family," Constantine said. "The American military has special planes for us."

Which was a good thing, too. They didn't want to fly commercial and risk exposing their magic to other passengers. The military pilots kept their cabin doors shut for a majority of the flight.

"If you're so nervous, why don't you just teleport us there, like when you stuck us in that cell?" Andrei asked with a mischievous grin.

Her cheeks colored, and she twirled the frosted pink tip of her black ponytail. "I don't have the ability to teleport far, just a few hundred feet at best, and my magic doesn't always work. We got lucky that time."

Tor rubbed the lamp, and Jezebeth burst out in a puff of smoke. The lamp tumbled to the floor. She hovered over Constantine, giving him a pointed look until he moved to the seat beside Tor. Tatiana quickly switched to Constantine's window seat, leaving the center seat for the demon.

Jezebeth sat beside her daughter, the lamp following her toes across the floor as if it was a ball and chain.

"Your magic will grow stronger as you age." Patting Phoenix's arm, she bestowed on her a motherly smile. "I will teach you how to wield it."

Tatiana froze. The thought of Jezebeth tutoring a young, impressionable girl didn't sit well with her. The climate in the cabin instantly changed, tension radiating off the shifters in an almost palpable way. Obviously, nobody else thought it was a good idea, either.

Magnus leaned toward them with a menacing snarl. "Will you teach her how to put curses on shifter hearts, too?"

Jezebeth turned up her chin. "Only if they deserve it."

"Tell me," Magnus asked, "did those humans Sami killed deserve it?"

"Magnus," Tor warned. "Now is not the time."

"When is the time? After she's polluted my sister's mind?"

Phoenix looked horror-struck. "What humans?"

"Your mother didn't tell you?" Magnus drummed his fingers on the armrest. "The reason Vidar and Sami were evil, the reason I was left with no choice but to kill Vidar, was because Jezebeth placed curses on their hearts."

"They took my child from me!" Jezebeth shrieked, jumping from her seat and hovering over Magnus like a possessed windsock.

Magnus shook his head. "I can't imagine why they didn't want a demon raising their child."

"They wanted to kill my baby!" Jezebeth screeched like a ghoul in the dead of night, her face turning deep crimson.

The plane rattled and shook as if it had hit turbulence, but Tatiana suspected Jezebeth was the cause.

"Everyone calm down," Tor said, rising to his feet.

"Then why didn't they?" Magnus sneered at Jezebeth, ignoring Tor. "Why did they take her to live with nuns?"

Jezebeth rolled her eyes. "I don't pretend to know what went on in their heads."

"What humans were killed?" Phoenix asked again.

"I didn't know them," Magnus said. "I only found their pile of skulls. Hundreds of them. Migrants, probably, who'd come here in search of a better life. Instead they were sucked into a nightmare created by your mother." He pointed at the djinn. "She turned Sami into a man-eating werewolf."

Tor stepped between Jezebeth and Magnus, holding out his hands in a conciliatory manner. "That's enough."

"I'm only getting started," Magnus said.

"I said enough!" Tor boomed, his deep protector voice taking over. "Can't you see you're upsetting your sister?"

Tatiana reached across the seat to rub Phoenix's back. She'd curled into herself like a frightened animal.

"She needs to be made aware of who her mother is. *What* her mother is," Magnus said between clenched teeth. "Maybe she has feelings for you. Maybe she even loves you, as much as a demon can love anyone. She is wicked and will make you wicked, too, if you allow her to influence you."

"Magnus," Tor said harshly. "You have two seconds to go sit at the back of the plane before I throw you there myself."

Magnus squared his shoulders, giving Tor a look that would've made a lesser wolf cower. "I never thought I'd see the day when the Amaroki's greatest chieftain sided with a vindictive demon."

"There are no sides! There is only my need to save my child. Now go!"

Tatiana continued rubbing Phoenix's back. "Are you okay?"

She shook her head. "I feel sick."

"Just ignore him, Phoenix." Jezebeth let out a grating laugh. "He is a hardhearted fool like his fathers."

Phoenix looked at her mother. "Did you turn Sami into a man eater?"

Jezebeth shrugged. "He got what he deserved." Either Jezebeth was oblivious, or she didn't care about her daughter's feelings.

"What about all the humans he killed, Mother? Did they deserve it, too?"

She waved away her daughter's concern. "They were only weak humans. They had no magic and couldn't retaliate."

Clearly, Jezebeth was missing the point.

Phoenix shot up, back as stiff as a board. "'Rescue the weak and the needy; deliver them from the hand of the wicked.'"

Jezebeth was puzzled. "Where have I heard that before?"

Phoenix gave her mother a look of derision. "The Book of Psalms."

Jezebeth snorted. "Curse your fathers for sending you to live with nuns."

Phoenix wilted. "I'm tired and need rest."

Tatiana didn't know how else to offer Phoenix comfort, so she simply held her hand and gave her a supportive smile. Phoenix gave her a weak, appreciative smile in return.

Tor opened a compartment above them. "Do you want a pillow and blanket?"

"Please." Phoenix groaned. "It's been a long few days."

Tatiana helped her arrange things and did her best to stay upbeat. "You can put your head or your feet on my lap."

"Thanks," Phoenix said, resting her feet on Tatiana's legs.

Jezebeth, seemingly unaware of her daughter's despair, said, "Do you wish me to tell you a bedtime story, my dear?"

"No, Mother." Phoenix turned red-rimmed eyes on the djinn, her tone as cutting as a razor's edge. "I don't think I wish to hear anything else from you. In fact, I'd rather you went back into your lamp."

Jezebeth gasped. "But my darling Phoenix."

She turned away and punched the pillow into submission. "And please don't call me your darling."

Magnus's laughter echoed from the back of the plane, and Tor growled until Magnus went silent. Jezebeth disappeared into the lamp with a dramatic flourish.

This fight is far from over, she told her mates.

I know. Constantine grimaced. *And I've got the sinking feeling we're about to be dragged into the feud.*

TATIANA LIFTED PHOENIX'S feet from her lap and stood, stretching her sore back. Constantine and Andrei had fallen asleep, as had her father. She thought it odd that all her guards were sleeping. Did this mean her father trusted her now? Drasko was still awake in back, playing solitaire under a dim overhead light. Luc slept across from him, feet hanging over the armrest, his neck turned at such an awkward angle, she knew he'd be sore when he woke up.

Drasko shot her a sideways look. "Do you need something, sister?"

So much for her father trusting her. Drasko was on duty. But that was okay; she didn't trust the demon inside her either.

"Using the toilet, if that's okay."

He shrugged, flashing a sympathetic smile. "You need to get more sleep. You won't be resting much in the forest."

She walked down the aisle toward him. "I know. Just have a lot on my mind."

"I know you do, and I'm sorry."

She got the feeling his apology was for carrying the axe and not because she was stressed. She looked at her hands, dismayed when she saw the edges of her nails were curling and splitting. When had that happened?

Drasko had been her favorite brother growing up. She'd been his little shadow, following him everywhere. He'd taught her how to ride a four-wheeler, fish, and fire a gun. She adored him, but one day she became possessed by a demon, and next thing she knew, her idol was following her around with an axe. She was crushed.

"How are you?" he asked.

"Ready to get this demon out of me."

Tatiana, my love.

Her attention was instantly drawn to Dimitri, who was sitting in the back row, eyeing her intently.

She turned pleading eyes to Drasko. "May I talk to him for a moment?"

His lips twisted. "Make it quick. We can't have a repeat of what happened last time."

She cringed. "It won't, I swear."

When Drasko nodded his approval, she moved toward the back of the plane, her legs feeling suddenly weak, her tongue heavy. What was she going to say to him? She missed him.

He looked at her with such intense longing, she knew it would haunt her nightmares for years.

How are you? she asked telepathically, preferring to keep their conversation private.

He dragged a hand over his face, and she noticed his nails were splitting, too. *Just missing you, iubita mea. How are you?*

Same. Wish I could talk to you more.

We will soon.

She glanced at Dejan, who slept upright, turned into the window, his back to Dimitri. She hadn't once seen the brothers interact during the flight.

Did you and Dejan have a fight?

Bitter laughter bounced around in her mind. *You could say that.*

She frowned at that. Was Dejan pulling away from more than just her? *I can't speak to him anymore.*

What do you mean?

I can't sense him in my head, and he doesn't answer when I call to him.

He sat up, back rigid. *Are you saying the bond is broken?*

Clutching the back of a seat, she frowned at her hands. *If it is, I wouldn't know how to fix it.*

Do you want *to fix it?*

Heat flamed her cheeks. *Of course. Why would you even ask that?*

He eyed Dejan through sideways slits. *He hasn't been there for us, Tatiana.*

He's here now, isn't he? she said, though her words lacked conviction. What if he was only here because he had to be? What if he no longer cared about them?

Physically, yes, he said. *Emotionally, no.*

She desperately tried to find the right words, more to convince herself than Dimitri. *That is your demon talking,* she finally said. *When they're gone, we'll feel differently about Dejan.*

His lips twisted into a scowl, as he cast another furtive glance at Dejan. *I hope you're right.*

I have to be, she said, too overwhelmed with grief to say anything else on the subject. *I need to rest. So do you. I love you.*

And I love you, iubita mea, he said. *More than anything.*

She wished she could throw herself in his arms and never let go. She cast one last woeful look at him before forcing herself to walk away, feeling as if she was leaving her heart and soul behind.

TATIANA SHOOK THE GIRL awake. "Phoenix, we're here."

She rolled over and opened her eyes. "Where is my mother?" she asked and yawned.

Tatiana nodded toward her father's backpack, which he'd set on the center seat while he removed carry-on bags from overhead. "In her lamp."

She scowled at the bag. "Good."

Tatiana sat beside her, noticing how sickly her skin looked compared to the warm glow of Phoenix's healthy complexion. But now wasn't the time to focus on herself. This poor girl had just discovered her mother was a cruel demon. "You okay, Phoenix?"

"I'm confused and horrified. All those humans killed, and she didn't seem to care." She wiped moisture from her eyes. "Maybe some of those humans stopped at our mission on their journey. The sisters were always taking in travelers."

That must have made it even harder for Phoenix to bear. As much as Tatiana felt sorry for the girl, at least Phoenix had a heart. Had she cruel inclinations like her mother, the world would not be safe. "I'm sorry you had to find out like that."

She wiped moisture from her eyes. "Now I understand why Magnus hates me."

Tor handed Phoenix a box of tissues. "He doesn't hate you," he said.

"He does." She dabbed her eyes, then blew her nose. "He thinks I'm like her."

Tatiana didn't know what to say to that. Magnus had exited the plane the minute the doors opened, not bothering to check on Phoenix.

Tatiana gave her arm a reassuring squeeze. "But you're not like her."

Tatiana remembered Jezebeth telling her that she was the creator of the shifter race, something she had yet to bring up to her father. She wasn't sure if she ever wanted to tell him. If it was true, it would only create more tension among their family when they needed to focus on healing.

"When Omar's men attacked my village," Phoenix said, turning her gaze to her hands fisted in her lap. "I lost control. I set fire to everything. I was trying to save them, and I ended up making things worse. Some humans may have died because of my actions." She hung her head. "That's why they think I'm a demon now. I panicked when I sent you to that cell and disoriented you in the garden. I didn't want a repeat of what happened in the village." She looked up at Tatiana with apologetic eyes, her expression as if her entire world hinged on Tatiana's forgiveness.

"You did the right thing." She patted the girl's hand. "We're alive because of you."

"I won't be like her." She looked out the window. Everyone else had disembarked except for Constantine and Tor, who had gathered their bags and were patiently waiting by the door.

"You won't be," she said. "Shall we go?"

Phoenix got up. "I don't want to see her again."

Tatiana winced. Jezebeth would curse Magnus for turning her daughter against her. "You might change your mind later."

Her face hardened. "I won't. Tor already told me my mother is helping you because you saved me."

"Yes."

"She should have helped you anyway."

They exited the plane while troubling thoughts ruminated through Tatiana's mind. While she was afraid Jezebeth would be a bad influence on Phoenix, she also feared the genie's wrath should Phoenix never forgive her. They walked a fine line with a vengeful demon. Either choice they made could have negative repercussions.

They walked outside to a winter wonderland of fresh snow dusting the small, European cars and old buildings and air so cold, she could see her breath.

After Tatiana hugged her mates' grandfathers, Klaus, Nicolae, and Novak, she got in the back of Klaus's car, with Phoenix on one side of her and Andrei on the other. Constantine sat up front, filling in Klaus on the gory details of the past few days. Tatiana wondered if her father had gone in another car to give Phoenix a reprieve from having to stare at his backpack. Tatiana still hadn't forgotten what Phoenix had said, how her mother should've helped her without having to bargain.

Releasing a slow breath, she prepared to finish their conversation. Not that she wanted to keep talking about Jezebeth. "Phoenix, your mother made a bargain to save her child's life. Any mother would've done the same. She loves you." She dropped her voice to a barely audible whisper, having a difficult time meeting Phoenix's eyes. "And speaking of what happened to me and my mate, you do know I have a demon in me, right?"

"Yes." She grimaced. "It's kind of obvious. No offense." She nodded at Tatiana's hands.

She rubbed her sore fingertips. The nails, which were cracking down the middle, made her fingers ache as if they'd been smashed by a hammer. "No offense taken. I don't normally look like this." She forced a smile. "The point is every day she tries to plant dark seeds in my heart, and every day I fight her influence. I refuse to let her destroy whatever good there is left in me. I will not let her destroy my wolf's heart." Taking a chance, she pressed her hand to Phoenix's heart. "You have a wolf's heart, too."

She looked on the verge of crying again. "How do you know?"

"I know," she said. "We wolf girls are loyal and compassionate, but we are also strong and fierce when we need to be. We will not let others dictate who we are." She chose her next words carefully, instinct telling her Phoenix needed to hear them. "I recognize another wolf heart when I see one."

"Thank you." She heaved a sigh, looking as if the weight of the world had been lifted from her shoulders. "You have no idea what that means to me."

"But I do know." Her throat constricted, making it hard for her to speak. "Because they are words I long to hear, too." She paused to steady herself and force the words out. "There are some who think my demon is winning, who underestimate my power." She fought the urge to turn and look at the car behind her, knowing Dejan was there.

Phoenix clasped her hand. "Only a fool would underestimate you, Tatiana."

Chapter Thirteen

DUSTING SNOW OFF THEIR boots and coats, Constantine and his family piled into their bunic's house, and he was instantly hit with nostalgia. Though this house had been rebuilt after the Devoras had driven a truck through it, his grandfathers had restored everything to nearly its original design, a traditional Romanian house with a long front porch and a low ceiling. He remembered hitting his head on it numerous times during his teen years after first learning how to shift into a protector. The sitting room walls were plastered with family pictures. The old floral furniture was covered with homemade quilts, and the nearby hearth always had a roaring fire in winter. The adjoining kitchen, though tight, was used for large family gatherings. The long oval table had been in their family for generations. After the Devoras had destroyed it, his bunics had painstakingly pieced it back together, sanding the rough edges and making it almost as good as new. When he inhaled the smell of roasting meats and pastries, he realized how much he'd missed this place. How much he'd missed Romania.

Bunic Anton and Bunica gave them warm hugs and insisted they sit and have tea and cookies. Anton helped Phoenix set up her rabbits in a warm spot beside the hearth, then gave her a guest of honor spot at the dining table which was usually reserved for the elders. As they worked to serve everyone, he noticed the lines around their eyes and mouths. Their fathers, Boris, Geri, and Marius, came over with their stepmother Eilea and their two baby brothers, Artem and Odin. Other than the oldest baby, Artem, blissfully playing with his blocks on a rug beside the table, a heavy gloom settled in the room, and not just because of the demons possessing Tatiana and Dimitri or the danger that awaited them in the Hoia Baciu. Father Jovan wasn't there, his absence a hole the size of the Black Sea, filling up every empty space in the room.

They gathered around the dining table, the elders and Phoenix sitting while the younger shifters stood behind them. Klaus sat at the head of the table, Tor at the other end, still holding the backpack. Despite Tatiana's protests, Phoenix insisted she take her chair. When his mate lowered herself into the chair, he heard her bones creaking as if she was an eighty-year-old woman. His family must've heard, too, because they all gave her looks of pity, and Anton doted on her more than anyone, insisting she eat several cookies and drink an extra cup of tea.

Constantine tried to put his worry for her out of his mind. Nothing he could do about it yet, but fear gnawed a hole in his gut anyway. Once they expelled her demon, he prayed she'd fully recover. Hopefully, his stepmom would be able to heal her if not.

Phoenix stood beside Tatiana, shifting nervously from foot to foot, her arms wrapped around herself, her eyes continuously darting to her rabbits in the other room. This would've been a good time for Magnus to give his sister comfort, but he hung back in the kitchen, glowering at Tor's backpack.

When Klaus cleared his throat, the room went silent. Even Artem had gone quiet, lying in his playpen with a bottle and snuggling his blanket.

"When do you go into the forest?" Klaus asked, pouring a hefty dose of vodka into his tea. He rarely saw his grandfather drink, but he understood the need for it.

Dejan was in the kitchen, stirring a big pot on the gas burner, his back to everyone, which he thought odd. He should've been with them at the table. "As soon as possible, Bunic."

Klaus nodded, deep lines on his brow. "Rest today, and we shall prepare for your entrance tomorrow before dawn."

Dimitri pushed in front of their fathers, his skin so deathly gray, it looked as if his body had been drained of all blood. "With all due respect, Bunic, we rested on the flight. I'm ready to get this demon out of me now."

"I agree," Boris said. "They should go now."

Constantine heard the urgency behind his father's words and suspected Boris wasn't telling them everything.

"The sun will be setting soon." Klaus stood, resting his knuckles on the table. "You must wait for the cover of darkness. The Albescus have been watching us."

Constantine let out a low growl. "Why now?" That pack had been harassing his family since before his grandfathers had taken over the chiefdom. It wasn't their fault the Albescus had made terrible leaders. The Romanian tribe had seen many improvements under the new leadership.

"They know your fathers' pack is weaker without a second alpha." Klaus nodded at Boris. "We think they are planning to take back the chiefdom."

"Hasn't Jovan nursed this grudge long enough?" Constantine grumbled. It had been three months. He didn't understand why Jovan hadn't reconciled with his pack. He refused to live in the same house with them or have anything to do with baby Odin, his son, all because he was still angry with Eilea for fighting demons without him. He'd always respected Jovan, but his ego was out of control. Would he really ruin their chiefdom over this? Destroy the family?

"I'd rather not talk of him," Boris said, sounding strained. "We need to focus on ensuring your survival."

"Before you go into the forest," Eilea said, rocking baby Odin in her arms, "I will cast a spell on each of you to ward off the burn."

Constantine heaved a huge sigh of relief. "That would be most appreciated." He remembered the welts his brother and mate had suffered after returning from the forest. Knowing they wouldn't have to suffer the distractions of demon burn could increase their chance of success.

Boris addressed Tor. "Are you sure this djinn can expel the demons?"

Tor tightened the hold on the backpack. "She said she could."

"If she does not, I will never forgive her."

All eyes turned to Phoenix, who'd been quiet till this point.

"Thank you, child," Klaus said with a smile. "We have heard much about you, that your magic is more powerful than anything we've ever seen."

"It is powerful." Tor beamed at her, a look of fatherly pride in his eyes. "Yet she wields it with compassion. She is truly a blessing from the Ancients."

"She brought Tor back from the dead," Tatiana said, clasping Phoenix's hand.

Gasps and murmurs rose around the table.

"Then you are indeed a blessing." Klaus lifted his glass to her, then tossed back the contents. Burping into his hand, he slammed the glass on the table. "We welcome you to our tribe."

There were cheers and claps, and Constantine's family hugged and shook hands with the girl.

"Thank you." Her smile was radiant. "I appreciate your welcome more than you know."

"You are more than deserving and long overdue for a kind welcome," Tatiana said, surreptitiously glaring at Magnus. He colored but said nothing. Phoenix and Magnus had a lot of healing to do. Constantine hoped the stubborn alpha was wolf enough to admit he'd been wrong about her.

"You must have more tea and cookies, dear." Anton hovered over her like a mother hen, sliding in a chair next to Tatiana and forcing the girl to take a seat before shoving a plate of cookies in one hand and a teacup in the other. "We will be serving supper soon. You hungry, da?"

She eagerly nodded. "Thanks!"

Constantine's chest warmed as Phoenix and Tatiana laughed and pressed their knees together like long lost sisters. At least one positive thing had come out of this mess. They'd recovered another lone wolf, one who had great potential to help their tribe.

Boris tugged on his arm, and Constantine followed him outside onto the porch. His father shut the door behind them.

Constantine tucked his hands in his armpits, hiding them from the icy winter wind. It was a sharp contrast to the Guatemalan and Texas heat.

Grasping his elbow, Boris took him to the far end of the porch. "Listen, there's something you should know. And for the love of the Ancients, do not tell your stepmother what I'm about to tell you."

His heart rate quickened. Instinct told him his father had bad news about Jovan. "What is it, Father?"

The stricken look on Boris's face nearly took Constantine's breath away. He had several new gray hairs, and the lines framing his mouth and eyes had deepened significantly. His short beard was more gray than blond. He was a shell of the strong alpha Constantine had once known.

"We have reason to believe Jovan has gone into the Hoia Baciu."

He blinked. "You must be mistaken. Why would he do that?"

"We do not know." Boris's lips flattened into a grim line. "Geri tracked him to the edge of the veil."

"Who else knows about this?"

"No one but you, me, and Geri, and we hope to keep it that way." He looked around and over Constantine's shoulder. "He entered from the backside, far away from the village."

He felt as if his heart would fall right out of his chest. Jovan had so much to live for—a new bride, a new son. "I still don't understand why he'd do that."

Boris looked ready to be crushed under the weight of his stress. "He changed after the demon battle."

"But to this extreme?"

"I know. It doesn't make any sense," he said on a groan, dragging a hand down his unshaven face. "I've been wracking my brain, trying to come up with a reason."

"What do we do if we see him there?"

"You will be carrying axes." His expression was hard, unforgiving. "Do what must be done."

Great Ancients!

The bitter wind numbing his skin paled in comparison to the knife cleaving his chest.

Boris grasped Constantine's shoulder. "He went in three days ago. You know time passes more slowly behind the veil. Three days is a lifetime. There is no way he will return unchanged."

Boris's haunted expression before he left was etched into Constantine's brain, and he stared at the door that slammed behind his father. He was barely aware of his lips and fingertips losing feeling as he stood on that porch for what felt like an eternity, the biting wind whistling in his ears. How could he go back inside now? How could he face his brothers, knowing that he'd been charged with bringing the axe down on Jovan's head?

THOUGH TATIANA LOVED visiting her mates' Romanian family, one of the downsides of their home was they had only one bathroom. Fortunately, that also made it easier for her to corner Dejan. When she saw him go to the upstairs bathroom, she decided to follow. She needed to speak with him before they went into the forest. If he had any doubts about their love, any reason to separate from her, she needed to know now. She would not let him risk his life for her if he didn't love her anymore.

She leaned against the lavender floral wallpaper outside the bathroom, seeing for the first time that the pattern was a repetition of five entwined flowers and knew the grandparents had deliberately chosen it to represent their pack. Her heart ached when she thought of her pack; only four entwined flowers if Dejan continued to pull away from them.

When he finally came out, his eyes downcast, he almost ran into her.

"Hey!" she said.

He stopped, looking at her as if she was a ghost.

"H-how are you feeling?" he stammered.

"I want this demon gone," she said tersely, unable to shake her annoyance at his reaction to her. Was she truly that frightening? "How are you doing?"

"Okay." He wiped wet hands on his jeans. "But how I'm doing doesn't matter."

"Of course it matters," she snapped, unable to hide her anger.

He lifted his palms in a gesture of surrender. "My suffering is nothing compared to yours."

"What would you know of my suffering, Dejan?" She jabbed his chest, instantly regretting it when her nail cracked and fell off, leaving her finger exposed and raw and in pain.

He looked at her nail on the floor. "I can see your suffering."

"But can you hear it?" She gazed at him through a sheen of tears. How could she have a serious conversation with him when her body was literally falling apart? "Can you hear me calling to you?"

"I don't hear anything, Tatiana." He stepped back, pressing his shoulders into the wall. "I haven't heard your thoughts since you stabbed Dimitri."

She swiped at her tears, angry for crying, pissed at Dejan for pulling away, and furious with that fucking spider for invading her body. "Do you know why?"

"No," he answered, turning his gaze to his feet.

Her chest ached from the blade of his rejection, twisting deep in her heart. "Were you ever going to say anything, or were you going to keep pretending everything was normal?"

"I was hoping the disconnect was only temporary, that when we expelled the demon, things would go back to normal."

"Dejan, you can't even look at me."

He did then, though it seemed to take an effort, and the discomfort in his eyes was like a dozen knives in her heart. "It's so hard seeing you like this."

"Imagine what it's like living in this body." She pounded her breastbone, then flinched when her bones ached in response. "I'm being slowly turned into this hideous creature, knowing I repulse my mate."

He released a slow breath, the chasm between them growing wider though they were close enough to touch. "You do not repulse me."

"Your lie is insulting." She backed away, looking at him as if he was the one possessed by a hideous creature.

"Tatiana, I love you." He reached for her. "I have never stopped loving you, and no matter what happens, I always will."

"Not enough." She smacked his hand away.

He pulled back. "Then what is?"

"You need to show me you love me." She pressed a palm to her aching heart, resenting him for piling on her torment. "You need to be there for me."

"I'm here for you." But his words were empty, a sharp contrast to the horror in his eyes.

"No, you're not."

Unable to bear his presence a moment longer, she ran downstairs and outside, ignoring the sting of the wind on her skin. She ran through the snow until she reached the barn, where she stumbled and fell to her knees, crying out at the pain that shot through her, but it was nothing compared to the agony she felt at the realization that she had lost Dejan.

Throwing back her head, she cried to the rafters, wishing she could howl and despising the bracelets that trapped her wolf.

You won't be able to live without him, Morana taunted. *Surrender to me. I will take away your pain.*

You will make my pain worse.

No. Your soul will disappear into the abyss. It will be as if you never existed, never felt heartache or rejection.

She bit down on her knuckles, her heart rate quickening. How tempting it would be to give in. Then she thought of Constantine, Dimitri, and Andrei, the three mates who still loved her. And what of Tor? He'd risked his life to save her. What would he do if she gave up now?

Rising on shaky legs, she squared her shoulders. "Fuck you, demon! You will not break me!"

"Tatiana."

It was Constantine. When he held his arms open, she ran to him and let him rock her.

"You will not win, Morana," she whispered.

Morana's laughter echoed in her skull. *I'm already winning.*

UNDER THE THIN LIGHT from the crescent moon, Tor paced in front of the Hoia Baciu, cursing when he saw a shadow run behind the veil, the wall of mist that separated the living world from the demonic forest. Ancient scrolls described the dark forest as a portal to hell, which was probably the most accurate description, considering the strange demons that lived there. Human eyes couldn't see the portal. They walked past it, though most humans avoided this forest because of the bad luck that followed them. They knew the woods were cursed, but here he was, preparing his daughter and son to go inside this perilous place. What kind of father was he to risk their lives?

He handed Drasko and Constantine, each in protector form, large weapons that looked like scythes. He gave Andrei and Dejan smaller silver axes. "You must carry these at all times."

"I'm not using it on my mate." Constantine's deep protector rumble sounded like distant thunder as his white, furry brow dipped low over his eyes.

"And I'm not using it on my sister," Drasko said.

"Quiet!" Tor shot them a look so severe they were compelled to look away. "There are other beasts there, some with venom that will melt your eyes out of your sockets."

Drasko visibly swallowed and tightened his hand around the axe like a lifeline.

"Drasko," he said to his son, "are you sure you want to go inside?"

"I'm sure. This is my sister's life we're talking about."

Constantine turned to him. "But you're a lot older than us."

Drasko's furry face flushed. "Not that much older."

"Almost ten years." Tor rethought letting Drasko go. "The older the wolf, the more chance of disorientation."

"They need more than one protector," he said stubbornly.

Magnus stepped forward. "I'll go in your stead." He held out a hand to Drasko. "Give me the axe."

Clutching the axe in a white-knuckled grip, Drasko backed up, suspicion in his narrowed eyes. "I don't think so."

Tor was not surprised Magnus had volunteered. In fact, he'd been wondering when the Texas chieftain was going to step up. No doubt Magnus had been waiting for the right opportunity. "We can't ask that of you."

Magnus's eyes darted to the backpack Constantine carried. Tor was no fool. He knew exactly why Magnus wanted to go. "You are right. They need more than one protector."

"You've already done so much for us," Constantine said. "That forest will change you."

"I know." The veins in Magnus's neck looked like rising tributaries. "Either I fight beside you now, or I risk having to fight all of you if you come back as unholy monsters."

"I-I'd rather have Drasko," Tatiana stammered. She didn't trust him and for good reason.

"Magnus, a word in private." Not waiting to see if he would follow, Tor dodged frozen pine branches and walked sideways down a snow-covered slope until he came to the lip of a ravine with a slow-moving icy stream at the bottom. They were well out of earshot of the group.

He spun around to face Magnus, who was only a few paces behind. "Do you think I'm an idiot?"

Magnus blinked in surprise. "I have the utmost respect for you."

He wasn't about to play fucking games when his daughter's life was at stake. "Listen to me, Magnus. I do not blame you for seeking revenge against the wrongs done to your fathers, but you must swear to me you will wait until she has cast those demons out of Tatiana and Dimitri."

Straightening, he looked directly into Tor's eyes. "I swear it."

A look of understanding passed between them, then Tor headed back up the hill. Snow had begun to fall. One more thing they didn't need. He called over his shoulder, "If you return from that forest alone, I will cut you down."

A LIGHT SNOW FELL AS Tatiana and her family stood in a clearing of pine trees, not far from the pulsing white mist of the haunted forest's veil. The snow wouldn't affect them beyond the veil. The Hoia Baciu had its own climate, a harsh, stifling one with air that burned her lungs, reminding her they were in hell. Her gut twisted with dread at the thought of going back.

Surrounded by her mates, Eilea handed Boris a jug of blue water. "Hold this, please," she asked, kissing his cheek.

She was wrapped in a white wool coat, her thick black hair piled in many intricate braids on top of her head, no doubt the work of Bunica, for she was a master at braiding hair. Despite Eilea's fresh glow from conceiving Geri's child, sadness clung to her like a shroud. Tatiana could read it in the downward curve of her full lips and the pain in her eyes. She missed Jovan. Tatiana had asked about him, but Constantine refused to discuss it. All she knew was that her mates' second alpha father had left the pack because he still harbored a grudge against Eilea. What if Dejan followed the same path?

Eilea came over to Tatiana and latched onto her wrist with a gloved hand. "Are you ready?"

She tensed, the reality of their situation settling in her stomach like a lead brick. "Not really."

"We will keep a light on for you," she said. Big flood lights, running on a generator, had been set up and aimed at the veil so Tatiana's party could find their way back. "Remember, you don't have to go deep into the forest. The jorogumo can't come back out without a human host."

Still in protector form, Constantine's brows drew low over his eyes. "You sure about that?" He held the backpack like a purse.

"Yes," she said. "Once ousted, don't let it reattach."

"How do we do that?"

"The djinn will know."

"What if she deceives us?" Tatiana asked.

"She won't." Phoenix joined them, speaking to the backpack. "But if she does, Eilea can teach me the spell, and I'll go back in with you and get it out."

Constantine looked at Eilea. "Can she do that?"

Eilea gave the girl an appreciative look. "I don't see why not. She is part demon, after all."

Tatiana grimaced. "I don't think your mother wants you going in."

Phoenix smirked. "And that is why she'd better not deceive you."

Tatiana smiled at her friend and mouthed her thanks. Demon blood or not, the Amaroki were indeed lucky to have found her.

After Eilea recited a protection spell, and sprinkled water on their arms and legs, Tatiana felt tingly as a surge of energy pulsated though her in deep waves. She looked around at her family and knew they would only have to wait a few minutes for them to return. Time passed much more slowly behind the veil, and what felt like a week there was only about twenty minutes here. She hoped they wouldn't need much time to extricate the demons. Speaking of which, Morana had gone suspiciously quiet.

The jorogumo was scared. Good.

She and her mates said goodbye to their parents and Klaus. They'd already said goodbye to the others back at the house. Drasko and Luc took turns kissing her and wishing her well.

"Thanks, guys," she said, her throat constricting, "for everything you've done for me and Dimitri. You're awesome brothers."

Drasko frowned. "I only wish we could've done more."

She shook her head. "You've done so much already." She was no longer upset with her brother for carrying that axe. She knew he had no choice.

Drasko had a few silver hairs by his temple, she noticed for the first time. Though she didn't want to admit it, it was for the best that Magnus took his place. Though he was only a few years younger than Drasko, those few years could make a difference when it came to survival.

Tatiana took Phoenix's hand, wishing she never had to let go. Just the act of touching her brought her peace. She thought she caught a subtle whiff of lavender. She wondered how Phoenix was able to relax her and if Eilea could replicate the spell.

"Where we are going is very dangerous. Are you sure you don't want to say goodbye to your mother?" Tatiana asked the girl.

Phoenix turned up her chin, her eyes flashing with defiance. "I'm sure."

"Okay." Tatiana sighed, pulling her new friend close for a hug. "Stay close to Eilea. You might learn some new magic."

When Tor came to her, it took all her willpower not to break down. She'd come close to losing him, and now she risked losing not just him, but everything and everyone she loved.

His eyes gleamed with pride. "You're a brave, strong young woman."

She waved away his compliment, pretending it meant nothing, but it meant everything. "That's because I've had a wonderful role model. You're the best father a girl could ask for."

"Please keep my daughter safe," he said to Constantine after they hugged.

Constantine held out a furry hand to Tatiana. "I will, or I'll die trying."

They walked toward the veil, her other mates and Magnus following them. Andrei now carried the backpack with the lamp. He winked at her and mouthed *I love you*. She mouthed it back, wishing she could offer him more for his bravery.

Dejan hung back, an axe hanging limply in his hands as he dragged his feet like they were made of concrete blocks. He didn't want to be here. She almost told him to stay behind, but she had a feeling it would do no good. He would not allow himself to be cowardly. Neither would his brothers.

Dimitri walked beside him, his eyes hollow, darkness clinging to him like a second skin. When she turned away, afraid to look at him a moment longer, she suddenly understood how Dejan felt.

When they reached the edge, Constantine swept her up in one arm, holding his huge axe with the other.

"Close your eyes," he whispered and ran into the light.

Chapter Fourteen

AFTER TRAVELING ONLY a few yards into the haunted forest, Andrei had an entirely new appreciation for what Tatiana and Dimitri had endured behind the veil. The skeletal, barren trees reminded him of lifeless corpses, bending at odd angles, their peeling gray bark revealing charcoal-colored cores. The ground was hard and unforgiving. The thirsty soil wasn't just cracked and parched. It was dead. Ash and stone. Nothing more. The tops of the trees were obscured by darkness, as if a giant thumb had blotted out the sun. Or maybe there was no sun here. Other than the dull red glow surrounding them, the only other light came from the big lights rigged outside the mist covering the forest.

The air was thick, so heavy it pressed on his lungs and made speaking, much less breathing, difficult. It burned his throat like he was inhaling smoke from the lit end of a cigarette. A dark gloom settled in his heart, eating away at him. If his family hadn't needed his strength, he would've fallen to his knees and bawled like a baby. He kept looking at Dejan, who was heavily frowning, eyes dark and depressed, shoulders sagging. His younger brother wouldn't last long in the Hoia Baciu.

"I think this is far enough," he called to Constantine.

Constantine stopped as if in a daze and scratched his furry head. He carried Tatiana on his hip like a mother carrying a toddler and dragged the heavy axe with his other hand.

Magnus stomped over to Constantine, his dark brown fur a sharp contrast to the Lupescu snowy white. "We should go a little farther."

Constantine set Tatiana down. "Why?"

He paused as if trying to think of the right words. No surprise, as this forest dulled Andrei's brain, too.

"We don't want the jorogumos finding their way back out," Magnus finally said.

"Eilea said they can't go past the veil without a human host," Dimitri said, rubbing his amethyst bracelets. There were red welts around his wrists.

Had they been there the entire time? Yet he hadn't complained once. He'd carried a tremendous emotional and physical burden, and Andrei wondered if he would ever recover.

Magnus pointed his axe at a decaying copse of trees in the distance. "I've heard there are rivers of lava here that are portals to hell."

Dimitri crossed his arms, narrowing his eyes at Magnus. "Da."

"I would feel better discarding the jorogumos there," Magnus said to Constantine, as if their opinions were the only ones that mattered. "I know you would, too."

Constantine rubbed his furry chin, his eyes nearly crossing while he looked lost in contemplation. "You're right."

With laborious steps and an equally heavy heart, Andrei trudged after them, his movements becoming more awkward and unsteady. What was this place doing to him? Dejan was falling behind. He let out a sharp whistle, and the others stopped. "We need to wait for Dejan."

Dimitri's eyes flashed red. "Hurry, Dejan!" he snapped. "I knew you'd be a hindrance. We should have never brought you."

Constantine said, "Easy, brother."

Dimitri turned heated eyes on Constantine. "I speak the truth, and you all know it."

Dejan had caught up by then, chest heaving and sweat dripping down his forehead. "This would be easier if I were a wolf."

"I'm sorry, but you need to carry your axe," Constantine said. "These demons can only be slaughtered by a silver blade. Wolf fangs aren't enough."

Dejan sighed, resigned. "I understand."

When Dimitri made a noise of disgust, Tatiana grabbed his forearm. "This is your demon talking. Don't let him win."

"It's so hard," he almost whined.

She kissed his cheek, and it suddenly occurred to Andrei that Tatiana and Dimitri's complexions were similar in color and texture to the petrified trees.

They walked for another five minutes, or perhaps it was five hours. Andrei had no concept of time in this place. All he knew was that he ached as if he had been pummeled by a protector, and he was thirsty. So damned thirsty.

They reached a red stream of lava about three meters wide, cutting through the forest like an exposed artery, bursts of fire randomly spitting at the sky. Andrei shuddered at the thought of getting hit by one of those fireballs.

When Tatiana wandered too close to the river, he lurched forward and yanked her back. "Watch your step."

She looked at him with glassy eyes. "Thanks. I forgot what I was doing."

When she latched onto his arm, he was mortified to see her fingernails had split open like rotten fruit. They had to get that fucking demon out of her. He thrust the pack at Constantine. "Let's get this over with."

Constantine unzipped the pack, retrieved the lamp, and rubbed it. Jezebeth appeared. "We're here. Magnus has upheld his end of the bargain. Phoenix is safe. Now cast out their fucking demons."

She twisted her lips derisively. "Do you think I just blink my eyes, say hocus pocus, and they're gone?"

Angry mutters issued from everyone.

Constantine shook a fist at her. "You said you could expel their demons."

"I did and I can," she said, "but I will need a tool to complete the extraction."

"What tool?"

"A fang from a fully formed jorogumo."

Magnus was pissed. "Why didn't you fucking tell us this from the beginning?"

She gave a sideways grin. "You didn't ask."

"She's lying," Magnus raged. "I knew she'd try to trick us."

"Do you want the demons out or not?" she drawled, unmoved by his anger.

She was punishing Magnus for turning Phoenix against her. The problem with that was that by doing so she punished Tatiana and Dimitri, too.

"Where will we find a jorogumo?" Constantine demanded.

She looked at Tatiana. "Where did you find the last one?"

Tatiana shared a look with Dimitri before answering. "It found us."

"Exactly." The djinn let out a grating laugh. "They aren't clever, but they will find you soon enough."

Magnus picked up the lamp. Andrei moved toward him, hackles raised.

"What are you doing with that?" Constantine asked, the fur on the back of his neck standing on end.

"Putting her back," Magnus said. "I don't want to look at that bitch's face." He closed the lid to the lamp, and Jezebeth slid back inside trailing smoke. Shoving it inside the pack, he offered it to Constantine.

He took it and stomped off to sit on a petrified stump. Tatiana sat on his lap.

Andrei rested on the scorching ground. Even though his ass burned, his feet hurt worse; he'd chosen the lesser of two pains.

Magnus ripped a tree out of the ground, exposing dead, black roots, laid it down, and motioned for Andrei to sit there instead.

He thanked him and ignored the rough splinters that poked his ass. His other two brothers sat beside him. Magnus was the only one who did not join them. He paced along the lava stream, cursing and muttering. Andrei had an uneasy feeling about him. When he'd held the lamp, there'd been a scary gleam in his eyes.

An odd howl, sounding part wolf, part demon, echoed in the distance.

Clutching their axes, they shot to their feet.

"What the hell was that?" Tatiana hissed, grabbing Constantine's arm.

"Something about it sounds familiar," Andrei whispered. He wasn't sure where he'd heard it before, but somehow he knew that demon.

Tatiana's eyes bulged. "We should go before it finds us."

They heard it again, closer this time.

Andrei scented the air. "I think it already has."

TATIANA PACED THE LENGTH of the fallen log, keeping an eye on the distant trees. Her attention kept drifting to Dimitri, who sat on the end, hanging his head. At one point she'd thought he was crying, but she had to have been mistaken. Her strong alpha wouldn't cry.

Yesss, Morana hissed, *because he knows the demon is winning. You should surrender, too.*

Fuck you, Morana.

Her laughter grated on Tatiana's nerves. *You no longer have until the next full moon. I can take over your body faster here.*

You'll be gone before then, she answered. At least she prayed she could rid herself of the unwelcome parasite.

She fought the urge to scratch a growing rash on the back of her neck, knowing she could lose the rest of her fingernails. She hated it here, and not just because of the overwhelming depression that threatened to consume her. She was uncomfortably hot and itchy, had the BO of a rotting corpse, and she was damned thirsty. They'd already gone through half their water supply, but nothing quenched their thirst.

Though she heard movement and occasionally saw sets of white and red eyes blinking at them, none of the demons came forward. She didn't know if they were jorogumos anyway. Aggravated, she clutched the roots of her hair and was dismayed when huge clumps came out in her hands.

She turned to Constantine, hopelessness washing over her. "This is taking too long. We should've been out of this fucking forest already."

"Hang on." He overturned the backpack, and she saw two lengths of rope next to the lamp, no doubt to tie up Dimitri and her should they lose control.

Jezebeth appeared in a plume of smoke, her lips twisted in an irritated scowl.

"Jezebeth, no jorogumos have come. Is there anything we can do to speed this along?" Constantine asked.

She gave him a long, cool look before answering through a sigh. "They respond to the smell of the blood of other jorogumos. If your brother or your mate cut themselves, they will come."

Magnus glowered. "Why the fuck didn't you tell us this hours ago?"

"Why?" She morphed into an ugly demon, and her voice dropped into a lower, more threatening register. "Because the minute you spill their blood, there will be chaos. You will not only battle any jorogumos that find you, you will also have to restrain *them*." She gestured at Tatiana and Dimitri.

Magnus flung sweat from his furry brow. "We have to do it, Constantine. We can't keep waiting."

Dimitri stood on shaky legs. "You didn't see what my demon did to Luc."

"We should cut Tatiana," Constantine said. "We can restrain her more easily."

Jezebeth clucked her tongue. "Female jorogumos are more powerful than males."

"Fuck!" Constantine roared.

She went to him. "Cut me and get it over with. Look at me. I'm changing faster than Dimitri." She held up a clump of her hair to emphasize the point. "We have no choice."

Constantine's face fell. "Let's do it." He looked apologetic. "We'll have to tie you up first."

"The ropes won't hold us," Dimitri said.

Constantine grimaced. "But they will slow you down."

She scanned the forest for sturdy trees. Though they all looked like decaying shells, she found two that were bigger around than the rest. "Tie us to these," she said, pointing.

Constantine scooped a length of rope off the ground and barked orders. "Dejan, help me tie up Tatiana. Magnus and Andrei, tie Dimitri."

Tatiana went to the tree closest to her, averting her eyes as Dejan approached. His hands were shaking like leaves in a windstorm. Was he afraid of the battle to come or terrified of her?

"I'm so sorry," he whispered.

She saw heartbreak and despair in his eyes. "It's not your fault."

He wiped moisture from his eyes before binding her hands. "It sure feels like it is."

She got the feeling he wasn't only talking about having to tie her up.

Constantine helped restrain her, then pulled a knife from the items that had been dumped from the backpack. "How much blood do I need to draw?" he asked Jezebeth.

The djinn inspected their work. "Not much. Adult jorogumos can scent a drop of blood from miles away."

Constantine grimly nodded. "Ready?"

"Do it." She turned her head, unable to stomach the sight of blood she thought might be as black as the roots of the petrified trees.

The moment the blade sliced open her skin, Dimitri's howl filled her brain like the beat of a thousand drums.

Save me, Amon, Morana cried. *Kill the wolves before they kill us!*

The ground shook, and Tatiana was horrified when Dimitri pulled out the tree he was tied to and swung it around as if it weighed no more than a bag of bricks.

"Guard her!" Constantine yelled to Dejan and Andrei.

They stood with their backs to her, axes raised, trembling. She could practically taste their fear and hated the demons even more.

Constantine and Magnus charged Dimitri and knocked him back. He fell to the ground, then ripped apart the ropes. She screamed when Constantine rammed him, sending him dangerously close to the embankment of the lava stream.

Dimitri tore the leather and chain amethyst bracelets from his arms like they were mere bandages. His gray skin bubbled and boiled as if his insides were made of molten liquid. His eyes rolled back, and he shifted into a giant spider demon covered with brown fur. Fangs dripping venom sprouted from a barely recognizable face. He let out an ear-piercing screech and advanced on Constantine on eight spindly legs.

"Great Ancients, no!" she cried.

Morana's laughter echoed all around her, as if her essence had leeched into the very air she breathed. *He's turned. It's too late for him now.*

Tatiana screamed when Constantine swung his axe at Dimitri's face. "Don't kill him!" she cried, but nobody was listening to her.

Magnus drove his axe into one of Dimitri's legs. He let out an agonizing wail, and her heart split in two.

He needs our help, Morana cried. *Shift now!*

No! Her blood bubbled and boiled as she fought the urge to surrender to the demon.

Constantine buried his axe in Dimitri's face. Blood black as tar splattered the ground, and one white fang spiraled through the air into Magnus's outstretched hand.

Spinning on his heel, he thrust the fang at Jezebeth. "Time to hold up your end of the bargain."

Taking the fang from him, she thrust it into the air and chanted in an unknown tongue. "Do you know this demon's name?" Jezebeth called.

"Dimitri's is Amon and Tatiana's is Morana," Constantine said.

Morana's piercing shrieks echoed in Tatiana's brain when Jezebeth called out Amon's name.

Dimitri's eight legs buckled, and he cried out. He kicked, then curled into himself. Jezebeth appeared to be tugging on an invisible cord, dragging Dimitri toward her. He left a trail of black blood in his wake.

Don't let her hurt him, Morana cried, releasing burning poison into Tatiana's veins. *Shift now and fight!*

No! Gritting her teeth, she fought back with every last ounce of her strength.

Floating over Dimitri, Jezebeth whispered something to him in a foreign tongue. Though she didn't understand what the djinn was saying, one word stuck out: *Detrudo.*

Jezebeth's features shifted to that of a ghoul again, her crimson, skeletal face reminiscent of the angel of death. She drove the fang into his back. The spider flopped on the ground like a fish out of water, squealing as smoke leached from its legs and mouth.

Morana cried out as if in agony.

Dimitri spun so fast, he created a funnel of blood and dust. After the debris settled, the spider was gone. In its place was her beloved mate, covered in cuts and bruises, the cursed fang lying in the dirt beside him.

"Dimitri!" She called when he didn't move.

"Is he dead?" Constantine asked.

"There's no time to find out." Jezebeth pointed at her. "Your mate's jorogumo is about to take over."

Tatiana tried to argue she wouldn't let it when blinding pain suddenly wracked her so badly, she was near to passing out. Something was crushing her head, squeezing so hard, she thought her skull would crack. Surrendering to the pain, a scream that sounded like the screech of a prehistoric bird tore from her lips. The djinn stabbed her, the fang piercing the skin just above her heart.

She fought the pain, snapping her restraints with a roar. Strong hands held her down, driving her to the ground when she broke the tree she was tied to, holding her there. Her life force spilled on the dirt. Great Ancients, she was dying!

CONSTANTINE CARRIED Tatiana's still body over to Dimitri, laying them side by side. Neither moved, and he could barely feel their pulse. Andrei and Dejan fell to their knees beside them, begging them to wake.

Dejan looked at Jezebeth with red-rimmed eyes. "Are they dead?"

"No. They are reborn." She floated over them, blowing what looked like glitter from her palm. It rained down on them like gently falling snow, sparkling brightly even in the gloomy forest.

"What are you doing?" Constantine demanded, sorely tempted to toss the lamp in the lava stream.

"Waking them up before they come."

"Before who comes?" Magnus asked.

She tossed a glance over her shoulder. "The other jorogumos."

Constantine froze. How could he fight the spider demons and protect Tatiana and Dimitri? "We need to get out of here," he said and picked up Tatiana. "Carry my brother," he said to Magnus as they suddenly heard what sounded like rushing water.

Jezebeth bounced on her smoke tether. "They come."

She disappeared when Andrei threw the lamp inside the backpack and they all ran to the stream. Constantine and Magnus easily hopped over it. When his brothers hesitated, Constantine laid Tatiana down and jumped back over and fetched them.

No sooner had he safely landed than an army of at least three dozen spiders descended, rushing toward them like a herd of wild horses, kicking up dust, pincers opening and snapping shut. Some had eyes that glowed red, while the larger ones had blinding white eyes and big, red abdomens. Constantine shielded Tatiana.

He let out a predatory howl and waved the axe over his head. "Come closer, and I shall hack off your limbs."

The spiders, ranging in size from large dogs to small cars, pushed forward until a smaller one fell into the lava, going under with a guttural wail beneath the bubbling liquid. A big spider covered in brown fur also fell in, scalding his backside before he flew back out with a screech.

They clacked their mouths and hissed. Just when Constantine thought they were in the clear, one of the large ones flew into the air, shrieking. He buried his axe in her abdomen, turning his head when her guts exploded all over his neck and chest. He spun, flinging her into the lava. She went down with such a high-pitched cry, he had to cover his ears for fear they'd rupture.

The remaining spiders retreated, the large, hairy one limping after them, his backside leaking on the ground, leaving a trail of goo behind him. There was something eerily familiar about the hairy spider's scent, but Constantine didn't have time to ruminate on it. His mate and brother needed him. He groaned in relief and sank to his knees as the spiders disappeared into the darkness. His relief was short-lived. They had to return that way. What if the spiders were simply waiting for another chance to attack?

He flung sweat and goop off his neck and chest while his brothers checked on Tatiana and Dimitri. He thanked Magnus when he tossed him a towel from the backpack, then crawled over to Dimitri and Tatiana.

His brother was the first to wake. "What the fuck happened?" His skin was a healthy pink and Tatiana had a beautiful golden glow.

Andrei said, "What happened is we got those fucking spiders out of you."

Dimitri sat up and looked at his hands, which looked like *his* again. "Thank the Ancients." He winced, hissing when he looked down at a huge gash in his leg. Andrei added antiseptic to it and bandaged the wound.

"The Ancients weren't here to help us," Magnus complained. He peered at Tatiana. "Is she going to be okay?"

Dejan stroked her smooth cheek. "I think so."

They all heaved collective breaths of relief when she opened her eyes and blinked at Dejan. "Darling," she whispered. "I had a dream you stopped loving me."

Dejan colored. "I'd never stop loving you, Tatiana."

She draped an arm across her eyes. "That's good. What a nightmare."

Dejan sat back on his heels, wiping away tears. Then he stood and turned his back to everyone. Dimitri, who was sitting up, shot eye daggers into Dejan's back. Even if they escaped this hellacious place, his pack still had a lot of healing to do.

Some of Tatiana's nails were still missing, leaving her flesh red and raw, but already the cracks in those remaining were closing. "*Iubita mea*, can you sit up."

Her brows knitted together in confusion. "Where are we? Why is it so hot?"

He looked to Andrei for help. Dimitri crawled over to her, took her hand in his, and kissed her knuckles before collapsing by her side. "I think we're in the Hoia Baciu."

She let out a terrified scream and scratched at her skin. "The demon! I have to get it out of me!"

Constantine stilled her hands. "It's okay. The demon is gone."

Wrapping her arms around his neck, she shivered against him. He whispered words of love into her ear until she calmed.

"What the fuck do you think you're doing?" Andrei unexpectedly hollered.

"What must be done," Magnus said. "Back up."

Constantine let go of Tatiana and jumped to his feet, hollering to Magnus, whose heels were dangerously close to the edge of the lava stream. "Magnus?"

Magnus held the lamp above his head. "I am avenging my fathers and sending this bitch back to where she came from. Tell Andrei to back off."

"Magnus, no!" Tatiana cried and stumbled to her feet.

Constantine said, "Stay out of this, Tatiana."

"No!" Her legs trembled as she pushed past him. "Jezebeth just saved me and Dimitri!"

Magnus leveled her with a dark look. "Only because we bargained with her."

"Please think of Phoenix."

Constantine's heart broke for the girl, but if Jezebeth had cursed his fathers, he would've tossed her into the lava, too.

Magnus laughed when he heard Jezebeth yelling inside the lamp. "Phoenix wants nothing to do with her mother now that she knows what an evil bitch she is."

Andrei raised his axe, but Magnus knocked it out of his hands and sent it tumbling into the stream.

Stand down, Constantine projected. *I will not have you lose your life over a demon.*

It's not right, Andrei answered, but he stepped aside.

When Tatiana moved another foot forward, Constantine stopped her. "That's far enough."

Her spine stiffened. "You don't right a wrong with another wrong." Her voice cracked with emotion, her eyes turning a deep gold.

Fuck. Her wolf was awake. Why did Constantine get the feeling this wouldn't end well? He wrapped an arm around Tatiana's waist, whispering in her ear. "Leave it be. Magnus needs this closure, and it's best for Phoenix."

"How is this wrong?" Magnus looked like a man possessed, his upper lip pulled back. "She turned Sami into a monster who feasted off hundreds of humans. What about *their* families? This demon belongs in hell, where she can't hurt anyone else."

He let out a maniacal laugh and tossed the lamp at the stream. It flew through the air in a graceful arc, the tarnished bronze glowing red as it reflected the lava.

Tatiana shifted so fast, Constantine didn't have time to grab hold of her. She jumped into the air in wolf form, twirling with her jowls open like a dog catching a frisbee. Time seemed to slow to almost a standstill as the clank of her teeth hitting the metal ricocheted in his skull. She landed on the other side of the stream with a yelp, her tail hitting the edge of the boiling liquid. Constantine swore his heart stopped beating when she stumbled back, nearly falling into the stream. With a roar, he raced after her, flying through the air and landing on the other side with a crack.

Magnus landed beside him, waving his axe threateningly. "Give me the fucking lamp!"

Constantine gave him a hard shove. "Stand down."

Andrei landed beside her in wolf form and licked her scorched tail. Dejan followed him. The three of them sped into the forest.

"Come back!" Constantine hollered, then cried out when Magnus pushed him, and he nearly fell into the lava. He howled when steam shot up and singed the fur off his back.

Magnus pulled him away from the deadly stream.

He fell to his hands and knees, the agony in his burning back nearly unbearable. "We don't have time to fight, you *idiotule*!" He tried and failed to stand, the pain so intense, he was afraid he'd pass out. "My mate is running through the forest without a protector!"

As if reading his mind, Dimitri appeared in protector form, limping slightly, blood dripping down his leg and clumping in his white fur. "Brother, you are injured."

Panting like a trapped animal, he tried to block out the pain. "I don't care." He pointed to his axe, which had fallen beside him. "Go get her!"

Dimitri picked up the weapon and took off.

Constantine couldn't believe how much he hurt. "How bad is it?"

"Bad." Magnus frowned. "I'm sorry."

"The fuck you are," he seethed and passed out.

Chapter Fifteen

TATIANA, WHERE ARE you going? Andrei sprinted after her in a panic.

Away from Magnus, she replied tersely. She ran, her russet tail dripping blood, the sweatshirt she'd been wearing as a human clinging to her back like a loose blanket.

Behind him, Dejan whimpered but didn't say anything.

He couldn't help his whimper when a shadow appeared overhead. *But what about the spiders?*

What spiders? she asked.

Fuck. *You don't remember?*

She stopped, her limp tail leaving a blood-splattered crescent shape in the earth. She gripped the rusty lamp handle between her teeth. *No.*

We don't have any weapons. Another shadow passed above them. Or perhaps it was the same creature gliding from branch to branch, waiting for the right moment to strike. He nudged her with his snout. *We have to return to the protectors.*

Her ears flattened against her skull. *I will bite off Magnus's balls if he tries to destroy this lamp.*

Okay, okay. Just calm down. I'm sure it won't come to that. Let's return to the others. There's something following us.

Watch out! Dejan yelled.

A hairy spider the size of a buffalo slid to the ground in front of him on a glistening rope, its pincers clacking as he feinted toward them.

Keep moving, he said to her. *Don't provoke it.*

I'm trying not to.

Dejan snarled at the spider, trying to scare it away.

Constantine! Dimitri! Andrei called, hoping they were close enough to hear him.

The spider lunged, and a familiar scent hit Andrei. Where had he smelled that before? Could it be? No. He was losing his mind or the jorogumo was playing tricks on him.

When the spider let out a wolf-like whimper, his blood turned to ice.

Something whooshed above his head, and Dimitri appeared, waving an axe at the spider. "Get the fuck away from my family!"

The spider retreated, letting out that familiar little noise again. That's when Andrei noticed the injury. Its entire backside bubbled with green ooze that dripped on the ground like melting wax. He suddenly recognized the spider as the one that had fallen into the lava. Why did he smell so familiar? The monster fell to the ground, curling into itself.

Dimitri raised his axe.

Brother! he blurted, his mind spinning. *Don't kill him! That's our father, Jovan!*

That can't be him, he said in disbelief.

Dimitri, I know his scent.

The spider let out a pitiful whimper, and for a moment, its eyes turned blue and the familiar scent struck him again.

Dimitri's nostrils flared. *Great Ancients, what has happened to him?*

He's turned into a jorogumo.

Tatiana shifted into a human. Kneeling on the ground, she was almost totally naked with the exception of a tattered shirt ripped down the middle, exposing the swell of her breasts. She rubbed the lamp, and Jezebeth sprang out in a cloud of smoke.

"Can you save him?" she asked the djinn.

Crossing her arms, the djinn scowled down at her. "He wasn't included in our bargain."

Fucking bitch! Andrei howled in anger.

Tatiana jumped to her feet. "I just saved your ass!"

"I know." Jezebeth slanted a wicked grin. "But I am a demon, after all."

Tatiana let out a string of curses, shaking a fist at the lamp. Andrei shifted into a human, crouching on all fours. "What is it you want?"

She looked at his nude body with an appreciative smile. Pressing a finger to her lips, her smile grew wider.

"Don't fucking think about it!" Tatiana said.

A roar sounded behind them. Magnus barreled into the clearing supporting Constantine, who staggered like a drunk. Magnus released him when he saw the spider.

When Magnus raised his axe, Andrei held out his hands. "Don't hurt it! That's our father, Jovan!"

Magnus's jaw dropped. "What in Ancients' name?"

Constantine dropped to his knees. "Tatiana! Are you okay?" Before she could answer, he fell forward, shuddering, his face planted in the dirt.

Andrei exclaimed when he saw Constantine's back. It looked like burned hamburger meat. He crawled over to him and felt his pulse; weak but steady. "We have to get him to Eilea." He looked at the djinn. "Will you help us, or should I tell Phoenix that you let our father perish?"

Jezebeth twisted her lips into a scowl. "First I want Magnus to swear he will not harm me."

"Magnus, by the Ancients," Dimitri said, chest heaving, "you must swear it."

"Damn you all! She destroyed my family!"

"And now our family will be destroyed, too," Andrei cried, "if you don't help us."

Magnus screamed, then ripped up a nearby tree and threw it. His eyes were blinding gold. "Fine, I swear I will not harm you if"—he exhaled noisily—"she swears to stop cursing the Wolfstalkers."

"Fine. I will stop cursing the Wolfstalkers." Jezebeth placed a hand on her curvaceous hip, looking at Dimitri and then Andrei. "And you wolves must take my daughter and me to live with your family in Alaska."

"W-what?" Andrei stammered.

"It's clear I'm not safe with Magnus's family," she said, "and he won't treat my darling Phoenix well."

Damn her, she was right. "Okay!" Dimitri threw up his hands. "We'll do it. Please get this fucking demon out of my father!"

"I need another fang," she said calmly.

"Fuck!" Andrei spun around, trying to scent the last one they'd used.

"We're wasting time," Magnus said. "Let me cut a fang off the spider." He jutted an axe toward the demon that was once his father.

"No!" Andrei and his brothers roared in unison.

Andrei shifted into a wolf and went hunting for the spider fang. He found it in a nearby clearing and hurried back, wincing when the hot ground burned his paws.

He dropped the fang at the djinn's feet, then held his breath as she floated over the spider.

"Do we know this demon's name?" she asked.

Andrei shared a look with Dimitri. "No. We didn't even know he was possessed."

She grimaced. "It may be harder to oust the demon."

"Can you do it?" Andrei asked, his voice cracking with emotion. They couldn't lose Jovan. His family would be devastated.

She shrugged. "I'll try."

He stepped back with a nod, praying it would work.

Chanting in a foreign tongue, she drove the fang through his back before yanking it back out and tossing it on the ground. The spider bucked and seized, flopping on the ground like sizzling bacon before it finally went deathly still. Then it shriveled up, looking like a giant, blackened boulder.

Andrei cautiously approached, sniffing at it.

Dimitri said, "What happened?"

They jumped back when the spider remains split open, revealing a naked man. Dimitri helped Jovan out of the shell. "Let's get out of this miserable place."

Andrei howled his agreement.

DRAGGING BECAUSE OF sore feet, Tatiana implored, "Can we please rest a moment?"

Large silver eyes vacantly gazing into the distance, Dimitri stopped as if he'd hit an invisible wall. His fur, wet with sweat, stuck to him in matted clumps. "Only for a moment." He gently laid Jovan on the ground. Their father still hadn't awoken from a deep slumber. She prayed the exorcism had worked. He was no longer a spider, so that was a good sign.

"Thank you," Tatiana said and checked Jovan's pulse again. It was strong, and she was thankful.

After the cursed earth had scorched her paws, her mates had located her torn clothes and shoes, and she'd shifted back into human form. Dejan and Andrei were humans, too, so they could help carry the pack and axes. Though Tatiana and her mates loved their wolves, the thick fur was too stifling in this heat. The protectors didn't have a choice. They had to remain big, furry beasts to drive away any demons that came near, and several more did attack them. Magnus and Dimitri's blades were crusted with blood by the time they returned to the lava stream a third time.

"We're walking in circles," Andrei groaned, scanning the forest. "I thought our fathers were supposed to shine beacons through the veil." He sank down beside Tatiana.

Dimitri frowned. "They were."

Without a beacon they were lost. The forest's evil magic could easily disorient even the most experienced wolf, forcing them to wander forever.

Magnus heaved Constantine to the ground, propped him up against his legs, and helped him drink from the last of their water. Though Tatiana appreciated the care Magnus showed Constantine, she couldn't forget it was his fault he'd been injured.

Andrei kept sweeping the area. "Where are the beacons?"

Tatiana tried not to take it personally when Dejan sat next to Magnus. Jezebeth floated above them, searching for the light, too.

"Is someone going to put the bitch back in her lamp?" Magnus asked.

Biting back a tart reply, she said, "She's helping us look for the beacons."

He snorted. "She does nothing unless it benefits her."

The Djinn sniffed. "I want to leave this cursed place and your company, too."

Tatiana thought about all Jezebeth had done to his family and understood why he'd tried to cast her down to hell, but she had no regrets. If she hadn't saved Jezebeth, she wouldn't have been there to cast out Jovan's demon.

"You must understand I've been conditioned only to do for others when they do for me first."

Her gaze snapped to Jezebeth, who was looking down at her with a frozen smile. "Whatever makes you feel better about yourself."

Clasping her hands to her chest, Jezebeth batted her lashes. "I'm going to give you something without being asked and without expecting anything in return."

Her voice was so sugary sweet, Tatiana wanted to vomit. Did she really think Tatiana would fall for her false sincerity? "I didn't ask you to give me anything."

"I know," she cooed. "But I want to show you that I can change. That I mean to become a better demon."

Magnus chuckled dryly. "There's no such thing as a better demon."

"All right," Tatiana said, tired of their banter. "What do you want to give me?"

"I looked into Morana's soul when I pulled her from you. I saw what she did to you after you stabbed Dimitri."

"What she did to me?" Fuck. Did she leave her with another curse?

"She was angry with Dejan for going for help," Jezebeth continued, "so she severed the cord in your soul that tethered you to him."

"Ancients, no," she breathed. "How do we restore the connection?"

"I said I'd give you one thing, not two."

"Really, Jezebeth?" She was furious with the Djinn.

Dejan jumped to his feet, clearly in pain. "All this time I thought the bond was broken because you didn't want me."

Tears welled up in her eyes. "I thought the same."

He swiped tears from his face. "And the nightmares. Constant, unrelenting. Maybe she planted those to drive me away."

She tilted her head. "What nightmares?"

She wasn't reassured when he turned away, heaving a shuddering sob.

"Jezebeth," Andrei asked, "How do we restore the bond?"

She gave them a long look, the slightest of smiles tugging at her lips.

Magnus jumped to his feet. "I promised I wouldn't harm her," he said to Dimitri. "But *you* can throw her in the lava."

"Okay!" she shrieked. "It's simple, really. Just repeat the bonding ceremony. Since he can't take your virginity again, you will need to draw blood another way."

Embarrassment made her flush. "I'm sure we'll figure it out. Thanks."

Dejan refused to look at her. What nightmares did he speak of? Were they of her? That would explain why he avoided her.

"Will you tell Phoenix I helped you?"

Her gaze shot to Jezebeth, whose smile was still plastered to her face. "Is that the only reason you helped us?"

"To win back my daughter's affection. Isn't that a good reason?"

Her mates and Magnus swore.

She was tired and wanted to go home. "Sometimes people help others because it's the right thing to do, and it makes them feel good."

"Yes, well." The Djinn rolled her eyes. "You can't expect me to turn into a saint overnight."

Dimitri pointed to two pinpricks of light deep in the forest. "The beacons!"

TOR PACED IN FRONT of the veil as a mighty protector, no longer caring if they were discovered by hunters in Romania's forest. Besides, humans rarely wandered this close to the veil. The Lupescus stared into it, their faces masks of worry. Eilea leaned against Boris, repeating a low chant under her breath. He had no idea if she was casting a protection spell or praying to the Ancients. Either way, he hoped it worked.

Ten minutes had passed and still there was no sign of Tatiana and her mates. Ten minutes on this side of the veil was like two or three days on the other side. Why would it take so long to expel a few demons? He was about to go out of his mind, but he had to remain calm for his sons' sake. Drasko and Luc were riled enough.

Drasko's golden eyes shone like twin suns. "We need to go in, Father."

"Give them a few more minutes."

"A few more minutes! They could be dead by then!"

He loved Tatiana with all his heart, but if Constantine and Magnus couldn't handle whatever was in that forest, neither would Drasko and Luc. He wouldn't risk losing two more children.

"Someone's coming," Klaus said, looking toward a pair of headlights.

Four trucks parked behind theirs, and Atan Albescu and his brothers and sons, plus several cousins, got out, immediately shifting into wolves and protectors and stalking up to them belligerently. The alphas carried axes. These wolves had come to wage war.

Atan pounded his chest, his white fur blending with the snow that swirled around them. "We thought we'd find you here."

Klaus moved to stand between his family and the Albescus. "What do you want, Atan?"

Atan pointed at the white wall of mist. "One of our betas saw Jovan go beyond the veil."

Klaus said, "You lie."

"Do I?" Atan laughed. "What does your instinct tell you?"

Klaus turned to Boris, his expression one of horror and grief. "Tell me they lie."

Boris didn't answer. Klaus turned back around. "What did you do with Jovan?"

Atan had a serpentine gleam in his eyes. "We did nothing with your son." He looked at the twin spotlights. "What's all this for?"

Boris said, "That's none of your concern."

"On the contrary, it *is* my concern and that of the tribe." Atan slapped his chest, then turned to his family, who all grumbled their agreement. "Why are the Thunderfoots here, and where is their daughter and your grandsons?" He glanced at Phoenix, who stood silently next to Eilea. "And who is this? Another lone wolf?"

Eilea wrapped an arm protectively around the girl.

"Again," Klaus said, "none of your concern."

Atan's family moved forward to cover his back in a show of force. "The forest changed your grandson and his mate, didn't it?" When Klaus didn't answer, Atan continued. "That was why our ancestors beheaded anyone who returned from the forest. We should not have broken from tradition. I will bring this before the council—after we take care of whoever comes back through the veil."

Tor, who had been listening without comment, finally spoke. "You will have to go through me first."

Atan grinned. "With pleasure, Thunderfoot."

The two groups faced off against each other, bristling with anger, weapons raised. Tor was about to charge when he was overcome by an overwhelming sense of fatigue. He fell face-first into the snow while around him, his sons suffered the same fate. Unable to keep his eyes open, he succumbed to darkness.

EILEA CHECKED EACH fallen family member, dusting snow off their fur and checking for injuries, relieved when the worst she saw was a nick on Boris's wide forehead from his axe. Not that he didn't deserve it for lying to her, for she knew without a doubt he was harboring a terrible secret about Jovan. Why would her mate have entered the haunted forest? Was he so angry with her that he'd rather live a cursed life than watch his son grow up?

Though she did her best to push such despairing thoughts from her mind, she couldn't help the overwhelming surge of fear that threatened to split open her heart.

"How did you do that?" Phoenix asked, trailing behind her.

She moved on to the Albescus. Atan still had a pulse. Too bad. Pressing her fingers to his temple, she recited an incantation, then projected a new memory into his mind.

"It was a simple spell," she finally answered. "Targeted only toward the male gender," she added with a wink.

"Can you teach it to me?"

Eilea looked at her with a smile. "Of course." Though her first instinct was to be suspicious of the girl for wanting to know a sleeping spell, she liked Phoenix, demon blood or not.

She went to each of the Albescus, making sure they still breathed and altering their memories. They wouldn't be happy when they woke up, but it served them right for all the trouble they'd caused.

She returned to Boris, uncorked a bottle of enchanted peppermint oil, and held it under his nose. He sat up with a grunt, fanning the oil away from his face.

She handed the vial to Phoenix. "Please wake the rest of our family. Let the Albescus be for the moment."

Phoenix nodded and went over to Klaus.

"Wha' happened?" Boris asked, his words slurred.

"Sorry." She wasn't sorry at all. "I wasn't about to let you all butcher each other."

He gaped at her and then at the rest of their family, still lying in the snow. "The Albescus?"

"Sleeping." She could tell he hadn't yet decided if he wanted to swear at her or sweep her into a passionate embrace and give her a big kiss.

"They won't be happy when they wake."

"I took care of that," she said.

His jaw dropped. "What spell did you put on them?"

She smiled. "They will believe it was their sons, not ours, who went beyond the veil."

He laughed heartily. "Ha! Perhaps we should show up at their door with axes."

"Leave them alone. They should wake up within the hour and will be too frightened to cause further problems." She frowned. "Boris, they said Jovan went into the forest." She desperately searched his eyes for any signs of deceit. "Please tell me they lie."

"I'm sorry, my love." His shoulders and face fell as he let out a mournful sob. "They do not."

Stunned, she fell on her ass. "Great Ancients. Why?"

She was struck by the cold reality of their situation when her big alpha's eyes watered. "I don't know, darling. I don't know."

She fell into his arms, sobbing against his chest until her body ached and her tears ran dry.

When the others stirred, she pulled herself together and stood. She didn't have to do much. Phoenix's calming presence helped them all awake with smiles.

Klaus pointed to the spotlights that had somehow fallen over. "The beacons! Get them back up!"

Eilea cursed herself for having missed that. She spotted the problem immediately. Drasko's foot had gotten tangled in the cords and pulled them over when he went down. After putting the lights back up, she nervously chewed her nails, praying their children hadn't lost their way.

"Look!" Phoenix pointed to five moving shadows beyond the mist.

Eilea clutched her throat, her heartbeat coming to a halt as she watched the shadows slowly approach. Why were there only five when six had gone in?

Her breath caught as their family finally emerged, and five shadows turned into seven.

Tatiana raced into Tor's arms, her brothers surrounding them with hoots and howls.

Eilea screamed and ran to Dimitri, who carried a naked Jovan in his human form. "What happened?"

"He was possessed by a jorogumo, too," Dimitri said.

"Over here." She pointed to Boris's truck, and Dimitri laid him in the bed on a sleeping bag. Her other mates surrounded them, urging him to open his eyes.

Taking the oil from Phoenix, she held it under his nose, but he did not wake. She pressed a hand to his neck. This wasn't ordinary slumber. He had a pulse, but she couldn't sense his soul. He was like an empty shell, a living, breathing body with no spirit. Had the jorogumo forced him to pass to Valhol?

"Jovan?" she cried, rubbing his arms. "Please come back to me!"

"Do you mind?" Phoenix asked, appearing beside her. Eilea stepped aside. Phoenix pressed a hand to his heart. "There is a great darkness here." Closing her eyes, Phoenix ran her hands over his arms and back to his forehead. "There is light here, but it's trapped, and I don't sense his wolf at all."

Eilea bit down on her knuckles to keep from crying out. Boris, grasped her shoulders, offering her his quiet strength while pressing into her back.

"Can you free it?" Eilea asked. This magic was beyond her skills. She'd healed bruises and broken bones, even cancer, but she'd never recovered a lost soul.

"I'll try." She pressed her palms to his face. A glow emanated from them and soon encompassed his entire head. The glow spread outward, spiraling around Phoenix and Jovan before fading to a dull, pulsing light.

When Phoenix stepped back, trembling, Jovan's eyes opened. He looked at Eilea. "My love. I was afraid I'd never see you again."

She flung herself on top of him, and he held her tight, whispering soothing words in her ear. His brothers patted his back, welcoming him back to the realm of the living.

"Why didn't you tell us you were possessed?" Boris asked him.

He looked at his family. "You wouldn't have been able to save me."

Eilea wiped her eyes, thanking Phoenix when she gave her a tissue to blow her nose. "I thought you hated me."

"Never, my love." He nuzzled her neck. His eyelids grew heavy. "I'm so tired all of a sudden."

"Healing magic takes energy," Phoenix said.

He quirked a brow. "Do I know you, child?"

She blushed. "I'm new around these parts."

Eilea reached for the girl's hand. "She's a blessing sent by the Ancients."

"Are the demons gone?" Jovan asked.

Dimitri patted his father on the back. "Da, and I pray we never have to go into that cursed forest again." He drew their attention to Constantine, whose back was badly burned.

After Eilea healed him, as well as burns and cuts on the others, the Lupescus threw back their heads and howled in relief. The Thunderfoots joined them. Phoenix howled with them, smiling.

By the time they finished, Constantine sat up, rubbing his eyes. Tatiana was immediately by his side, stroking his face and kissing his forehead.

"Anyone care to explain what happened with the Albescus?" he asked. Snowflakes had settled on their white fur, making them look like an assortment of glittery wolves and sparkling abominable snowmen.

Eilea laughed. "Guess all this excitement wore them out."

Chapter Sixteen

TATIANA AND ANDREI ate chicken and vegetable soup. Dimitri sat across from them, nearly falling in his soup, he was so tired. Constantine and Andrei finally helped him upstairs. She was exhausted and couldn't wait to go to bed, too, but she had to stay awake long enough to celebrate with her family.

They had so much to be thankful for. Not only had she and Dimitri rid themselves of those awful demons, but Phoenix and Jovan had been recovered. Phoenix was a blessing to their tribe, and already Tatiana thought of her as a little sister.

She sat on the carpet of the front room, her rabbits crawling on her lap while she fed them apple pieces. She was kind and incredibly gifted. Other than having to put up with her mother, the Amaroki were lucky to have her.

She was thrilled for Eilea to have her mate back. They'd only stayed long enough to drink one toast and then the two of them had slipped out the back door.

Tatiana couldn't deny feeling a stab of jealousy when Jovan looked at his mate with longing in his eyes. If only Dejan wanted her that way. He had no more reason to be repulsed by her appearance. Her skin had its usual healthy glow, her back no longer looked like a wire brush, her stomach wasn't a hideous boil, and Eilea had healed any lingering injuries.

Yet despite her transformation, Dejan had kept to himself after they returned to the house, insisting he help the other gammas in the kitchen, despite their protests. Tatiana suspected he was hiding from her rather than confront this unease between them.

Tor sat beside her. "You look tired."

"I am, Father," she said, stifling a yawn. "I'll be off to bed soon."

"Good. You need rest." He stood, kissing her forehead.

Constantine returned. Andrei was still upstairs, and she heard the water running. A shower sounded good, too, but later, when she could think straight again.

Constantine's brows were drawn. "Tor, I must speak with you."

"What about?"

He lowered his voice. "We had to promise Jezebeth that we would take her and Phoenix to live with us in Alaska."

Tor nodded. "I was hoping we could take Phoenix back with us anyway."

"You want me to stay with you?" The girl came up behind him, holding a rabbit. The vulnerability in her eyes tugged at Tatiana's heart. She understood all too well the feeling of not being wanted.

Tor extended a hand to her. She took it. "Child, why wouldn't I? It's the least I can do after you saved my life. Besides, my mate and youngest brother have been beside themselves since Tatiana left the den. They would love to have another daughter to spoil."

"It's true." Tatiana laughed. "And you will be spoiled rotten."

"I would love to go with you." She hid her face in the rabbit's fur. "But I'm not sure about taking my mother."

"We cannot break a promise to a Djinn," Constantine said.

When Phoenix winced, Tatiana added. "Despite her flaws, she does love you. She went into that forest to ensure your safety, knowing we could've left her."

She could tell by the look in Phoenix's eyes the girl was not impressed. Rocking side to side, she rubbed her cheek against her rabbit's silky white ears. "I was hoping Eilea could show me some of her magic."

"I think Eilea needs some time to reconnect with Jovan," Tor said. "She will be visiting us for a month this spring. She can mentor you then."

"Come with us, Phoenix," Tatiana pleaded. "We can hang out in my old bedroom. I left all my books, movies, and about a hundred shades of nail polish there."

Phoenix flashed a bashful smile. "Okay."

Tor gave Tatiana a pointed look. "You need time to reconnect with your mates, too."

"I know," she said, casting a furtive glance in Dejan's direction. He had his back to her, his spine ramrod straight while he rolled out dough on the counter. Would there be anything left to salvage in their relationship?

"We want to return to Alaska tomorrow," Tor continued. "Your mother and Amara have been beside themselves with worry, but not nearly as much as Arvid and Rone. They are driving the family crazy."

Constantine nodded to Boris, Geri, and Marius, who slipped out the back door like wayward children sneaking out of the house. "I think my fathers and stepmother need alone time anyway." He chuckled.

"So do we," Andrei said, kissing her cheek when he returned to his seat.

Tatiana's stomach roiled when she thought about spending time with her mates. Not that she didn't long to be with them, but she had no idea what to do with Dejan. Would he join them? Did she want him to join them?

Tatiana flushed when her father mumbled something about young pups before going into the living room. Phoenix followed and sat on the floor with her rabbits. Tatiana briefly wondered if those rabbits knew their mother was a wolf, then realized she was probably able to control them with the soothing magic she used on everyone else. If only Tatiana had the power to use such magic on Dejan.

Constantine leaned across the table. "What is it?"

"Nothing." She didn't want her mates to get into a confrontation with Dejan and risk them fighting. She'd deal with him on her own.

Is it Dejan? Andrei projected.

She refused to answer. "Can we please change the subject?"

"When we return home," Constantine said, "we'll do the bonding ritual again."

Dejan was attacking the pastry with the rolling pin as if he wanted to pound it into oblivion. "What if it doesn't work?"

Constantine drummed his fingers on the table. *It will work.*

She looked away from him, angry with herself when moisture pricked the backs of her eyes. *Not if he doesn't want to bond.*

Why wouldn't he? Andrei asked.

She was too afraid to look in Dejan's direction again, worried he'd turn around and she'd see rejection in his eyes. *He's been avoiding me.*

Do you want me to talk to him? Constantine asked.

No. Deciding it was time to go to bed, she rose on shaky legs. Anything to end the conversation. *I want him to talk to me.*

DEJAN WOKE WITH A SCREAM, sweat drenching his clothes and hair despite the frigid outside air that crept in through the cracks in the windowpane beside the narrow sofa that served as his bed.

Constantine ran down the stairs, clutching the banister. "You okay?"

"I'm fine," Dejan spoke through a shaky voice while trying his best to purge the dread from his soul. "Just a nightmare."

"The forest will do that to you. Want some coffee?"

"Not right now." The nightmares had nothing to do with the forest. This was the same recurring dream he'd been having for days where a spider version of Tatiana drained his blood like a vampire. He'd hoped it would stop after they returned from the Hoia Baciu, but if anything it felt more real than before. He clutched his neck, the phantom pain of her fangs crushing his windpipe lingering.

It wasn't real, Dejan. Get yourself together.

Tatiana came downstairs, cinching the belt of her robe around her waist. His grandparents were nowhere to be seen. Tatiana's brothers, father, and Phoenix had spent the night at his fathers' house, which meant he'd have to interact with her. How was he supposed to face her when he couldn't get the image of her killing him out of his mind?

She sat on the sofa across from him. "How did you sleep, Dejan?"

He knew she'd wanted him to sleep upstairs in their room, but that bed was small, and he didn't care to sleep on the floor.

"He had a nightmare," Constantine said and handed her a cup of coffee.

"That's too bad." She gave him a cool look from over the rim of her cup. "I slept like a baby."

Jealousy twisted Dejan's heart when Constantine sat next to her, nuzzling her cheek. He heaved a sigh of relief when he didn't scent sex on them. Certainly he would've heard them if they'd indulged. He was sure they'd fuck like rabbits when they returned home, and what was he supposed to do while they honeymooned without him?

He stood, his knees cracking like he was an old man. His neck had an uncomfortable kink and he ached like he had run a marathon. Despite his exhaustion, he hadn't slept much last night. His brothers and Tatiana would expect breakfast though. He went to the kitchen.

He was cracking eggs in a bowl when Constantine joined him and leaned against the small ancient fridge. "We have to do another bonding ceremony."

Dejan didn't know how to answer. He wasn't ready, but he didn't know how to tell them that without crushing Tatiana.

"Don't bother, Constantine." She came in and poured cream in her coffee. "It's obvious he doesn't want to restore the bond."

Dejan winced, feeling the slap of her words deep in his soul. "I didn't say that," he whispered.

"You don't need to say it." She leaned against the counter while palming the flowery, porcelain cup. "Your actions say it for you."

Dejan gripped the whisk as if it was a lifeline. He loathed himself for the hurt he saw in her eyes. "I want our pack to heal. I want us all to be together again."

"But do you want me?" she asked, her voice cracking like that porcelain cup shattering on a wood floor.

He swallowed back his fear, searching her eyes, his heart aching at the vulnerability he saw there. These past few months, they'd shared so many loving memories together. Was he willing to throw that all away over a few nightmares? Over something totally out of her control?

"Of course I want you," he said tightly.

"Well, I don't know yet if I want you. You hurt me. You weren't there for me."

Dejan suddenly felt like he was back in the dream, and she was draining his blood again. "I've been here for you this whole time, despite what you did to Dimitri." The words popped out before he could take them back. He hadn't meant them, had he?

"That was the fucking demon, you dick!" Constantine grabbed his collar and lifted him off the floor, his eyes shifting to brilliant white.

The sound of the whisk hitting the floor ricocheted through his brain like a crack of thunder, but oddly enough, he wasn't afraid of his brother. It felt like this was happening to some other *idiotule*, because there was no way the real Dejan would've said something so heartless to his mate.

"Constantine, please don't," Tatiana begged, grabbing his arm. "He's not worth your anger."

When Constantine released him with a grunt and a shove, and he fell against the counter, pain shot up his side.

"Thank you for finally telling me how you feel, Dejan," she said coldly. "I must have invited that demon to set up shop inside me, right? All my fault? You jerk."

Dejan hated himself so much for pissing her off. "I know it's not your fault, but I cannot get that nightmare out of my head." He wished he could drive the memories away. A thought occurred to him that he could ask Eilea for a memory spell, but he didn't want to involve his stepmom and fathers in this. Besides, it was wrong of him to ask for a spell that would make him forget while his brothers and mates held on to those awful memories. "I can't sleep anymore. Whenever I close my eyes, I see you turning into a spider and draining my blood."

Constantine's chest heaved. "You should leave."

"And go where?"

"I don't care." His eyes and nose lengthened, fur sprouting from his ears and forehead. "Just fucking leave."

Dejan pushed off from the counter and went past them. In the living room, he looked at Tatiana one last time, his heart breaking all over again. "I'm so sorry."

Constantine pulled her into his arms and glared at Dejan over the top of her head. His chest caving inward as if a protector was crushing him, he threw open the door, the bitter winter wind instantly stinging his flesh. He sprinted into the barn in search of heat, dreading the prospect of being alone with his dark thoughts. He'd never hated himself more than he did at that moment. What had he done? Tatiana would never want him back now.

DEJAN HAD BEEN TRYING to warm his hands by a trashcan fire all morning, without much success, and the rest of him was nearly frozen through. He kept stamping his feet to keep the blood moving. He was also hungry, as he'd had no breakfast before letting his self-hate drive him from the house.

Dimitri was screaming for him. The cold air biting his nose and cheeks, he skulked back to the house.

Crunching snow under his boots, he passed Drasko and Luc who were warming up the trucks and giving him murderous looks. Constantine had told everyone, most likely. His sweet Tatiana wouldn't cause him trouble. Except she wasn't his sweet Tatiana anymore, was she? What a fuckup he was.

Bags were piled by the front door. His fathers, grandfathers, and Tor were somberly standing around in the kitchen. Tatiana, Eilea, and Phoenix played with Artem on the carpeted floor.

"Get your shit, Dejan." Dimitri slammed into his shoulder as he went by. "Oops."

Dejan kept his mouth shut. He deserved to have his shoulder bumped and far worse. Shoving his hands in his pockets, he planted himself by the bannister. "I'm going to stay here a while longer."

Tatiana went over to him. "Please don't do this."

He didn't know if he should feel relief or panic that she wanted him to go with her, but he dug in. He was making the right decision. "The last thing I want to do is hurt you. You'd be better off without me."

"You will not separate," Eilea said, balancing Artem on her hip. "When Jovan left us, it nearly killed me."

When Klaus cleared his throat from the kitchen doorway, everyone stopped what they were doing, giving the older wolf deference. "You will go home with your mate and brothers and work it out. Understood?"

"Da." Dejan hung his head in shame.

How were they going to work it out when they clearly hated him? When he couldn't even stand himself? Tatiana deserved better, and he wasn't sure he was wolf enough to give her what she needed.

Chapter Seventeen

DEJAN AWOKE TO TATIANA lying beside him, gazing at him with luminous brown eyes.

"Good morning," she said. "Did you sleep well?"

He gently touched her cheek, sighing his contentment. "Da."

She sat up, letting the blanket fall, and a ray of sunlight struck her long neck and beautiful, full breasts. His dick instantly hardened.

He reached for her. "Come here, Tatiana."

She rolled into him with a laugh. He ran his fingers through her silky hair and down her back before cupping her ass. She was perfect, absolutely perfect. When she straddled him, his hips rose to meet hers, searching out her wet heat.

"Not now." She giggled.

"But why?"

"I have to be sure you love me first."

"I do love you, Tatiana!" He reached for her as she slipped off him.

"You love me when I'm perfect," she said. "You have to also love me when I'm not."

She trailed her fingers over her stomach, and he saw the faint trace of a raised, red scar no bigger than his thumb.

He got up on his knees. "Tatiana."

A shadow fell across her, and she disappeared into darkness. Had he lost her forever?

"Wake up, idiotule! We're home."

His eyes shot open. Dimitri was scowling at him. He looked out the window at the snowy field beyond the tarmac. The beautiful Alaskan mountains loomed in the background, painted in brilliant crimson hues by the setting sun.

"Home," he breathed. Still groggy, he watched Tatiana and his brothers gathering the luggage.

Feeling like a fifth wheel, he helped but lagged behind, remembering bits and pieces from the dream he was having when he woke up. Tatiana hadn't been a monster! She'd been his sweet, broken-hearted mate. Did this mean he was finally healing and ready to rebond with her?

Except... what if that was no longer a possibility?

DEJAN FOLLOWED HIS brothers and Tatiana into their temporary cabin, a three-bedroom home at the edge of the Thunderfoot property usually reserved for guests from other tribes. Even though their place was still being built, this one felt like home to him. It smelled like pine, cinnamon, and his pack. *His pack.* How long would he be able to say that?

He was grateful for the pot of stew, cornbread, and fresh pie waiting for them on the counter, with a welcome home note from Rone Thunderfoot. There were also two breakfast casseroles, chili, and a platter of cookies in the fridge from Arvid. Dejan was still exhausted from their ordeal and didn't feel like cooking. Besides, he wasn't sure his brothers and Tatiana would want him to cook them anything, anyway.

Tatiana stopped at the bottom of the pine staircase and stretched, her shirt rising to expose a beautiful, flat stomach with no ugly red boils. "Ahh, it feels good to have this demon out of me. I need to take about a thousand showers."

Dimitri wrapped his arms around her. "I'll take one with you."

"Dimitri, stop." She giggled, then tilted her head so he could feast on her neck.

When he dragged his teeth across her skin, she let out a moan that made Dejan's dick swell to painful proportions. He wanted her badly, but he had no right to her body.

His cheeks heated when his other brothers joined Dimitri to run their hands all over Tatiana. Feeling like a creepy voyeur, he forced himself to look away. "Is anyone hungry?" he asked, though he wasn't sure why. Maybe he just wanted to remind them he was still in the room.

Ignoring him, they raced upstairs.

"I've lost my appetite anyway," he mumbled, wishing he hadn't let Eilea talk him into returning to Alaska when it was obvious his pack no longer wanted him.

TATIANA STOPPED AT the top of the stairs, fighting Dimitri when he tried to drag her to the master bedroom. She couldn't go there. She dug her heels into the carpet. "Can we use a guest bedroom? I don't think I want to go into that room."

Andrei went ahead, pushed open the door, and peeked inside. "It's okay." He waved them forward with a wolfish grin, his eyes smoky with desire. "It's been cleaned up."

"I-I don't know." She backed up until she pressed into a big wall of muscle. Craning her neck, she looked up at Constantine.

"It's over," he assured her. "No more demons. Just us."

She trembled. "I'm afraid."

Dimitri invaded her personal space. "There's nothing to be afraid of." He flashed a lopsided grin. "We kicked demon ass."

She followed him on shaky legs but was still reluctant. "Okay."

When he pulled her into the bedroom, she was relieved to see no trace of the attack. The floors had been replaced with dark hardwood and the walls repainted. Even the furniture was new. It was a completely different room.

Constantine and Andrei sat on the bed, waggling their brows while taking off their shoes.

Dimitri pulled her toward the bed, kissing her tenderly, his lips delicately tracing hers like teasing wisps of smoke. "I've missed being inside you, *iubita mea*," he said and peeled off her shirt.

Her head lolled to one side while he feasted on her neck. She was so damned horny. "But I need a shower." Though she was loath to pull away, she ducked under his arm and slipped into the bathroom, hearing his footsteps behind her. "Your bunics' house had terrible water pressure." She took off her shirt and unbuckled her jeans.

He followed her, closing the door behind him and muffling the protests of Constantine and Andrei. His eyes turned to silver slits as he slipped off his shirt, revealing a wide, hard chest. "Is it pressure you want?" He swept her into his arms again and slid a hand under her panties to probe her with a thick finger. She groaned her delight, her legs instinctively falling open.

He lifted her and set her on the bathroom counter. "You smell fine to me."

She wanted to fight him, but desire had turned her resolve to putty. He unsnapped her bra and threw it to the floor, then took a breast in his mouth, sucking the nipple until she thought she'd explode.

"Taste fine, too," he murmured and slipped off her underwear.

"Oh, Dimitri," she cried, burying her fingers in his thick hair. "I've missed this so much. I've missed *you* so much!"

She had no idea what Constantine and Andrei were doing, but she appreciated them giving her and Dimitri alone time. After what happened the last time they had sex, they needed this to erase ugly memories and create beautiful new ones.

He pushed her panties aside and toyed with her slit, driving his finger into her with rapid, shallow thrusts until she was on the verge of a powerful orgasm.

"Dimitri!" she cried. "Please make love to me. Please!"

He tore off his jeans and underwear in record time while she tossed her panties to the floor. He grabbed her ass, and she wrapped her legs around his waist.

"The wait is killing me," he rasped, raking his teeth down her neck.

"Then don't wait," she pleaded, her lips searching out his. "Take me. Claim me."

He buried himself in her heat in one smooth thrust, a low feral growl escaping his throat as he panted into her hair. She cupped his face, looking into his silver eyes before opening her mouth for a kiss. He bent her over the counter, pressing her back against the mirror, his tongue swirling with hers while he pumped into her, slowly at first, but it didn't take long for them to find the perfect rhythm. She opened her legs wider for deeper penetration, crying out each time he banged into her sweet spot, making her swell and swell until she teetered on the edge of oblivion.

Dimitri! she cried, digging her nails into his back. *Please don't stop loving me. Please.*

Never, iubita mea. He pounded her harder, faster. *No demon and no curse will ever stop me from loving you.*

They both went to the end of the world together, finding perfect bliss in each other's arms.

By the time they came up for air, she was drenched in sweat and their combined fluids. She draped an arm over his shoulder with a lazy smile. "Now I *really* need a shower." She laughed.

"Yeah," he said, nibbling her bottom lip. "Not sorry."

He helped her into the shower. "Shall I send in another brother?" he asked with a wink.

She brushed her lips across his. "Please."

She thoroughly cleaned herself and wasn't surprised when Andrei came in. She had a feeling Constantine would wait to take her last. Something about the smoldering looks he'd given her on the way home told her he wanted to make love to her long and slow in their bed, which suited her just fine.

Andrei pulled back the curtain. "Room for me?"

She crooked a finger at him. "Always."

Water droplets slid down his lean, toned body. He looked far more feral than he had when they first bonded, the angles of his face sharper, his stomach concave, his hips narrower, and his muscles more defined. He had the perfect tracker body, and she had so much more appreciation for his sacrifices after going on a mission with him.

She ran a big soapy sponge across his chest, a chill going through her when he gazed at her with a predatory gleam. Fuck, he made her so horny. She cleaned every inch of him, except for that one large appendage jutting from him, standing at attention like a good soldier. She knew to save the best for last, choosing instead to clean his erection with her hands. She threw down the sponge, playfully batting her eyes while sitting on the edge of the tub. She lathered him up, stroking up and down his shaft and massaging his balls with soapy fingers.

He swore while she pumped him like a piston. When his flesh swelled and his balls lifted, she rinsed him off and took him in her mouth. He lifted a leg, resting a foot on the side of the tub, biting his lip every time she swallowed him, sucking and slurping until his cockhead burst, spilling into the back of her throat. She greedily swallowed every last drop until he sagged against her with a groan.

When she slowly slid off his cock, batting her lashes, he cupped her chin, rubbing her lips with the pad of his thumb. "I didn't get to give you pleasure, *iubita mea.*"

"That's okay. We have all night."

They dried each other off and parted with a sweet kiss, then she brushed her teeth and returned to the bedroom with nothing but a towel wrapped around her.

Constantine was waiting on the bed, his body glistening with moisture, his wet hair slicked back.

"So that's why I lost water pressure," she teased.

A fire was roaring in the hearth, chasing the chill from her bones, though she suspected the flushing of her skin was due to Constantine's virile scent and smoldering looks.

He held out a hand to her. "Come here. Let me properly make love to you."

She eagerly threw off the towel and crawled onto the bed, sighing when he held her in a warm, loving embrace. They held each other a long while, stroking, petting, and tenderly teasing.

His eyes were blue with silver specks, and her heart felt near to bursting with love. "Thank you for being an amazing protector."

He wrapped a strand of her dark hair around his finger. "It's my job."

"Don't act like it was nothing, Constantine," she said. "You protected me from demons, bandidos, and even my own family."

"I would die protecting you." His eyes shone with sincerity. "Without you, my life is nothing."

She touched her nose to his, her heart so full, she wanted to wrap him in a cocoon of love and never let go. "And with you, my life is everything."

"Come here, my sweet mate," he said and rolled her onto her back. "Let me love you."

She lay on her back, and he loomed over her before settling between her legs. She loved the feel of his skin pressed against hers and sighed when he slid into her.

They made love slowly, bodies and souls entwined. Her mounting passion mimicked the overwhelming love in her heart. They crested together, suspended in orgasmic bliss for several heartbeats. She snuggled against him, and he stroked her hair and back, whispering tender words. Then they made love once more, taking their time adoring each other while working toward that magical pinnacle of release.

They held each other for a long time, watching the brilliant lights of the Aurora Borealis through the huge window. Though Tatiana wanted to lie here all night, her growling stomach had other ideas.

When her stomach made an especially loud protest, he gave her a sideways smile. "You sure we got rid of those demons?"

"These are my food demons." She patted her blessedly smooth and boil-free stomach. "They require moose burgers and brownie sundaes or I turn into a raging bitch."

He stroked her arm, sending delightful shivers across her skin. "I don't know about burgers, but I smelled stew and pie."

"That'll work, too."

Loath though she was to leave the comfort of their bed, she got up and changed into warm pajamas and a flannel robe, then slipped into a pair of white bunny slippers, which reminded her of Phoenix's pets and made her smile. She hoped the girl was happy tonight.

"You ready?" he asked.

Nervous energy destroyed her post-coital lassitude when she thought about having to face Dejan. She refused to be a coward, though. They were eventually going to have to deal with the fallout of their broken bond. But as the memory of him blaming her for stabbing Dimitri replayed in her mind, she wasn't sure she wanted to see him. Her other mates would only add to the tension by picking on him. After what they had survived, she was ready to put strife behind her, but she wondered if that was possible.

TATIANA AND HER MATES stuffed themselves with stew and cornbread. Dejan hadn't eaten yet, and she worried there wouldn't be enough left over for him. The moment she mentioned it, Andrei and Dimitri finished off the cornbread and pie with shit-eating grins. She wanted to tell them they were behaving like children, but she remembered from old stories how the forest changed those who'd survived even the slightest brush with the veil, leaving them in sour moods for weeks. She hoped that's what was happening and they'd soon be treating their youngest brother with affection. She couldn't deny she still felt on edge after their time in the Hoia Baciu.

She put the remaining stew in the fridge for Dejan and curled up with her mates in the living room, alternating between watching an old movie and stealing glances at the guestroom door to see if Dejan would come out.

The movie was only half finished when all three of her mates passed out on the sofas. That's when Dejan finally emerged, skulking around the kitchen like a stray cat.

After extricating herself from a tangle of muscular arms and legs, she went to the kitchen, discouraged when panic flashed in his eyes. He was handwashing the dishes with the tap barely running.

"Let me help," she said, taking a clean bowl from him and drying it with a towel.

"I got this," he said. "You need rest."

She wondered if he cared for her health or simply wanted her to leave.

"I don't mind," she said, tugging another bowl from his hands. "I slept on the plane."

"That's good." He turned back to the dishes. "I did, too."

After all they'd shared, was it that hard to look her in the eye?

She took a chance and placed a hand on his arm, relieved when he didn't pull away. Progress.

His shoulders fell, and the dark circles under his eyes were more pronounced. "I haven't slept well since...." He trailed off.

"I know." She squeezed his arm and then let go, not wanting to push too far, too fast.

She wondered how often he thought of the stabbing when all she'd tried to do was block it from her mind. He'd seen it through a totally different pair of eyes. Tatiana hadn't fully been there mentally after Morana took over. Perhaps he'd experienced things that had left scars on his soul that were too deep to heal.

"I've had the same nightmare every night since it happened."

When her gaze shot to his, a knife of guilt sliced open her chest. "I'm so sorry."

His eyes softened, and he touched her cheek, his hands damp from dishwater. "If anyone should be sorry, it's me. I didn't make things easier by pulling away. None of this was your fault."

She wanted to melt into him, but she couldn't. She was still too afraid of being rejected by him. A thought occurred to her. What if he was only being sweet because of pressure from his brothers?

She stepped back as fear and self-loathing washed over her. "That's not what you said this morning."

"Please don't pull away," he begged. "I wasn't blaming you."

"It sure felt like it." She refused to come closer. "Was the dream about me?"

He wiped his hands on his jeans. "I can't control my dreams."

"So it *was* about me." She turned to the window. The northern lights were still dancing across the sky. "Was I a demon?" she asked and held her breath, afraid to hear the answer.

"Not this last time. I think maybe I'm past it."

A small flame of hope kindled in her heart. "I'm just trying to understand your rejection. "

"I love you, Tatiana, more than anything." He grabbed both of her hands and pulled them to his chest, his eyes radiating warmth and love. "You have to believe that."

She was slightly stunned by the admission. Could it be true?

"I-I want to." She still had an overwhelming fear he would reject her. She pulled away and busied herself drying dishes.

"When the spider broke the bond, I think she also planted that fear in me," he said to her back.

"That makes sense," she said, too choked up to say more. It didn't matter how much he loved her. They could never restore the bond if he was afraid of her. After running out of dishes, she wiped silverware that had long since dried.

"I think I'm over it." He gently touched her shoulder. "I don't fear you anymore, *iubita mea.*"

She dropped the knife she'd been wiping, and the sharp tip accidentally cut her finger. "Ouch! Damn."

"Let me see." He examined her thumb. "Come on. We need the first-aid kit."

He led her to the hall bathroom, the same place where they'd discovered that horrid red boil on her stomach. She didn't want to go in there. What if the memory of her hideous transformation repulsed him?

He took bandages and antiseptic out of the cabinet. "Does it hurt?"

She shook her head. "I know I traumatized you," she blurted, "and I'm sorry."

"You have nothing to be sorry for. It was your demon. I was blinded by fear. I swear it will never happen again."

She nodded, not sure what to say. He pressed gauze to her finger, then turned over her hand and placed a delicate kiss on her wrist. A tingling sensation raced down her spine and into her toes.

He trailed kisses across her palm and stopped at the tip of her injured finger. Realization dawned when he looked at her as if he needed permission to keep going.

She uncurled her finger and rested it under his full, sensual lips. He unwrapped the gauze and drew the tip of her finger into his mouth, sucking. Every nerve ending in her body lit up.

Can you hear me? she projected.

"Da," he answered with a broad smile, "but I don't think you can hear me yet."

His face lengthened and sharp canines extended from his mouth. He bit his thumb, puncturing the skin deep enough so that the blood pushed up like a spring.

When he held it out to her, she took it in her mouth, sucking.

Can you hear me?

She smiled. *Yes.*

He let out a howl, took her in his arms, and twirled her.

You sure this is what you want? she asked after he set her down.

He pressed her against the wall until her chest was flush with his and his erection could be felt through his tight denim. *How could I not want my brave, sweet, beautiful mate?*

Do you think we can put the past behind us? The events of this week had left her tired and heartsick. All she wanted was to curl up with her mates by the fire.

I'm more than ready if you are.

I want things to go back to the way they were.

His eyes were two silver pools of sincerity. *They may never go back exactly how you want them, but know that I love and adore you.*

As long as you love me, I'll be happy.

He swept her into his arms. *Let me show you how much.*

Yes, please. She needed to feel him inside her to complete their bond and ease their battered hearts.

He carried her into the guest bedroom and shut the door with his foot. Then he tenderly laid her down on the bed, as if she was a fragile flower he was trying to preserve.

He peeled off their clothes, whispering words of love, and then settled between her legs. They kissed, their touches tentative and feather soft, but soon their kisses became more passionate, more urgent, and she was begging him to make love to her.

By the time he finally slid into her wet heat, she was desperate. They crested together, two souls stranded out to sea riding a wave that carried them to paradise. He made love to her again this way, and she fell apart in his arms two more times. After he cleaned them both, he slipped under the covers with her, holding her until she fell asleep in his cocoon of love.

Epilogue

TATIANA RAPPED ON PHOENIX'S bedroom door, smiling at the girl when she let her in. "Hey, mind if I get a few of my books?"

She looked around the room, noting there hadn't been many changes other than the bunny pen in the corner, complete with a litterbox, tunnel, and wooden castle.

"Sure." Phoenix motioned to the white bookcase by the computer table. "You have quite the collection."

Tatiana ran a finger across a few spines. It had been years since she'd opened some of the books, and she needed something to read.

"I loved to read when I was your age," she said, noticing the dusty oil lamp that was wedged between two books. Tatiana's mother had told her Phoenix refused to release Jezebeth or even talk about her. "Still do. I'm out of stuff to read at the guest house." She dug for the naughty books she kept in the back and pulled out the one she wanted, determined to slip it under her coat when Phoenix snatched it from her.

"*Academy for Misfit Witches?* Ohh! It's got dragon shifters!"

Heat crept into her cheeks. "I hope you haven't read it."

"Not yet." Letting out a low whistle, Phoenix turned it over in her hands. "Is it bad?"

Tatiana snatched it back from her. "It's not appropriate for girls your age."

Phoenix rolled her eyes. "I've seen a lot, Tatiana."

"I know," she said, shoving the book in an inside pocket of her jacket. "But my parents would kill me if I let you read it. Sorry. How are you liking it here?"

She felt horrible that this was the first time she'd visited. The girl had been living with her parents for two weeks. She'd just been so busy with her mates. When they weren't fucking like rabbits, she was acting as a buffer between Dejan and his brothers.

"I love it. Drasko is teaching me how to fish." Phoenix's smile practically lit up the room, and Tatiana was filled with an overwhelming sense of calm. She should've brought her feuding mates along.

"That's awesome," Tatiana said. "Sorry I haven't been around before."

"That's okay." Phoenix shrugged. "I know you had to reconnect with your mates."

Reconnect. Hmm. That was an interesting choice of words. She thought of all the times her mates' tongues had reconnected with her pussy and their cocks had reconnected with her mouth. Yeah, definitely a lot of reconnecting going on.

"Sure." She loosened her collar as a sudden wave of heat washed over her. "But things are pretty much back to normal, so if you want, I can hang out here more often."

Though she missed Constantine and Andrei, she couldn't deny feeling relief when they'd gone back to work yesterday morning. Earlier today Dimitri had actually thanked Dejan for passing him the butter. She hoped Dejan would be welcome in their bed soon, because she was tired of sneaking into his room in the middle of the night.

"Maybe you can go fishing with Drasko and me tomorrow. "

That was just what she needed. She hadn't seen him since they'd returned from the forest, and she missed his sharp wit and snarky jokes.

"I'd love to," she said. "I'm really happy you're here. "

Phoenix beamed. "Me, too."

Tatiana was relieved things were working out. She wasn't sure how much longer they'd have Phoenix. In the not-so-distant future, she would discover her fated mates and move out. She wondered how they'd react to having a half-demon mate.

She jumped when she heard an unexpected cry from the bookcase.

Phoenix shrugged. "She bugs me sometimes."

That wasn't good. She couldn't imagine the awkward family conversations when Phoenix brought dear old demon mama home for supper.

After they said goodbye, she ran down the stairs and right into Dejan's loving arms. She sent a silent prayer to the Ancients that one day Phoenix would find caring mates, too, ones who loved her unconditionally, demon blood or not. Gaining a mate's acceptance wasn't always easy, but in the end, it was so worth it.

THE END.

Books by Tara West

Eternally Yours
Divine and Dateless
Damned and Desirable
Damned and Desperate
Demonic and Deserted
Dead and Delicious
Something More Series
Say When
Say Yes
Say Forever
Say Please
Say You Want Me
Say You Love Me
Say You Need Me
Dawn of the Dragon Queen Saga
Dragon Song
Dragon Storm
Whispers Series
Sophie's Secret
Don't Tell Mother
Krysta's Curse
Visions of the Witch
Sophie's Secret Crush
Witch Blood
Witch Hunt
Keepers of the Stones
Witch Flame, Prelude

Curse of the Ice Dragon, Book One
Spirit of the Sea Witch, Book Two
Scorn of the Sky Goddess, Book Three
Hungry for Her Wolves Series
Hungry for Her Wolves, Book One
Longing for Her Wolves, Book Two
Desperate for Her Wolves, Book Three
Tempted by Her Wolves, Book Four
Fighting for Her Wolves, Book Five
Fated for Her Wolves, Book Six
Defending Her Wolves, Book Seven
Saving Her Wolves, Book Eight (TBA)
Academy for Misfit Witches
(Set in the same world as The Fae Queen, but 2,000 years later)
Academy for Misfit Witches, Book One
School for Stolen Secrets, Book Two
Academy for Courting Curses, Book Three
The Fae Queen's Warriors
The Fae Queen's Warriors, Book One
The Fae Queen's Captors, TBR
The Fae Queen's Saviors, TBR

About Tara West

Tara West writes books about dragons, witches, and handsome heroes while eating chocolate, lots and lots of chocolate. She's willing to share her dragons, witches, and heroes. Keep your hands off her chocolate. A former high school English teacher, Tara is now a full-time writer and graphic artist. She enjoys spending time with her family, interacting with her fans, and fishing the Texas coast.

Awards include: Dragon Song, Grave Ellis 2015 Readers Choice Award, Favorite Fantasy Romance

Divine and Dateless, 2015 eFestival of Words, Best Romance

Damned and Desirable, 2014 Coffee Time Romance Book of the Year

Sophie's Secret, selected by The Duff and Paranormal V Activity movies and Wattpad recommended reading lists

Curse of the Ice Dragon, Best Action/Adventure 2013 eFestival of Words

Hang out with her on her Facebook fan page at: https://www.facebook.com/tarawestauthor

Or check out her website: www.tarawest.com

She loves to hear from her readers at: tarawestwriter@gmail.com